IN THE COMPANY OF FOOLS

IN THE COMPANY OF FOOLS

Tania Bayard

This first world edition published 2020
in Great Britain and the USA by
SEVERN HOUSE PUBLISHERS LTD of
Eardley House, 4 Uxbridge Street, London W8 7SY.
Trade paperback edition first published
in Great Britain and the USA 2020 by
SEVERN HOUSE PUBLISHERS LTD.

British Library Cataloguing in Publication Data
A CIP catalogue record for this title is available from the British Library.

ISBN-13: 978-0-7278-8941-6 (cased)
ISBN-13: 978-1-78029-678-4 (trade paper)
ISBN-13: 978-1-4483-0382-3 (e-book)

All Severn House titles are printed on acid-free paper.

Severn House Publishers support the Forest Stewardship Council™ [FSC™],
the leading international forest certification organisation.
All our titles that are printed on FSC certified paper carry the FSC logo.

Typeset by Palimpsest Book Production Ltd.,
Falkirk, Stirlingshire, Scotland.
Printed and bound in Great Britain by
TJ International, Padstow, Cornwall.

ACKNOWLEDGMENTS

Thanks to R. C. Famiglietti for graciously answering questions about the court of Charles VI; Sara Porter, my editor at Severn House, for skillful editing and perceptive comments; Josh Getzler, my agent, for unfailing support; and my husband, Robert M. Cammarota, for making invaluable suggestions and providing editorial expertise.

Now is a time of cowardice, weakness, and decay, senility, greed, and slander. All I see are fools, both men and women. Truly, the end is near.

Eustache Deschamps (c. 1340–1404), *Ballade 95*

PROLOGUE

The young woman followed the man in the black cloak through dark streets and even darker alleyways that reeked of urine and garbage. Clouds hid the moon, and sudden gusts of wind threatened to extinguish the flickering glow from a taper wavering in the man's hand. Rain soaked her cloak and boots, and a large black dog loped along beside her, shaking himself and spraying her with more water. Somewhere another dog howled. He answered with a sharp yelp that ricocheted off the walls of the houses they passed.

The silent figure she followed slipped in the mud and hitched himself up before he could fall. She slipped, too. But when she tried to steady herself by grabbing on to the man's cloak, he stretched out an arm and pushed her back so violently that she lost her balance and stumbled over a motionless body lying against a shuttered door. Was the person dead or alive? She didn't know. She heard shuffling sounds behind her. Was someone following them? She was afraid to turn and look.

The man stopped at a house she could barely see in the weak light of his taper, seized her hand, and pulled her to him as he put his shoulder against a door. The door swung open, and he dragged her through it into a dark hallway. He gave a muffled shout and stood motionless, waiting for someone to answer. The dim glow of another taper appeared high above them.

'Have you done what I asked?' he called out.

'Everything is ready,' came the reply.

The man put his foot on the bottom stair of a narrow staircase with cracked steps and a banister that seemed to disappear in mid-air and started climbing, pulling her up behind him. At the top, he moved toward a shadowy figure that gradually turned from a specter into a tiny hunchbacked old woman in a long black dress and a mass of disheveled white hair that nearly obscured her face. Without saying a word, the woman led them into a darkened room.

She could see nothing, but she smelled mold and rot, and she heard the rain pattering against a window. When her eyes became accustomed to the darkness, she saw a small fireplace where a few logs hissed and spit as they tried to work themselves into a blaze. The old woman threw something into the fire, and soon a fetid smell like rotten meat filled the room. She felt sick, and she started to fall. The man in the black cloak caught her and laid her on the floor.

Her head felt light, her feet left the ground, and she was flying above the city's shadowy streets, out over the countryside. The sun rose, and she looked down on the tops of trees whose leaves shimmered in its rays. Rivers of silver slithered through emerald fields, and meandering roads sparkled like gold. The towers and spires of distant towns turned rose pink, and the houses beneath them shone snow white. Tiny figures moved about, their feet hardly touching the ground as they danced and leapt, throwing their hats into the air, where the sun turned them to fire. She wanted to call out to them, but when she opened her mouth to speak, no sound came. The sun disappeared, the air became thick, and she struggled to breathe. She smelled something rotten. She choked. Then she slept.

Someone was shaking her. She opened her eyes. Daylight filtered in through a grimy window, and the diminutive woman she'd seen the night before stood over her, motioning for her to rise. She struggled to her feet, put out her hand to brace herself against a blackened wall, and looked around for the man who'd brought her to this dismal place. He wasn't there, but on the floor where she'd been sleeping lay her cloak and, beside it, a coin.

The old woman took her hand and led her to the fireplace. There were no flames, only blackened ashes, but the sickening smell she'd noticed the night before still filled the room, and she started to gag.

'You will be away from here soon,' the woman said, her voice shrill and grating. She bent down, her misshapen body contorting as she crouched and twisted her head so she could look up at her. She pointed to something on the ground. 'This is what you came for. You know what to do with it.' She lifted the corner of a ragged blanket. Under it was a baby. The child, tightly wrapped in a tattered, oil-stained cloth, gazed at her with huge eyes protruding from a skeletal face, one side of which was covered with an ugly black mark.

She could hardly look at the baby, it was so thin and its face so disfigured. Dazed and confused, she tried to understand. Then she remembered, and she drew back in horror. The grotesque little woman struggled to her feet and grabbed her wrist. 'It's too late to change your mind now, *ma petite chérie.*' She pulled her to where her cloak lay on the floor. 'Don't forget this.'

She picked up the cloak and threw it over her shoulders. The old woman drew her back to the fireplace, lifted the baby in its greasy covering, and thrust it into her arms. She handed her the coin and pushed her toward the door. 'It's light now,' she said. 'You can find your way.' She shut the door, leaving the young woman to creep alone down the crumbling staircase and out into the street as the dawn broke.

ONE

The people of France were greatly dispirited by the king's illness . . . for when the head is sick, all the limbs feel it.

Froissart, *Chroniques*, Livre IV, 1389–1400

Paris, late March–early April 1396

C hristine put down her pen and contemplated the book she was copying for the Duchess of Orléans. She'd come to the story of the fox and the grapes, and she took a moment to savor it. Aesop's fables provided a welcome respite from her worries.

She worked in a room at the top of a tower, a sunlit space in the residence the Duke and Duchess of Orléans occupied across the street from the other buildings of the royal palace, the Hôtel Saint-Pol. She went to an open window and looked out at those buildings, reflecting that somewhere in one of them her pitiful king paced the floor, tearing his hair and biting his fingernails.

The king had been mad for nearly four years. He had periods of sanity, but he always relapsed, succumbing to a mysterious illness that periodically enveloped him in darkness and despair. Then he would become a poor caged creature who tore at his clothes and howled words that should never issue from the mouth of a monarch. He would forget he was king, flee from the queen, and rage around the palace in such a blind fury that his retainers had to bolt the doors to keep him from running naked out into the streets of the city. Even his intervals of lucidity were filled with horror, for the knowledge that his illness would return preyed on his mind. King Charles the Sixth of France was a broken man, and the whole country suffered as a result.

The king's doctors tried to explain his illness in various ways. Some said he'd inherited the derangement from his mother. Others claimed that his humors were unbalanced and that he had too much black bile. Many attributed the problem to the excesses he'd committed in his youth. But all their efforts to cure him had failed, and sorcerers had been summoned. These charlatans claimed the king was bewitched, and they pointed their fingers at one person, his brother's wife, Valentina Visconti, Duchess of Orléans, who, they claimed, had to be a sorceress since she'd come from Italy, a country rife with witchcraft and poisons. People became convinced that Valentina was like her father, Duke Gian Galeazzo of Milan, a sorcerer reputed to have the ability, even from afar, to cause the King of France to die. Then, they said, the king's brother, Louis, would ascend to the throne, and Gian Galeazzo would have achieved his objective: his daughter would become queen of France.

Christine didn't believe any of this, but she knew one thing for certain: the king's affliction was sickening the whole country. During his periods of madness, the task of governing fell to Louis, who was thwarted at every turn by his uncles, Duke Jean of Berry and Duke Philip of Burgundy. The Duke of Burgundy, greedy for power and wealth, was especially destructive, and he was urged on by his malevolent duchess, who'd started the rumors that Valentina was a sorceress. France was in turmoil, and everyone waited for open warfare to break out between those who supported Louis of Orléans and those who backed Philip of Burgundy.

Christine sighed, turned to resume her copying, and found she was being watched by four creatures who seemed to have sprung from the book of fables. An owl stared at her with large unblinking eyes, a dolphin fixed his small round eyes on her as he wallowed on the floor, a fox peered at her down a long nose, and a lion gazed at her through a mane of tawny hair. A monkey squatted on her desk, grinning. The duke's fools had come for a visit.

Hanotin, the fool with the unblinking eyes, picked up the fables of Aesop and showed it to the monkey, a real monkey that usually perched on his shoulder. 'Can you read this?'

The monkey made a squeaking noise and reached for the book. Hanotin pulled the book away and laid it carefully back on the desk. 'Books are not for you,' he said. The monkey climbed onto his shoulder and yanked at tufts of hair growing above the fool's ears.

'You didn't think I could read, did you?' Hanotin asked Christine.

'Can you?' she asked.

'No.'

'I can't either,' said Coquinet, the fool who looked like a fox. 'But I can do other things.' He bent over backwards until his head touched the floor. Then he jumped up, balanced on one foot, and raised the other foot over his head. 'I can stand on my elbows, too. And make myself so small you can stuff me into a little box.' He twisted himself into a knot. Christine wondered how he could contort his tall body into such impossible shapes.

'I won't tell you whether I can or not,' said Blondel, the dolphin, round and fat, with a smooth, bland face and a shiny bald head. He rolled around the room, something he did a lot because that seemed to come more naturally to him than walking, and started to laugh. The laughter began as a giggle, turned to guffaws and then a roar, and went on and on until Christine thought it would never stop. The other fools started to laugh, too.

Giliot, the lion, tossed his head, sending his tawny hair flying around his face. He tugged on his voluminous beard, wiggled his nose, and said, 'You don't know whether we're fools or madmen, do you?'

In truth, she didn't. All she knew was that the fools belonged to the duke but were more attached to the duchess, who had no fool of her own. The duke didn't seem to mind. In fact, he didn't pay much attention to them. This didn't surprise her; Louis was preoc-cupied with other things, especially his affairs with women. Valentina was often lonely and sad, and the fools made it their business to cheer her. And when the duchess was too busy to bother with them, they came to amuse the woman sitting by herself in the tower with her copying, claiming she was too solitary and serious for her own good. She enjoyed their company; they brightened the melancholy atmosphere of the duke's residence, where everyone was downcast because of the accusations swirling around the duchess.

'It's possible to be both a fool and a madman,' Giliot said.

'But it doesn't matter what we are today,' Hanotin said. He could make his voice seem to be coming from the monkey's mouth. 'Not today,' the monkey repeated, scratching himself furiously.

Giliot pushed his mass of tawny hair away from his face, pointed to the monkey, and said, 'Too much scratching hurts the skin.' He waved his hand at the other fools. 'Too much talking hurts the whole body.'

'Where's Fripon?' Christine asked, when she realized that one of the fools wasn't there. She missed the little man with curly black hair and eyes like black cherries who danced around as gracefully as any of the duke's courtiers and always carried a supply of balls, buttons, onions, eggs, or small stones that he produced at unlikely moments, tossed into the air, and made a great show of catching.

Hanotin waved his hands about in a beckoning gesture. 'You'll see. Come.' She had work to do, so she started to demur, but Hanotin nodded his head so vigorously that the monkey struggled to keep his perch on his shoulders. The fool put his hands together as if in prayer. 'It's important.'

Giliot did a little dance, slid to a stop at Christine's side, and said, 'We frolic, but our hearts are not as light as our heels. You must come and see why.' He raced to the door and came back to her side again, making a gesture as though he were pulling her along with a rope. She would have laughed, but he looked so solemn that she sighed, went to her desk, and while the fools stood staring at her hopefully, closed the fables of Aesop, placed her writing materials in her pouch, put on her cloak, and indicated that she was ready to go with them.

'Hurry. The hour flies,' Giliot said as he ran out into the hallway. Coquinet walked to the door on his hands, Blondel waddled after him, and Hanotin followed, with the monkey standing on his shoulders making shooing motions. Christine brought up the rear as they trooped down a winding staircase that passed the duke's library. She snuck into the room and hastily placed the book of fables on the desk where the librarian, Gilles Malet, would find it and put it away until the next time she came for it. Gilles was there, but he didn't notice her because he was watching a man on a ladder put the finishing touches to a fresco he'd painted on one of the walls. She wanted to stop and have a look at the painting herself, but the fools were waiting impatiently on the stairs and she hurried to join them.

As they passed a chamber where the duchess received visitors, she tried to hide behind fat Blondel so no one would see her, then breathed a sigh of relief when she realized the room was empty. At the bottom of the stairs they passed a kitchen. Someone had overturned a cauldron of water, and the cooks were busy cleaning it up, so no one paid any attention to the little band of four fools and one bewildered woman sneaking past. She breathed another sigh of relief.

The fools scampered to the door of a storeroom. Inside, large barrels of wine covered nearly every inch of the floor, and jugs of oil crowded the shelves along the walls. In the half-light that worked its way in through a dusty window, she saw at the far end of the room the fifth fool, Fripon, standing next to a barrel with a pile of rags on top.

Hanotin wove his way through the barrels to Fripon's side. The monkey leaned down from his shoulder, pointed to the pile of rags, made strange chirping noises, and gestured for Christine to follow.

Dust and mold clogged her throat, and the acrid smell of fermented wine leaking from old barrels made her gag, but she gathered up her skirts and followed, turning this way and that to prevent her clothes from catching on rough wood or loose staves. The other fools came after her, nearly stepping on her heels. When she got to Fripon, she leaned over the pile of rags and was met with a smell that sent her reeling back.

'You'll get used to it,' Fripon said. 'Look again.'

She stepped up to the barrel, held her nose, and saw that the pile of rags covered a baby. The child had no hair, and its bald head was covered with sores. One cheek was as black as the ink she used for her copying. She gasped. 'Who brought this child here?'

'Don't blame me,' Fripon said. He pointed to the other fools. 'They found it. I wasn't there.' He walked around the barrel, pulled three onions from his sleeve, and tossed them into the air.

'Where was it?' Christine asked.

'In the palace gardens,' Coquinet said.

'Beside the fishpond,' Blondel said.

'Where the nurses take the queen's baby to watch the ducks,' Hanotin said.

'Why would a baby be left there? I don't understand.'

'Take the queen's baby, leave another,' Giliot whispered, looking behind him to make sure no one had followed them into the room.

The child lay perfectly still, staring at them with huge eyes in what looked like the face of a very old person.

She shuddered. The queen's baby, stolen from its crib, and an ugly, disfigured creature left in its place – a 'gift' from the Devil. Many people, including her mother, believed such things.

'A different baby for the queen,' Blondel cried, rolling himself into a ball on the floor. 'But we got there first.'

Christine thought of the queen's baby, a little over a year old. The child that lay before her was probably older, but what did it matter? If the queen's daughter were stolen and this child substituted, the evil would have been accomplished: Valentina would be blamed.

The rumors about her had become so persistent that any shocking occurrence at the palace was attributed to her.

Giliot lifted the baby, wrapped the rags around it, and held it out to her. 'Take it,' he said.

Christine looked at the baby. It was so dirty and disfigured, she couldn't tell whether it was a boy or a girl. She wanted to turn her eyes away.

'So the duchess won't be blamed,' Giliot said. 'Take it to your mother.'

'Why my mother?'

'Mothers love babies.'

Christine wasn't so sure her mother would love this baby. 'My mother would believe this child was left by the Devil,' she said.

'Does your mother have a spiteful heart?' Giliot asked.

'Of course not!'

'Then she will love this baby.' He stood holding the bundle out to her. She was tempted to walk away. But instead, she moved closer and looked more carefully. All was not what it seemed. The baby stared at her with those large eyes, eyes that seemed to be pleading.

Christine looked at the fools, wondering whether they saw what she did. They stood with their hands in prayer. She lifted the baby from Giliot's arms, trying not to gag from its smell, and made her way through the forest of barrels to the door. She peered out to make sure no one was around, turned, smiled at the fools, and walked out into the street.

TWO

In spite of prayers and medicines, the king's illness never abated until it had run its course. When the doctors and sorcerers who attended him found their labors did no good, they announced that he must have been poisoned or harmed by certain herbs, and this gave rise to much speculation of evil among the nobility and the common folk. To make themselves more believable, the sorcerers claimed that the king had become deranged because of spells and charms . . . they said that Duchess Valentina of Orléans, daughter of the Duke of

Milan, was causing all this trouble so she could succeed to the Crown of France.

Froissart, *Chroniques*, Livre IV, 1389–1400

C hristine held the child under her cloak, tried to ignore the smell, and hurried down the rue Saint-Antoine. Several stray dogs trotted along beside her, sniffing, and an old woman with a market basket stopped and stared, nodding her head as though she knew there was something foul under the cloak. Christine glared at her. On the street leading to her house, more dogs emerged, some of them snarling menacingly. She resisted the temptation to run; she needed time to think about what she was going to tell her mother.

When Christine had first announced she was going to work as a scribe and had received a commission from the queen, her mother had been frantic with worry. Francesca had once lived at the palace herself because her husband, the noted physician and astrologer Thomas de Pizan, had brought his family from Italy to France so he could serve the present king's father, King Charles the Fifth. But things had changed. King Charles the Sixth had gone mad, and everyone believed he was bewitched. And now that her daughter had gone to work for the Duchess of Orléans, Francesca was even more concerned, for she knew what people said about Valentina, and she didn't want Christine to go anywhere near a woman who was reputed to be a sorceress. It didn't matter to her that Christine, whose husband had died a few years earlier, needed to support the family; Francesca's only concern was that her daughter would be touched by evil. *When she sees this*, Christine said to herself, opening her cloak slightly and gazing at the disfigured baby, *her first thought will be that I've brought the evil home*. But she could think of no way to soften the shock.

In the kitchen, Francesca stood stirring something over the fire and didn't look up when her daughter came in. 'Why has that girl not come back from the market?' she grumbled as she lifted a heavy pot from the pothook and carried it to the table. Christine was glad that Georgette, their hired girl, wasn't there, for she was even more superstitious than Francesca, and there was no telling what she would do when she saw the baby. She stayed in the doorway and waited until the pot was safely on the table before she walked into the room.

'She probably met someone on the way,' she said, thinking of Georgette's beau, Robin, one of the palace guards.

Francesca turned and looked at her. 'Why do you not take off your cloak?'

'I will in a minute,' Christine said, keeping the cloak tightly closed.

Francesca sighed. 'What have you done now?'

'You must keep calm. I have something to show you.'

'Another dog?' Francesca looked down at Goblin, the small white stray her daughter had brought home several years ago.

'No. It's not a dog.' Christine slowly opened her cloak and held out the child.

Francesca gasped. *She's going to faint,* Christine thought. She set the child on the table and put her arms around her mother to break her fall.

The baby lay motionless, its huge eyes fixed on Francesca. The black mark on its face seemed more disfiguring than before, and the strange smell permeated the kitchen. Goblin sniffed the air and growled.

Francesca stared at the baby, but instead of fainting, she reached out her hand and touched the child's face. 'Who did this?' she asked in a hushed voice.

Christine breathed a sigh of relief. 'So you see what I see, Mama.'

'Of course I see. Who could have done such a thing?'

'I don't know. The child was found in the palace gardens. That's all I can tell you.'

There was a sound at the door and Georgette, cheeks flushed and carrying a large loaf of bread and a jug of milk, ran into the room. 'I only stopped to talk for a moment,' she said as she set the bread and the milk on the table. She wrinkled her nose. 'There's a bad smell in here.'

Then she saw the baby. She shrieked, grabbed the child, and ran with it to the fireplace. Christine dashed after her and tore the baby from her arms just as she was about to drop it into the flames.

'Why did you stop me?' Georgette wailed. 'We have to burn it.' She was crying and shaking uncontrollably.

'I know what you're thinking, Georgette,' Christine said. 'But you're wrong. This is not the Devil's child.' She handed the baby to Francesca, took Georgette's arm and made her stand close. Georgette, her eyes wide with terror, tried to back away, but Christine grasped her hand and brought it to the child's face. 'Touch it,' she commanded.

'Never!' Georgette screamed.

'Stop this foolishness! Do you think my mother would stand there calmly holding a child of the Devil?'

Georgette looked at Christine with tears in her eyes. 'Please don't make me do it!'

Christine gripped the girl's hand tightly and pressed her fingers against the black mark on the baby's face. 'No!' Georgette shrieked. She fell to her knees. Christine raised her up and made her look at her hand. The fingers were black.

'You know what it is,' Francesca said.

Georgette smelled her fingers and looked at the baby in disbelief. 'Black grease!'

'Indeed,' Francesca said. 'It is meant to be put on the wheels of a cart, not on the face of a child.'

'You mean this is a real baby?'

'Of course it's a real baby,' Christine said. 'A real baby, disfigured and left in the palace gardens for someone like you to find.'

'Why?'

'So some ignorant, superstitious person would think it was the Devil's child, meant to be substituted for the queen's baby. And everyone would blame the Duchess of Orléans.'

Georgette looked at the baby and started to cry. Christine took her in her arms. 'You see, Georgette, how dangerous superstitions can be? What if you had succeeded in killing the baby?'

'I'd go to Hell,' the girl whispered.

'But you won't, because I stopped you. But you must promise not to tell anyone about this.'

'Will I go to Hell if I do?'

'Perhaps.'

'I swear I won't tell anyone.' The girl sobbed uncontrollably.

Francesca handed the baby to Christine, made Georgette sit on the bench by the table, went into the pantry, and came back carrying a cup of wine with pieces of valerian floating in it. 'Drink this,' she said. 'It will calm you.'

But instead of drinking the wine, Georgette got up, wiped her eyes, and went to Christine. Very carefully, she lifted the baby from her arms. By that time, the tattered rags had fallen away, and they could see that it was a girl. 'She's nothing but skin and bones!' Georgette exclaimed. 'We must feed her!'

'You are right,' Francesca said. 'But first we must cover her.' She took the child, laid her on the table, and wrapped her in two dish towels. Then she poured milk into a small pot and held it over the fire until it was warm. 'Here is the final proof that this is not a child of the Devil,' she said.

Georgette peered into the pot. 'I know,' she said. 'If this were the Devil's child, the milk would have curdled.' Christine put her hand over her mouth so they wouldn't see her smiling.

Francesca poured the milk into a cup and held it to the baby's mouth. When Georgette saw that the baby, who had until that moment not uttered a sound, made gurgling noises and swallowed a little of it, she clapped her hands. Then she began to cry again.

'You must stop that,' Francesca said.

The rags that had covered the baby lay on the floor. Christine bent down to retrieve them and several small bell-shaped objects, hidden in the folds of the cloth, fell into her hand. She held them up for her mother to see. Goblin, who had been lying at her feet, stood up and growled.

'Now I know what the strange smell is,' Francesca said. 'Those are the seed pods of a henbane plant.'

'Isn't henbane one of the poisonous plants you say you'll never grow in your garden?'

'That is so. Henbane is the Devil's plant. Whoever left this child in the palace gardens certainly knew that.'

Georgette peered at the seed pods and sniffled. 'Ugh!' she said. 'They smell awful.'

'Do not breath too deeply, or you will become drowsy,' Francesca warned. Georgette backed away.

'Is that why this poor child hasn't cried or moved around?' Christine asked.

'I am sure of it,' Francesca said. 'Henbane can dull your senses. Or worse. But look! She is beginning to stir now.'

It was true. The baby seemed to be fully awake.

'Who would do this terrible thing to a child?' Georgette asked.

'That's what I'm going to find out,' Christine said. 'But first we have to make her comfortable and see that she is fed.' She gave the baby another drink of milk.

Francesca dipped a cloth into a pail of water, wrung it out, and gently rubbed the child's face with it until the black mark was nearly gone. Then she went upstairs and came back down with two blankets. With one of these she lined a large basket. She drew the basket close to the fireplace, placed the baby in it, and covered her with the other blanket. Rocking the basket gently, she hummed a soft tune until the child fell asleep.

When the children came home from school, they were astonished to see their mother, grandmother, and hired girl hovering over a sleeping baby.

'Where did *that* come from?' Thomas asked.

Christine wondered how to explain. Marie, who was fifteen, disliked anything out of the ordinary, and she would certainly object to having a strange baby in the house. Twelve-year-old Jean, on the other hand, would probably treat the baby with all the compassion Marie lacked; while Thomas, who was eleven, would be more interested in knowing the gruesome details of what had been done to the child. Lisabetta, Christine's eight-year-old niece, would be sad when she learned the baby had been abandoned. She lived with Christine's family because her mother was dead and her father had gone back to Italy. She felt abandoned, too.

Francesca put her finger to her lips and motioned for the children to come closer. They tiptoed over and peered into the basket.

Thomas looked at his mother and said, 'You're always bringing strange people home. But why a baby?'

'She was left in the palace gardens.'

'All by herself?' Lisabetta asked.

'Yes.'

'Whose baby is it?' Marie asked in a whisper.

'I don't know.'

'Why doesn't she have any hair?' Thomas asked. 'And what are those sores?'

'Someone shaved her head.'

'And starved her. And put black grease on her face,' Francesca said, her voice rising in anger.

The baby woke up and stared at them. 'Can I pick her up?' Jean asked.

Francesca lifted the baby out of the basket and placed her in the boy's arms.

Lisabetta reached out and touched the child's cheek gently with her finger. 'Who would do such bad things to a baby? And then leave her all alone?' she asked. 'Didn't they know that a baby left all alone could die?'

Georgette started to cry.

'What's wrong with her?' Thomas asked.

'Don't tell them what I did!' Georgette blubbered through her tears.

'What's she talking about?' Jean asked.

Christine pushed Georgette down on to the bench, picked up the cup of wine and valerian, and made her drink. 'I'll never tell anyone, Georgette,' she said. 'My mother won't, either. But if you don't stop crying, you'll have to tell them yourself.'

Georgette wiped her eyes and sat up straight.

'Where did you get the idea that this could be a child of the Devil?'

'It's all the talk of witches and sorcery.'

'I see,' Christine said. 'I suppose you think the Duchess of Orléans is a sorceress. I suppose you think she's bewitched the king and made him lose his mind. Don't you realize that because people believe such rubbish, someone finding this baby in the palace gardens might have done exactly what you were about to do with her. Superstition! That's what is causing all the trouble around here.'

Her voice rose, and Georgette shrank away from her.

Francesca stood by the fireplace, hanging her head. 'I'm talking to you as well as Georgette, Mama,' Christine called out to her.

'I know you are, *Cristina*. But that is not fair. I knew right away this was not the Devil's child.'

'So you did. I'll give you credit for that. But now you must rid yourself of your foolish beliefs. Like the one about the Duchess of Orléans being a sorceress.'

'How else could the king go mad?'

'That's just what the people who are slandering her want everyone to think.' Christine went to Jean and took the baby from his arms. 'One of those slanderers left this child in the palace gardens so the duchess would be blamed.'

'Valentina's father is a sorcerer, *Cristina*. She could have learned from him.'

'Nonsense.'

Everyone gathered around and looked at the baby, who had fallen asleep in Christine's arms. 'The Duchess of Orléans is not a sorceress. It's all slander,' Christine said. 'Until now, the slander has not gone beyond mere words to defame her. But now someone has taken it further and nearly caused the death of an innocent child.' She rocked the sleeping baby back and forth.

'It was a monstrous act, and I intend to find out who did it,' she said.

THREE

Of all the women, Madame the Duchess of Orléans was the one whose presence was the most agreeable to the king. He called her his beloved sister and went to see her every day. Many people misinterpreted this predilection. Their suspicions, which seemed to me not at all justified, were based on the fact that in Lombardy, the duchess's homeland, there were more poisons and sorcerers than in any other country.

The Monk of Saint-Denis, *Chronique du Religieux de Saint-Denis, contenant le règne de Charles VI de 1380 à 1422*

Early the next morning, Christine walked up the rue Saint-Antoine, went around the Hôtel Saint-Pol to a side street, and entered the palace gardens. As she approached the stockade where the king's famous lions were kept, a boy ran out and grabbed her hand.

'Come in and talk to the real lions!'

'Not today, Renaut,' she said, laughing and remembering the time he'd caught her swearing at the stone lion on top of a pillar in the courtyard of the queen's residence.

The boy looked disappointed, but he brightened when she said, 'Simon told me you're doing a good job with those lions.'

'Just like my aunt,' he said.

Several years earlier, a deaf girl, Loyse, had been the lion-keeper's assistant. Thanks to Christine, she'd been admitted into the queen's entourage, and her nephew, Renaut, had decided he wanted to take her place in the lions' stockade. Simon, the *portier* at the entrance to the queen's residence, had persuaded Gilet, the old lion-keeper, to let him do this, and the boy had been there ever since.

Gilet himself emerged from the stockade and tousled Renaut's tawny hair. 'He's a real treasure, now that he's learned not to make a lot of noise and frighten the lions,' he said.

'Did you happen to see anyone pass by here yesterday carrying a baby?' Christine asked.

'Many people come to see the lions. Too many. The palace should be more closely guarded. But no, I didn't see anyone with a baby yesterday.'

'I saw someone!' Renaut cried. 'I saw a woman with something under her cloak. It could have been a baby.'

'What makes you think that?'

'The lions got excited. They smelled something.'

Gilet laughed and tousled the boy's hair some more. 'He has a great imagination,' he said.

'The lions don't imagine things,' Renaut said.

Christine watched the boy and the old man go back into the stockade and continued on through the gardens. It was a warm day, and she'd left her cloak at home, as had a number of other people who'd come out of the palace complex to enjoy the fresh air. Ladies in fur-lined *houppelandes* meandered along the graveled paths, their long skirts rustling over the stones, and men in tight-fitting hose and brocaded jackets with padded shoulders tossed their heads to draw attention to the peacock feathers in their hats. They wore *poulaines*, the latest fashion in shoes, and they swore as the long, pointed tips caught on the thorny branches of leafless rose bushes spilling out of the planting beds. Wanting to avoid these people, Christine stepped away from the paths and walked across grassy lawns to watch gardeners setting out grape vines and digging holes for young cherry trees and new rose bushes.

A boy bringing plants in a large wheelbarrow came toward her. 'What do you have there?' she asked.

The boy pointed to a plant with leaves shaped like arrows. 'That's cuckoopint,' he said, giggling. 'And there's lady's-mantle, oxlip, wallflower, and hawkweed. Aren't those names silly?'

She laughed and continued on. A yellow butterfly with black spots on its wings rested briefly on the handle of a shovel that one of the gardeners had left beside the path, and a white cat from the palace kitchens crept up to a sparrow hopping across the lawn. She clapped her hands. The cat looked at her reproachfully with large green eyes and slunk away. A bee circled her head, and the sparrow uttered soft chirps as it bounced through the grass, unaware that it had been saved from a gruesome death.

A blood-curdling shriek rang out. The gardeners jumped to their

feet, scattering grapevines and rose bushes and colliding with the
boy pushing the wheelbarrow, who cried out as all his plants tumbled
on to the grass. Cooks emerged from the palace kitchen, grooms
ran out of the stables, and the keepers of the hounds rushed away
from the kennels, followed by dogs whose pens they'd forgotten to
close. Everyone converged on a spot near the palace where the king
stood tearing at his hair and screaming, 'It's going to happen again!
Someone is pricking me with the point of a sword!'

'He thinks he's about to have another of his attacks,' said one of
the gardeners. 'I remember the last time this happened.'

'I was here,' said a cook. 'I was standing right on this spot. He
ran out of the palace and fell to his knees and beat his head on the
ground. His brother yelled at him. "You're Charles, King of France.
Kings don't act like that." And do you know what the king said then?'

'I know,' said the boy with the wheelbarrow. 'I heard him say it,
plain as day. "My name isn't Charles. My name is George." Can
you imagine that?'

'And it got worse,' the cook said. 'He pulled his *houppelande*
up to his neck and tore it in two. What a disgrace! The King of
France standing there in his undershirt and *braies*!'

'And he started screaming, "Don't touch me. I'm made of glass.
I'll break,"' said the first gardener. 'The queen came and tried to
tell him she was his wife, the mother of his children. "No!" he
cried. "I don't know who you are. I don't have any children." He
lashed out at her with his fists, and his chamberlains had to grab
his arms and hold them behind his back. They sent for the Duchess
of Orléans. She was able to calm him and get him to go back into
the palace. That attack lasted for many months.'

'The sorceress!' exclaimed the cook. 'She puts spells on him.
She's the only one who can take the spells away.'

A murmur of excitement ran through the crowd. Everyone was
waiting for the king to go mad again. But he didn't. He just stood
there with tears running down his face. His fool, Hennequin, ran to
him and pranced around, laughing and waving his arms. Charles
looked at him sadly. Hennequin gave up, sat down on the ground
with his head in his hands, and said, 'I'm a poor fool.'

The king said, 'I'm the poor fool, not you.'

The Duke of Burgundy came out of the palace, stepping gingerly
over the path so as not to dirty his gold-trimmed black velvet *houppelande*, and behind him came the Duke and Duchess of Orléans.

Valentina stretched out her arms and said gently, 'Come, Sire. You must go inside now.' He grasped her hand and followed her into the palace.

Christine sat on a bench and listened to everyone talk about Valentina. 'Send her back to Italy!' some said. 'Back to her father, back to the Viper of Milan,' said others. They proceeded to tell stories they'd heard about her family in Lombardy, the notorious Visconti, ruthless tyrants notorious for their greed and cruelty. They all agreed that with such a family, Valentina had to be a danger to the king. After all, her father had murdered his own uncle, so there was no end to the evil his daughter could do.

Christine knew that much of what people said about the Visconti family was true, but she couldn't believe the same of Valentina. As far as she could tell, the Duchess of Orléans was incapable of evil. If anyone was guilty, it was her husband. She was fond of Louis, whom she'd known since her childhood, but her feelings about him were variable. He was charming, learned, and eloquent, but at the same time unpredictable and sly, driven by his desire for money and power and the need to seduce any woman he met. She'd always been surprised that of the two brothers, Charles was the one who'd gone mad.

She was roused from her thoughts when she heard Queen Isabeau, surrounded by her ladies-in-waiting, come out of the palace. 'He has been so well lately,' the queen cried. 'Now he thinks he will have another attack. Oh, I can't bear it!' she wept.

Isabeau's ladies fluttered around, trying to comfort her. Marguerite de Germonville, loud and bossy, ordered the others to step back and give the queen room to breathe. No one obeyed. Little Catherine de Villiers pressed even closer, twittering like a bird. 'You don't know that it will happen,' she said. 'It's just that he fears it so much.'

Old Jeanne de la Tour said, 'I'm sure it won't happen. I feel it in my bones.' Symonne du Mesnil, younger than the others, nodded in agreement. Madame de Malicorne, who carried the queen's little daughter, grasped the baby's tiny hand and waved it in front of the queen's eyes, which made Isabeau smile. She took a deep breath and stood tall. 'I will be brave,' she said.

The queen's two fools, Guillaume and Jeannine, bounced up and down, clapping their hands. Guillaume's bald head glistened in the sunlight. 'You *are* brave,' he shouted. 'The bravest woman in the world.' The queen's minstrel, Gracieuse Allegre, played a joyful melody on her lute, and the queen's two mutes, Collette and Loyse, nodded their heads as though they could hear the music. Christine was glad to see that Loyse, the young woman who'd once lived with the king's lions, was happy.

The queen's dwarf, Alips, came to Christine's side. 'It's so hard for her,' she said. 'The king has been kind to her lately. Now she's afraid he's going to reject her again.'

'Did she see that it was Valentina who quieted him just now?'

'I don't know. I hope not. The Duchess of Burgundy tells her she should hate Valentina for being able to do that.'

Christine had seen this herself, because she often worked as a scribe for the queen, and she'd been with her when Duke Philip of Burgundy's arrogant and power-hungry wife, Margaret of Flanders, had poured forth her malicious lies.

'Valentina hasn't bewitched the king,' Alips said. 'She hasn't tried to seduce him, either, no matter what that woman says. No one knows why he calls for her all the time. Valentina laments this. Her dwarf, Jacopo, tells me all about it.'

'Her dwarf? I haven't seen him.'

'You will. He's quite a good-looking little man.'

Christine noticed that as Alips turned away to go back to the queen, she was blushing.

Before Isabeau and her entourage returned to the palace, Madame de Malicorne handed the queen's baby to two nursemaids. 'Keep her out in the fresh air a little longer,' she said.

The nursemaids carried a golden crib lined with satin cloth, and into this they placed the child. Then they walked on, carrying the crib between them. Christine followed them as they walked along the garden paths and meandered on to the lawns, stepping carefully around wheelbarrows, shovels, and scattered plants. They talked softly to each other, and the murmur of their voices mingled with the gentle rustle of their gowns sweeping over the gravel paths and the sighing of the breezes that shook the newly budded branches of the trees. When they came to a little fishpond where three ducks floated lazily on sunlit water, they set the crib on the ground. One of them had brought a piece of bread that she ripped into small pieces and threw into the water. The ducks flapped their wings and dove for the bread, causing the nursemaids to laugh and turn their backs to the little princess, who had fallen asleep.

This must be the place where the fools found the baby, Christine thought. *How easy it would be to remove one baby from its crib and substitute another.* She silently willed the nurses to turn around and pay attention to their precious charge, and she breathed a sigh of relief when they picked up the crib and headed back to the palace.

Beside the pond stood a grove of young pines. Christine thought she heard a voice call out, and she walked away quickly toward the lions' stockade, planning to tell the lion-keeper to call the guards because someone was hiding in the trees. Then she told herself not to be a coward, went back, and peered into the grove.

A young woman leaned against one of the pines. Her long blond hair hung loose over her shoulders, and her blue gown, tattered and covered with blood, barely covered her body. She looked at Christine and tried to say something, but choked before she could get the words out.

Christine stepped into the grove. With a feeble motion of her hand, the woman waved her away.

'I want to help you,' Christine said.

'No one can help me,' the woman rasped. She coughed, clutched the tree, and took a deep breath. 'Just tell me that the queen's baby will be safe.'

Stunned, Christine stared at her for a moment. Then she realized why the woman was there.

'She'll be safe,' she said.

'I am glad,' the woman said. She fell to the ground. Dead.

FOUR

If you put a laurel branch above a cradle where a frightened baby is being nursed, the child will be freed from fear.

Picatrix, ninth-century Arabic book on magic, translated into Spanish and Latin in 1256

'I told you not to go to the palace!' Francesca cried the next morning when Christine told her about the dead woman. She took the ladle out of a pot of beef stew she was stirring over the fire and shook it at Christine.

'You know I need the work,' Christine said. She sat on a bench, rocking the baby in the cradle her mother had made from an old basket and looking up at the ceiling.

'And find dead people all the time!'

'Not all the time.'

'What were you doing in the gardens?'

'I wanted to see the place where the fools found this child.' She pointed to the ceiling. 'Why is that branch hanging there?'

'It is not just any branch. It is laurel. The baby was crying. The laurel calms her.'

'Another of your superstitions.'

'It works. She is not crying now, is she?' Francesca lifted the pot off the pothook and set it down on the table with a bang. 'What is this about fools?'

'Didn't I tell you? The Duke of Orléans's fools found this child. They asked me to bring her home to you.'

'They do not know me!'

'They know about mothers. They said you would love her.'

Francesca thrust the ladle back into the pot and stirred so furiously that some of the stew splashed on to the table. 'Why do you not bring these fools home, along with all the other misfits you befriend?'

'You'd like these fools, Mama.'

'I do not want to know any fools!'

'Is that so? It seems to me there are fools everywhere these days.'

Francesca sighed. 'There is no arguing with you, *Cristina*. You are just like your father.' She sat down beside her daughter. 'You have told me how the child was found. Now tell me, what was the dead woman doing in the palace gardens?'

'She'd come to see whether the queen's baby was safe. She asked me about it, just before she died.'

Francesca rocked the makeshift cradle. 'Do you think she was the one who left this poor child there?'

'Who else could it have been?' Christine said.

'But why was she killed?'

'All I know is that someone stabbed her, probably in the street. Amazingly, before she died she managed to make her way to the spot where she'd left the child. The palace guards weren't able to identify her, so they took her to the morgue at the Châtelet.'

Francesca lifted the baby from the basket and hugged her. 'I am glad you were able to save this child,' she said. 'But you must stop bringing strange people home, *Cristina*.'

'I suppose you're thinking of Marion,' Christine said, referring to the friend Francesca objected to because she was a prostitute. Or, *had been* a prostitute; at least that was what she hoped her mother believed.

'Not just Marion. What about the midwife with the pockmarked face?'

'She helped me save a woman from burning at the stake.'

'And the deaf girl, the lion-keeper's assistant.'

'You know you loved Loyse. You worked hard to make her presentable so I could take her to the queen.'

Francesca held the baby up and studied her. 'She is putting on weight.'

'She's only been here a day.' Christine touched the baby's face. Hardly a trace of black grease remained. 'Don't change the subject, Mama. What about someone *you* brought home? What about Klara?'

Christine grimaced as she thought of the girl whose elderly husband had disappeared and who'd turned her household upside down with her petulant ways before the man came back to claim her.

Francesca sighed. 'Perhaps I should not have done that. But everything turned out all right in the end, did it not? And you got to keep the recipes and other things he wrote for her.'

'I wouldn't be surprised to find she's still making life miserable for poor Martin du Bois.'

'You do not know. People change.' Francesca handed the baby to Christine, picked up a knife, and began to cut crosses into the bottoms of some little cabbages.

'Why do you do that?' Christine asked.

'So any demons hiding in the leaves can get out before we eat them.'

Christine hid her face in her hands, then looked up as Georgette burst into the room with a pot of milk from the market. 'We already have milk,' Francesca cried. 'Why did you buy more?'

'We have to be sure there's enough,' Georgette said as she put the milk on the table. She sat down beside Christine, gazed at the baby, and started to cry. Christine put her arms around her.

'You didn't drop her into the fire, Georgette. You didn't know what you were doing, and I stopped you.' Christine looked at her mother. 'You see what comes of having those ridiculous superstitions?'

'Do not look at me, *Cristina*. I knew this was not the Devil's baby.'

'I'm sorry. I should have had more confidence in you. The duke's fools did.'

Francesca sniffed.

'What about the duke's fools?' Georgette asked.

'They're the ones who found this baby,' Christine said.

'Robin knows those fools. He thinks they aren't foolish at all. At least, not like a lot of other people at the palace.'

Robin is smart, Christine thought. *She's lucky to have found him.*

Georgette wiped her eyes. 'Can I hold her?' she asked.

Very carefully, Christine transferred the baby to Georgette's outstretched arms. The girl held the child carefully and started to cry again, which made the baby cry, too. 'Poor little thing,' Georgette whispered through her tears. 'You miss your mother.'

Francesca took the baby and held her under the laurel branch. The crying stopped. 'You see. It works,' she said.

Christine sighed, went to the pot on the table, ladled some of the stew into a bowl, and started to eat it.

'Why are you eating that now?' Francesca asked.

'Because I'm going to find out who the woman who died in the palace gardens was, and I may not be home in time for dinner.'

Francesca threw up her hands. 'You will be putting yourself in danger!'

Christine was out the door before her mother could say another word.

FIVE

If a prostitute has a body strong enough to do evil and suffer numerous blows and other misfortunes, she might use it to earn her living in a better way.

Christine de Pizan, *Le Livre des Trois Vertus*, 1405

She went down the rue Saint-Antoine to the place de Grève, the open space beside the Seine where the wine boats docked, and looked for Marion, who often went there to taste the wine criers' offerings. Marion knew all the street people in Paris, and Christine thought she might be able to identify the woman who'd died in the palace gardens. But Marion was nowhere in sight. She shook her head at the criers in their colorful breeches and jerkins and walked down to the rue de l'Arbre Sec, where she recoiled when she saw the bones of a thief hanging over her head; she'd forgotten about the wooden gallows standing at the crossing of that street and the rue Saint-Honoré. The bones had long since been plucked clean by crows, but that didn't make them any less revolting. She hurried past.

Marion lived in a room she rented in a small house farther down the rue Saint-Honoré. Unfortunately, the house was owned by Henri Le Picart, a man Christine didn't want to see. She cursed her luck as she turned a corner and found him standing in the middle of the street, looking as though he'd been expecting her.

'Ah, Christine,' he said. 'What brings you here?'

'Why bother to ask? You always know everything.'

Henri laughed. 'I can guess. You've come to see your friend Marion.' He was a small man with a little black beard who always wore a plain black cape with a long black hood and an ermine collar. He looked austere, but Christine knew that under the cape he would be wearing an elegantly embroidered jacket or a velvet *houppelande* trimmed with gold. Henri was a mystery, a man of contradictions. In spite of the fact that he'd once saved her life, she disliked and distrusted him.

'Is Marion home?' she asked.

'I think so. I'll come with you to see.'

'You will not!'

'I know what you're up to, Christine. I know about the dead woman in the palace gardens.'

Christine held her breath. *Does he know about the baby, too?*

'As usual, you can't let well enough alone. Now you're going to try to find out who the woman was, and you're going to involve Marion in some foolhardy scheme.'

She was angry, but at the same time relieved because he hadn't mentioned the baby.

'I suppose you think no woman should do anything other than stay home with her cooking and sewing, as my mother says.'

'That's exactly what I think.'

'You're wrong, Henri.' She turned and marched away to the house where Marion lived.

She found her friend seated at a table covered with pins, needles, thimbles, scissors, and scraps of cloth. For years Christine had tried to get Marion to change her profession, and now she had; she'd become a successful embroiderer. Because she'd been a prostitute, she would never be accepted into the needleworkers' guild, but that didn't bother her. She had many customers, including the queen, who bought her belts and purses for herself and her ladies. The royal embroiderers were not pleased.

Bolts of velvet, satin, and linen cloth – purple, creamy white, sage green, azure blue, and rusty red – lay at Marion's feet, and skeins of thread in all the colors of the rainbow spilled from a work basket on to the floor. But Marion herself, with her flaming red hair bound by glittering beads and her gown of dark rose pink embroidered with gold dragons and green parrots, was the most colorful object in the room. *Or perhaps the second most colorful object,* Christine thought when she heard a loud squawk and looked up to see a green parrot with a bright red beak and red-rimmed eyes looking at her from the top of a green cage.

'That's Babil,' Marion said.

'I never expected to see you with a pet.'

'I get lonely, now that I don't go to the brothel every day.' Marion held up her wrist, and the bird flew down and perched on it. 'He keeps me company.' Babil nodded his head and strode up and down her arm, talking to himself.

'How do you get any work done?'

'I manage.' Marion held up a blue belt embroidered with gold acorns. 'For the queen,' she said. 'She thinks the acorns will protect her in a thunderstorm.'

Christine smiled. It was well known that Queen Isabeau was terrified of thunder and lightning. She was almost as superstitious as Francesca. Alips, her dwarf, understood, and she humored the queen by bringing her whatever she needed to allay her fears – acorns to put on the windowsill, bells to ring, candles to light. She'd even sit with her and count the claps of thunder to see whether they foretold good or bad luck.

'The belt is lovely. Perhaps you'll make one for me,' Christine said.

'I already have,' Marion said as she reached into a basket and brought out another belt, this one embroidered with white dogs wearing gold collars.

Christine laughed. 'Goblin will like it,' she said. Then she remembered what she'd come for. 'I need your help, Marion.'

'Something to do with the palace again?'

'Yes. Have you heard about the woman who was murdered in the gardens?'

'No. What happened?'

'I'm going to tell you, but you have to keep it a secret. Especially from Henri. I met him outside, and, as usual, he started ordering me around.'

Marion wrinkled her nose. 'He does that to me, too. But sometimes he's useful. He got several of my friends out of the Châtelet when they'd been arrested for wearing gold belts.'

'I suppose the man has a good side,' Christine said. 'But I don't trust him. He was a friend of my father's, and Papa got into trouble because of some of his schemes.'

'Have you seen his house? There are weird animals carved on the door. Maybe he's a magician.'

Christine pondered this. Henri always seemed to know everything that went on, and he even seemed to be able to predict what would happen in the future. *Perhaps he really does have crystal balls and magic mirrors,* she thought. Then she realized she was thinking like her mother. 'There are more important things to discuss,' she said.

Marion stroked Babil's head. 'Tell me.'

'Some of the Duke of Orléans's fools discovered a baby in the palace gardens. Its head was shaved, and its face had been discolored with black grease.'

'God's teeth! Who would do that to a child?'

'Someone who knew everyone would think it was the Devil's child. The fools understood that, and they knew the Duchess of Orléans would be blamed. They took the baby away and asked me to take it home to my mother before anyone else could find it.'

Marion laughed so hard, she had to hold her sides, upending Babil, who squawked and flew back to his cage. 'You took a baby that looked like the Devil's child home to your mother?' Tears ran down her cheeks. 'I wish I could have seen her face!'

Christine laughed, too. Then she said, 'I'm sorry to disappoint you, Marion, but my mother didn't scream or faint dead away. Instead, she realized right away what had happened.'

'I don't believe it,' Marion said, wiping her eyes.

'It's true. It was Georgette who was fooled. She would have dropped the baby into the fire.'

'By saints Afra and Thaïs!'

'I stopped her before she could do it.'

Marion held up her arm and Babil flew back down. 'So what has this to do with the murdered woman?'

'I think she may have been the child's mother.'

'What mother would do that to a child?'

'I don't think she knew what she was doing. There were henbane seed pods in the baby's rags. My mother says that when henbane is burned, the smoke dulls the senses. I think that's what happened to her; someone drugged her and got her to starve the child, disfigure its face with black grease, and take it to the palace gardens. The duke's fools think it was meant to be substituted for the queen's baby.'

'And everyone would assume Valentina had done it.'

'Exactly.'

'But what has this to do with me?' Marion picked up the belt she was working on and resumed her needlework. Babil gurgled and squawked and tried to cling to her arm, then flew back to his perch when she didn't pay attention to him.

'No one at the palace had ever seen this woman before,' Christine said. 'You know so many people, I thought that – if you saw the body – you might be able to tell me who she was. She's at the morgue at the Châtelet.'

Marion frowned. 'I hate to go anywhere near the prison. Too many of my friends have been in there. But if it will help discover who did such a terrible thing to a baby, I'll do it.' She laid aside the belt, got up, and put on her crimson cloak.

SIX

There is no part of the body that does not smell of putrefaction.

Georges Chastellain (c. 1405 or c. 1415–1475),
Le Pas de la Mort, 1450

Christine, too, dreaded going to the Châtelet. The huge, fortress-like prison standing on the bank of the Seine near the Grand Pont was bad enough in itself, but what surrounded it was even worse, for it was a neighborhood of slaughterhouses, fishmongers' establishments, and butchers' shops. Even the cheerful pealing of the bells at the church of Saint-Jacques-la-Boucherie, the parish church of the butchers, couldn't soften the effects of sickening odors, gruesome sights, and hideous sounds. The cries of terrified animals rang out, rivers of blood flowed into the Seine, and the sour smell of rotting meat and decaying fish filled the air. Hooves, horns, and skins of slaughtered animals lay in piles outside the shops of the skinners and tanners, stray dogs wandered in and out of open doors, rats scurried into corners, and beggars searched through piles of garbage. To add to her loathing of the place, Christine had painful memories of the times when she'd visited the dank cell of a young woman who'd been wrongly accused of poisoning her husband. But she was determined to learn the identity of the murdered woman in the palace gardens, and since the morgue was at the prison, that was where she had to go.

Marion tugged on her sleeve. 'Hurry,' she said. 'Let's get this over with.' As they tried to push their way through the crowds on the rue Saint-Denis, an old woman stopped in the middle of the street and blocked their way. She put her hands on her hips and stared at Marion's crimson cloak, bright red hair, and strands of shiny beads. 'Strumpet!' she cried.

'*Va te faire foutre!*' Marion shot back as she raised the fool's finger. Christine was glad to see that her friend hadn't become completely respectable.

A mob of ragged boys rushed by, throwing stones at rats, and a group of beggars pranced up to Christine and asked why such a fine lady would be walking with a prostitute. One of the beggars, who wore dirty bandages on his feet, tugged on her cloak. 'Spare a coin to get me some shoes?' he pleaded.

'Get lost, Huguet,' Marion said. 'I know you've got shoes hidden in that alley over there.' She took Christine's hand and hurried her along to the vaulted passageway that ran underneath the prison and came out at the Grand Pont. The stench in this passageway was terrible, for it abutted a room where the bodies of people who'd drowned in the Seine or had been murdered in the street were laid out so friends or family members could come to identify them. Later, those that were not claimed would be taken away by the sisters of the nearby Hôpital de Saint-Catherine, to be washed, covered with shrouds, and carried to the cemetery of the Innocents and dumped into mass graves.

Two men wearing short jackets and *poulaines* with very long points stood in the passageway, taking turns peering into this room through a little hole in the wall. They nudged each other, laughing and making jokes. Marion tapped one of them on the shoulder. 'What's so funny?'

The man turned. 'Who are you to ask?'

Marion, who was already taller than either of the men, drew herself up to her full height and towered over them. 'Who are you to disrespect the dead?' She shoved them out of the way and looked through the hole.

'*Dieu!*' She drew back and stepped on the points of the men's shoes.

'*Putain,*' one said.

'*Salope,*' said the other. Marion turned on them so fiercely, they hung their heads and snuck away.

'What did you see?' Christine asked.

'Look for yourself.'

Christine held her nose, peered through the opening, and saw five nude bodies laid out on the floor with their clothes hanging on poles beside them. Two were men she thought must have drowned, for they were bloated, their eyes bulged, and their tongues dangled from their mouths. Two other men had been strangled. And right under the window lay a woman with long blond hair. Her blood-stained gown hung on a pole next to her, grisly evidence that she'd been stabbed. It was the woman she'd seen in the palace gardens.

She stepped back. 'Do you know her?'

'I do,' Marion said. 'Poor soul. She didn't deserve to die like that.'

'Who is she?'

'At the brothel we called her Fleur.'

'Could she have had a baby, about a year old?'

'Fleur never had a child. Are you thinking she's the one who left the baby in the palace gardens?'

'I'm sure she did.'

A fat man with a red face approached them. 'Let's get out of here,' Marion said.

They started to walk away, but the man called after them, 'Don't you recognize me?'

'Is he a friend of yours?' Marion asked Christine.

Christine thought she recognized the voice. She turned and looked at the man.

'You came to visit a young woman in the prison, several years ago,' he said. 'I was her guard.'

Then Christine remembered. 'How could I forget you, Hutin?'
she said. 'You were so kind to Alix de Clairy.'

'How could one not be kind to such a gentle lady?'

'More than kind,' Christine said. 'If it hadn't been for you, she'd
have burned at the stake.'

Hutin held up his hand.

'You saved someone else, too. Her sister, the deaf girl who was
left to die in her place.'

Hutin looked around fearfully. 'We must not speak of it,' he
whispered.

'I won't mention it again. But I want you to know, the sister is
now in the queen's entourage. The queen is very fond of her.'

'I'm glad,' Hutin said in a low voice. He pointed to the peephole
in the wall. 'Was the dead woman in there a friend of yours?'

Marion answered. 'I've known her for many years. She had a
hard life, and she didn't deserve to die like that.'

'No one deserves to die like that,' Hutin said. 'But we see so
many people here who have died unfairly. And I have to deal with
them.'

'Are you no longer a guard?' Christine asked.

'No. Now I receive the bodies you see in there. It's a horrible
task. And there are so many. Five were brought in just this morning.
Poor souls. Drowned or murdered in the street. Except for your
friend. She was found in the gardens of the Hôtel Saint-Pol. No
one at the palace recognized her, so they brought her here.' He
reached into his sleeve and took out something wrapped in a cloth.
'I found this clutched in her hand,' he said as he carefully uncovered
an object that exuded a foul smell and held it up.

Christine gasped, remembering the henbane seed pods she'd found
in the baby's rags.

Marion recognized it, too. 'There was an old woman at my brothel
who used to draw worms out of people's teeth by burning that,' she
said.

Christine couldn't help smiling. 'My mother believes that, too,
at least the part about the worms,' she said. 'It's another of her
ridiculous superstitions.'

'I'm not so sure it's just a superstition,' Hutin said. 'Once when
I had a toothache henbane smoke really did cure it.' He looked
around to make sure no one was listening. 'Of course, the person
who burned the henbane was a witch,' he whispered.

'I'm sure she was,' Marion said. 'That's a dangerous herb. The smell can make you drowsy. It can even kill you if you get enough of it.'

'My mother won't grow it in her garden,' Christine said.

'I wonder whether she knows it's burned in bathhouses, to rouse the clients' passions,' Marion mused.

'I doubt it,' Christine said.

'Then I'll have to tell her.'

'Don't you dare!' Christine said.

Some of the guards from the prison were coming through the passageway. Hutin bowed slightly and hurried off.

Marion peered through the opening in the wall again, stepped away, and bowed her head. 'We shouldn't be joking while poor Fleur is lying there.' She looked at Christine with tears in her eyes. 'Someone murdered her, stabbed her in the most brutal way. She didn't deserve that.' She put her hand on Christine's sleeve and said, 'Please, for me, find out who did it.'

'I'll try,' Christine promised. 'For all of us.'

SEVEN

If the child of a woman that is suspected to be a witch, be lacking or gone from hir; it is to be presumed, that she hath sacrificed it to the divell: except she can proove the negative or contrarie.

Reginald Scot (c. 1538–1599),
The Discoverie of Witchcraft, 1584

'Did you find out who this child belongs to?' Francesca wanted to know. The family had finished supper, and she sat at the kitchen table holding the baby in her lap. Georgette hovered over her, every now and then sniffling and wiping her eyes. The child was wide awake, and each time she moved, Georgette reached out to prevent her from falling, although there was no chance of that in Francesca's firm grip.

'No. But I found out it wasn't the woman who was murdered in the palace gardens.'

'How did you discover that?' Francesca asked.

'I took Marion to see her body at the morgue.'

Francesca jumped up, shaking with anger. 'I cannot believe you went to the morgue! And with Marion, too! What were you thinking, *Cristina*?'

Christine took the baby so she wouldn't drop it. 'I thought Marion might know who the woman was, and I was right. The woman was a friend of hers.'

'Another prostitute!'

'Don't you remember? Marion's changed her profession.'

'Then she should not be associating with prostitutes any more!'

'That's beside the point. Marion told me that her friend had never had a child.'

'But to go to the morgue!'

'Surely you've been there yourself, Mama.'

'Never!' She fiddled with the strings of her apron. 'At least, not without something to protect me from the foul air. If you had told me where you were going, I would have given you a sprig of rue. Or some garlic.'

The children had come into the room. 'Why did you go to the morgue?' Jean asked.

'I found a woman who died, and I took Marion to the morgue because I thought she might know who she was.'

'You're always finding dead people,' Thomas said. 'Take me with you the next time you go to the morgue. I want to see some dead people, too.'

'Stupid boy.' Marie sniffed.

'If the mother isn't the woman at the morgue, then she's alive!' Georgette said. She took the baby from Christine and rocked her in her arms. 'She's out in the street right now, searching for this child. She's wandering through the city day and night, crying and wailing, beating her breast, begging everyone to tell her where her child has gone.'

'You can't know that,' Marie sniffed.

'It's even worse,' Georgette continued. 'People think the mother gave her child to the Devil. They're chasing her in the street. Look! They've caught her! They're beating her! They're going to kill her!'

'Stop that, Georgette! You'll drop the baby!' Christine cried.

Georgette sat down on the bench. 'I'm sorry. I seemed to see it all so clearly.'

'At least this child's mother isn't the woman who was murdered,' Marie said. 'That woman must have been killed for a good reason. Perhaps she was a prostitute.' She made a face.

'Not all prostitutes are bad,' Christine said. 'Have a little compassion, Marie.'

'Your mother is right, Marie,' Francesca said. 'Even her friend Marion has some good qualities.'

I must remember to make sure Marion doesn't tell Mama about henbane in bathhouses, Christine said to herself.

'Then she shouldn't be a prostitute,' Marie said. She turned to Jean. 'Don't you agree?'

Jean laughed. 'You're always telling me I'm too young to have opinions.'

Lisabetta tugged on Georgette's sleeve. 'I want to hold the baby.'

'Sit down first,' Georgette said. Lisabetta settled herself on the bench and held out her arms. Georgette carefully transferred the child into her lap. Christine sat down beside Lisabetta and looked at the baby. The little girl had been at her house for only a short time, but now she had a bit of color in her cheeks, and the sores on her shaved head were healing. She thought she could even see some hair growing back. Someone might have exchanged this child for the queen's little daughter, a child who had never known anything other than golden cribs, dozens of nursemaids, and stout, kindly Madame de Maucouvent, who was in charge of all the queen's children, to make sure she wanted for nothing. At the palace, Christine had seen the satin pillows, fleece blankets, silk bibs, silver rattles, jeweled bracelets, and all the other finery provided for the royal babies. Surely the child lying in Lisabetta's arms had never had a wet-nurse, fine linens, or a silver rattle. Perhaps she'd never even had a crib. Instead, she'd been starved and disfigured and left where she could have been found by some superstitious person who would throw her into a fire or kill her in some other vile way without ever realizing she was human.

'We have to find her mother,' Georgette said.

'Yes, we do,' Christine said.

Francesca went to the fireplace and stirred a pot of nuts she was cooking for a preserve. It was getting dark, and she had to squint to see what she was doing.

'Why did you start cooking that so late in the day, Mama?' Christine asked.

'I was so worried about you, running off after murderers. I did not know what else to do.' Her lips moved as she stared into the pot.

'What are you saying?'

'A miserere. I am making a preserve, and I am boiling the nuts for as long as it takes to say a miserere. That is what you told me it says on one of those pages you brought home to copy, the ones Martin du Bois wrote for his wife before he disappeared.'

'I'd forgotten that recipe.'

'Do you still have what he wrote?'

'I do. Martin told me his wife wouldn't be interested, so he left everything here.'

'Ugh. Klara,' Thomas said. 'I wish you hadn't brought her here, *grand-maman.*'

'That's unkind, Thomas,' Christine said. 'And anyway, Klara wasn't here for very long.'

'I hope I never see her again,' Thomas said.

Christine's feelings about Klara were not as damning as the children's, but she'd been just as happy when the girl's husband, who'd disappeared because his life was in danger, had taken her back to his own house. Even Francesca, who'd felt sorry for the girl, had been relieved when she left. She and Christine had feared they might have to put up with her forever.

'The next time you see Klara, she may be different,' Francesca said to Thomas. 'Marriage changes a person.'

'She wasn't so bad,' Georgette said.

'But her husband is old!' Marie exclaimed.

'That doesn't matter,' Christine said. 'Martin du Bois is a kind man. Don't forget, he saved Klara and her brother after the sack of Courtrai. He brought them home to France and raised them. How many men would have done that?'

'What would have happened if the soldiers had taken them?' Thomas wanted to know.

'They might have been killed, or sold as slaves,' Christine said, not mentioning some of the other horrible possibilities, such as rape and mutilation. The French had committed unspeakable atrocities in the Flemish city of Courtrai fourteen years earlier.

'It doesn't seem right that Martin du Bois made Klara marry him, just because he'd raised her. Did he think she owed him something?' Marie asked.

She has a point, Christine thought. But she was certain Martin du Bois really loved his young bride.

'It is too bad Klara does not want to read what Martin wrote for her,' Francesca said. 'She could learn how to be a good housewife.'

'I don't think Klara wants to be a good housewife,' Christine said, thinking there were some things in Martin's manuscript that the girl would resent, such as the admonitions about obeying her husband in everything.

'At least she could learn how long it is necessary to boil the nuts when you are making a preserve,' Francesca said, taking the pot off the fire.

'The next step is to stuff the nuts with ginger and cloves,' Georgette said. 'I heard you discussing this with Martin du Bois, the night he came to take Klara home.'

The children, bored with the conversation, sat by the fire playing with Goblin, while Georgette sat quietly gazing at the baby on Lisabetta's lap. 'Poor little girl,' she whispered to the child. 'What happened to your mother?'

The baby looked up at her and smiled, which made Georgette cry.

'You have to stop that, Georgette,' Christine said. 'You didn't do it.'

'But I almost did.' The girl sniffled. She took the baby from Lisabetta and held her close. 'I'll find your mother, to make up for it,' she whispered.

Christine heard. 'How are you going to do that?'

'I have an idea.' Georgette handed the baby back to Lisabetta and jumped up. 'I'll tell you about it tomorrow.' She went into the hall and put on her cloak.

Whatever can she have in mind? Christine wondered as she heard the door slam.

EIGHT

The Duchess of Orléans, Valentina, had a son, a beautiful child the same age as the dauphin, the king's son. One time these two children were playing together in the Duchess of Orléans's chamber and an apple full of poison was thrown on to the floor toward the dauphin so he would eat it. But, by the grace of God, he did not eat it. The duchess's own child ran after the apple and as soon as he got it he put it into his mouth and when he bit into it he was poisoned and he died; nothing could save him. Those who took care of the dauphin took him away, and he never came to the duchess's chamber again. This caused a great noise and murmuring throughout Paris and elsewhere, and it was said that if the duke did not take the duchess away from the king's court, the people would do it themselves and kill her. People said she had bewitched the king and she would poison him and his children.

Froissart, *Chroniques*, Livre IV, 1389–1400

A s she walked up the rue Saint-Antoine to the palace the next morning, Christine noticed that all around her people whispered and gesticulated, agitated and angry. Two young women stood in the center of the street gesturing to each other, so intent on what they were discussing, they didn't notice the onions and cabbages spilling out of their market baskets and rolling on the ground at their feet. They didn't even see a group of rowdy boys pick up some of the onions and run about throwing them at each other. Christine ducked as an onion flew past her head and sauntered over to the two women so she could hear what they were saying.

'How did she think she could get away with it?' one asked. She wore a brown kirtle over which she'd thrown a white apron that she'd forgotten to tie.

'People like that never think they'll get caught,' said the other, shaking her head so vigorously that her white hood fell over her eyes.

What on earth are they talking about? Christine wondered. A third woman, struggling with a large crate of chickens, stopped beside her. 'The Duchess of Orléans's little boy, Louis,' she said, as though she'd read Christine's thoughts. 'The one who died.'

'But that was last year!' Christine exclaimed.

'But now everyone knows *how* he died,' the woman said.

'We've always known how he died,' Christine said. 'He had a severe case of the flux. My own children suffered from it at the same time. There was an epidemic.' She shuddered as she remembered the terrible days when she and her mother had struggled to keep everyone calm in a house full of children who couldn't control their bowels. But they'd been lucky; they had all recovered. The duchess's son, under the care of two of the best doctors in Paris, had not.

The woman sneered. '*That's* not how the duchess's son died. His own mother killed him.'

Christine stared at the woman, thinking she was as mad as the king. The other two women moved closer.

'The poor nursemaids. The queen thought her little boy would like to play with his young cousin,' said the woman whose apron was askew. 'So they took the dauphin to the duchess's chambers and put the two children together on the floor.'

'They were nearly the same age, you know,' said the woman with the chickens. She'd set the crate on the ground, and the chickens stuck their heads through the slats and clucked as though they were taking part in the conversation.

'And then the duchess threw the apple.' The woman with the white hood finally tired of pulling it away from her eyes and took it off, letting her long brown hair spill over her shoulders, which made her look as though she'd just gotten out of bed. 'She threw it to the dauphin, but it rolled along the floor, and her own son ran after it. Before she could stop him, he took a big bite out of it. And he died.'

All three women laughed. 'Too bad the sorceress's other child didn't die. He was only a baby. I guess he was too small to eat an apple.'

Christine put her hand on the arm of the woman with the untidy apron and squeezed, hard. 'What are you talking about?'

The woman turned to her. 'What do you think we've been talking about? The poisoned apple the duchess wanted the dauphin to eat, of course.' She looked Christine up and down.

'What poisoned apple?' Christine asked.

'The duchess got some poison and put it in an apple. Where have you been?'

'The duchess is Italian, you know. All Italians carry poisons in their sleeves,' said the woman with the white hood.

Christine clenched her teeth.

'The duchess meant for the dauphin to eat it,' the woman continued, dangling the hood close to the ground, where it attracted a stray dog that tried to snatch it out of her hand. A tug of war ensued, until the dog gave up and ran away. The woman smoothed the hood with her hands and went on with the story. 'The duchess's own son ate it instead.' She laughed, and Christine resisted the inclination to slap her.

'Who told you this?'

'Why, everyone knows it,' said the woman with the skewed apron.

'*I* don't know it,' Christine said. *But I know where the rumor came from*, she thought, remembering what she knew about the Duchess of Burgundy. 'It's not true,' she said. 'I can tell you because I know the doctors who treated the duchess's son.' She really didn't, but her husband had known them, and that seemed close enough to the truth.

The women looked at her with what she hoped was a bit of respect.

'As I said before, the duchess's son, Louis, died of the flux. The doctors knew it. Many children died of it at that time.'

'Then why is everyone saying it was a poisoned apple?' asked the woman with the chickens.

'Because there are people who want everyone to believe the Duchess of Orléans is an evil person.'

'She *is* an evil person,' said the woman in the disordered apron. 'She caused the king to lose his mind.'

'She's a sorceress, like her father,' added the woman who'd almost lost her hood. 'He's down there in Italy making wax images and sticking pins into them so our king will die. Then his daughter can become queen of France.' She put the hood back on her head and stuffed her hair under it.

Christine marveled that the women had no sympathy at all for Valentina, who'd lost her son. She thought about all the rumors plaguing her; people said she'd brought poisons from Italy. They said she worked magic spells to take away the king's mind. They said she had a steel mirror she used to summon the Devil. And now they said she'd tried to poison the dauphin. If the fools hadn't rescued the baby in the palace gardens, everyone would have said she'd put it there. The hatred of Valentina was so strong, people would believe anything of her.

She'd had enough of the women's chatter. 'You know, don't you, that there are people in high places who want you to believe this lie?'

'What people?' asked the one with the messy apron.

Christine hesitated. The story about the poisoned apple had surely come from the Duchess of Burgundy, but she knew it would be dangerous for her, a commoner, to level accusations at a member of the nobility.

The three women were looking at her suspiciously. 'Who are you, anyway?'

'Someone who's tired of seeing women slandered.'

The woman with the chickens picked up the crate and was about to walk away when she suddenly turned and set the crate down again. 'I know what you mean,' she said. 'It's always us women who get blamed when something bad happens. I heard a preacher say we're bad because we're descended from Eve.'

'Do you believe that?' Christine asked.

'We can't contradict the men.'

'Try it sometime,' Christine said.

The woman with the untied apron grabbed the arm of the woman with the hood. 'Such talk! Let's get out of here before we find ourselves in a lot of trouble.'

The three women walked away. Christine called after them, 'At least *think* about what I've said.'

At the palace, she tried to concentrate on her copying, but even the fables of Aesop couldn't take her mind off Valentina's troubles. She hoped the duke's fools would come to distract her. But instead, she heard two chambermaids talking outside the door.

'First she bewitched the king, then she tried to kill his son,' one whispered.

'What will she do next?'

'Have you seen the steel mirror she has by her bed?'

'She looks into it at night.'

'That's how she works her spells. She looks into the mirror, and the Devil comes to her and tells her what to do. Make sure you don't look into it yourself.'

Christine got up and strode to the door, ready to lash out at the women. But they were gone. *At least they don't know about the baby in the gardens, so they can't accuse Valentina of that,* she thought.

She went to the open window of her room, looked out, and saw Louis, accompanied by the fools, walking with the king. Charles seemed calm until a large brown dog came running down the street and brushed against him. He shrank back and clutched at his brother.

She was about to turn away when she saw three people ride up to the royal residence. Duke Philip of Burgundy in a crimson-purple *houppelande* embroidered with gold sat tall and proud on a big black stallion, and beside him, looking very small and uncomfortable on a huge white destrier, was his son, Count Jean of Nevers, wearing a short pleated black *pourpoint* that did not flatter his ungainly, almost dwarf-like body. The Duchess of Burgundy, her long, austere face frowning beneath an enormous jeweled and padded headdress, rode behind them on a little palfrey that was nearly hidden under her voluminous black cloak.

When the duke saw the king and his brother making their way slowly to the palace, he dismounted and greeted them, but Jean and his mother stayed on their horses, looking at Louis with hatred. Louis had all the qualities his cousin Jean lacked – a handsome face, a graceful body, and a winning manner that made him attractive to everyone, especially women. Jean, on the other hand, was loutish and disagreeable, with sharp features and a sour expression very much like that of his cruel and haughty mother.

Louis's fools pranced around Philip, who paid no attention until Hanotin's monkey jumped onto his shoulders. He brushed the creature off and stamped his foot in disgust. The monkey landed on the ground, did a somersault, and bumped into Coquinet, who was turning himself into a ball. Blondel lay down on the ground and rolled from side to side, helped along by Giliot and Fripon, who pushed him with their feet. Soon all the fools were laughing, and the king laughed, too. Fripon looked up, saw Christine watching, and tossed some small stones in the direction of her window.

Christine realized that someone was standing beside her. She turned and found the Duchess of Orléans. She started to kneel, but the duchess motioned for her to remain standing. *How different she is from the queen,* Christine thought. Isabeau usually sat on her ceremonial day bed, surrounded by her ladies-in-waiting and her entourage of fools, mutes, a minstrel, and her dwarf. Valentina, on the other hand, moved about constantly – talking to her retainers, listening to the minstrels and other musicians who frequented her court, greeting the many artists and writers she and the duke employed. She would take a book from the duke's library, look at it for a moment, put it aside, and rove through the rooms of her residence, her retainers trailing after her. Interested in everything, Valentina never seemed to sit still.

'It's so sad,' Valentina said as she looked out the window at the scene below. 'Charles really does think that if he falls, he'll break. I've heard that when he's having one of his attacks, he has his men sew iron rods into his clothes, like a cage, to protect him.'

'How horrible,' Christine said.

Valentina looked around the room. 'Do you get lonely up here, working all by yourself?'

'No, *Madame*. I like solitude.'

Christine heard a sound at the doorway and turned to find Valentina's two Italian maids, Julia and Elena, sisters the duchess had brought with her from her home in Milan. 'I've instructed them to come up here every now and then and bring you some refreshment,' Valentina said. 'They will be happy if you speak to them in Italian. They miss their home.' She said to the girls, 'You may go now.' They curtsied and left.

Valentina looked out the window and saw the fools capering around the king and his brother.

'They are so kind, the duke's fools,' the duchess said. 'It's hard to consider them foolish.'

'I don't think they *are* foolish,' Christine said.

'Perhaps you're right.' The duchess went to Christine's desk, picked up the Aesop's fables, and turned the pages. She wore a plain blue gown with a simple gold belt from which hung a large embroidered purse. No necklaces sparkled at her neck, and no jewels studded her starched white headdress. Christine knew she'd come to France with wagonloads of diamonds, rubies, emeralds, and other precious stones, but she'd never seen her wear any of them. *She's more elegant without them,* she thought as she looked at the duchess's long, aristocratic face. She couldn't help comparing Valentina, who was tall and lithe, to the queen, who was short, a little chubby, and, while very pretty, lacking in poise. She remembered seeing them riding together. Even on a horse, Valentina was graceful. Isabeau was an excellent horsewoman, but since Valentina had come to France, she preferred to be seen riding in a litter.

'This is one of my favorite books,' the duchess said. 'There is so much truth here. And it makes me laugh. There is so little to laugh about these days.' She laid the book carefully on the desk and went back to the window.

The king's fool, Hennequin, came out of the palace and pranced up to Charles and his brother. The duchess smiled. 'Hennequin never stops dancing,' she said.

Just then the Duke of Burgundy's son, Jean, who had his eyes closed and seemed to be asleep in the saddle, let his horse move close to the king. Charles screamed and flung his arms around Louis, who was knocked off balance and nearly fell.

'He did that on purpose,' Valentina said.

Hennequin reached up, grabbed the horse's bridle, and led him away from the king. Jean couldn't protest because he was pretending to be asleep. Then the fool did a little dance, agitating the horse, which reared up so suddenly that Jean had to open his eyes and clutch the saddle to keep from falling. Hennequin laughed, and the king loosened his grip on his brother and laughed with him.

'Hennequin has always been able to cheer him,' Valentina said. 'He wears out his shoes, and Charles is constantly buying him new ones.'

'It is the same with the queen's fool, Guillaume,' Christine said.

'At least there are some people here who can relieve the pain,' the duchess said.

One of the duchess's maids reappeared at the door. 'Perhaps you need my assistance now, *Madame*?'

'No, no, Julia. You and Elena may go down.'

'It helps to have people near who are from my own country,' the duchess said when the girl had gone. She took Christine's hand. 'I understand your family is from Italy, too.'

'Yes. I was brought to Paris as a child.'

'Do the people here accept you?'

'I have lived here most of my life, *Madame*.'

'Then I am sure you understand the French. I do not, even though I have been here for seven years.' She reached into the embroidered purse and took something out.

'I found this in my room this morning,' she said as she held it up for Christine to see. 'I don't know who put it there. But it makes me very afraid.'

It was a large red apple, fashioned in wax.

NINE

They make a great show of flattery and respect, but they gossip and spread scandal. They are just like the bad sheep who has mange and spreads it to the rest of the flock.

Christine de Pizan, *Le Livre des Trois Vertus*, 1405

After Valentina left, Christine tried to work, but she found it impossible. She went to the window, looked down at the street below, and saw the duchess come out of her residence with her entourage. Madame de Maucouvent carried Valentina's little son Charles, the maids Julia and Elena walked behind her, making faces at the baby so he would laugh, and the ladies-in-waiting followed, whispering among themselves. Christine supposed they were going to visit the queen, and she wondered whether Isabeau's attendants would allow the duchess and her child to be brought near the queen's baby. She had her answer when the queen's youngest lady-in-waiting, Symonne du Mesnil, came out of the palace and spoke excitedly to Madame de Maucouvent. Christine couldn't hear what she was saying, but she knew what it was because Madame de Maucouvent's stout body shook with indignation. Valentina and her entourage turned around and headed back to the duke's residence.

Several courtiers approached and made deep bows to Valentina. She acknowledged their obeisances graciously, and the courtiers smiled at her, but after she'd passed, the men put their heads together and smirked. Several noblewomen appeared. They, too, made sincere-looking gestures of respect that turned to grimaces when they joined the courtiers at the end of the street.

Valentina walked proudly, but her face was drawn and sad. The duke's fools came racing toward her, Hanotin in the lead with his monkey bouncing up and down on his shoulders. He made such a deep bow that he nearly fell, causing the monkey to lose his balance and fly into Valentina's outstretched arms.

The duchess's small white dog bounded over, barking at the

monkey; Coquinet stood on his elbows and waved his feet over his head; Blondel rolled on the ground; and Giliot shook his shaggy mane and wiggled his nose, making himself look more like a rabbit than a lion. Fripon tossed three small balls into the air and let them bounce off his head before he caught them. The monkey reached out from Valentina's arms, grabbed one of the balls, and threw it at the dog. Fripon hurled the other two balls at the monkey, reached into his sleeve, and produced three eggs. Valentina's dog ran to him and got entangled in his legs, causing him to stumble and drop the eggs, which fell to the ground and broke, delighting Coquinet, who pretended to skate on the sticky mess.

Valentina and the fools were nearly doubled over with laughter. The ladies-in-waiting, however, were not amused. They stood whispering together behind their hands, throwing disgusted glances at the fools, and drawing away whenever Blondel rolled toward them.

Valentina stopped laughing when she saw her husband come striding toward her with a frown on his face. *Perhaps he's angry with the fools for paying so much attention to his wife*, Christine thought. But it was Valentina he'd come to reprimand. He seized her arm and led her into their residence. The ladies followed, shaking their heads.

Too disturbed to do any work, Christine packed up her writing materials and prepared to leave. As she started down the stairs, she heard angry voices below. Louis was berating Valentina. 'What made you decide to go there when you know they think you tried to poison the dauphin?' he shouted.

'I wanted to find out who started that story. I wanted to tell them it is not true.'

'You are a fool. They would never believe you.'

'But I am not an evil person! I have to convince them of that.'

'There is no way you can do it, now that my uncle and his wife have taken against you.'

'But why? Why does everyone here think I have bewitched the king? You know I have no power to do that.'

'It's *me* they're after. They would like everyone to think *I* was the one who caused my brother's illness. But since they can't accuse me directly, they go after you instead.'

'But why do they hate you so?'

'You know about the court, Valentina. The jealousies, the power struggles. My uncle Philip has always hated me. My cousin Jean, too. Now that I am regent, their hatred knows no bounds.'

Christine thought she heard someone crying. She crept down a few steps and saw that on the landing the duke had dragged Valentina's maids, Julia and Elena, out from behind a large high-backed chair where they'd been hiding and listening. The girls were sobbing. Valentina put her arms around them. 'There was no need for that, Louis,' she said. He glared at her, and the two stood facing each other without speaking for a few minutes. Then Louis fell to his knees and buried his face in Valentina's skirt.

'I am so sorry,' he said. 'None of this is your fault.'

Valentina leaned over and touched his head gently, tears streaming down her face. 'What are we going to do?'

Louis didn't answer. He just stood, put his arm around his wife, and led her down the stairs. Julia and Elena followed, choking back their sobs.

Christine returned to her workroom and sat at the desk with her head in her hands. She heard voices, and the fools burst in, bringing with them a little man in a red velvet doublet, silver hose, and a pointed green cap with a large peacock feather. The man removed his cap, made a deep bow, and said, 'Jacopo, the duchess's dwarf, at your service, *Madame.*'

Blondel lay down on the floor, and the others sat beside him, rocking him back and forth with their feet. 'Jacopo has something to say,' Giliot announced.

'But first you must tell us about the baby!' Coquinet cried.

'She's safe,' Christine said. 'She's with my mother.'

'Did your mother wash the baby's face?' Hanotin asked.

'Yes. She knew what the black was. How did you know?'

'Fools know everything.' Giliot said. 'Mothers do, too. Jacopo here thinks he does. But you must judge for yourself.'

'It's about the duke,' Fripon said, standing up and tossing some nuts into the air.

'I don't believe it,' Coquinet moaned as he curled himself into a ball.

'I don't either,' Blondel wailed, turning his face to the floor and starting to cry.

'It can't be,' Hanotin cried. The monkey jumped from his shoulders and ran around the room chirping and scratching himself.

'It's lamentable, if it's true,' Giliot said.

'What do you have to tell me?' Christine asked the dwarf.

'Something most troublesome that you should know about, because you are wise.'

'Do you think I will be able to do something about it?'

'That we will find out,' the dwarf said. He drew himself up to his full height, which was about as high as Christine's waist, and began. 'As you see, *Madame*, I am of small stature.' He had a thick Italian accent, and Christine started to tell him it would be all right to continue in that language, but the fools interceded, shaking their heads and murmuring, 'Let him speak so we can understand.'

'I understand Italian,' Fripon said, juggling some dried figs.

'But we don't,' the others shouted.

'Being so little,' Jacopo continued in his broken French, 'I hear much, for the reason that people do not know I am there.'

Just like Alips, Christine thought. 'Go on,' she said.

'I am much disturbed when I hear the duke talking to the woman with the bare breasts.'

'Who is that?' Christine asked.

'Young flesh, food for love,' Giliot said, and the other fools laughed until tears ran down their cheeks.

Hanotin stared at her with his large, round, unblinking eyes. 'Don't you know? The duchess's lady, the one who wears her gowns cut so low you can see her breasts.'

'That is the one,' Jacopo said. He crossed his arms over his chest. 'I am much disturbed when I hear what the duke whispers to her.'

'We are disturbed, too,' Giliot said. 'Perhaps you should hold your tongue, Jacopo. If you don't say it, maybe it won't happen.'

The fools surrounded the dwarf and wrestled him to the floor. 'Don't say it!' they all cried.

'You brought him here!' Christine cried. 'Why do you not let him speak?'

Jacopo stood up and dusted himself off. 'I *will* speak.' He picked up his feathered cap, which had gotten squashed in the tussle with the fools, and turned it round and round in his hands until it had returned to its proper shape. When he was satisfied that everything was in order again, he waved the fools away and stood squarely in front of Christine.

'This is of great importance,' he said.

'If it's true!' the fools all cried together.

'If it's true, the sounds you will hear are our hearts breaking,' Giliot said.

'Please tell me what you are talking about!' Christine said impatiently.

'The duchess,' the dwarf said. He put his hands over his face and started to cry. Then he wiped away his tears and said, 'The duke has told the woman with the bare breasts that he will send the duchess away.'

TEN

There is no proof that such a noble lady could commit such a great crime, and no one has the right to accuse her of it. For my part, I am far from sharing the common opinion, spread about by fools, necromancers, and superstitious people, concerning spells. The doctors and the theologians agree that sorcery has no power and that the king's illness was caused by the excesses of his youth.

The Monk of Saint-Denis, *Chronique du Religieux de Saint-Denis, contenant le règne de Charles VI de 1380 à 1422*

Christine left the palace preoccupied with what Jacopo had told her. On the rue Saint-Antoine her friend, Brothel Michel from the abbey of Saint-Denis, strode toward her, his black robe swirling around his feet, his sandals slapping the ground. Deep in thought, he nearly passed her by.

She called out to him, and he turned so suddenly he almost fell. 'Ah, Christine. I didn't see you.'

'Obviously. What are you doing?'

'I'm thinking. We have a situation at the abbey that worries me greatly.'

'Can you tell me what it is?'

'We are hosting a criminal. I'm sure you've heard of him. He tried to kill the constable, the year the king went mad.'

'Pierre de Craon? He was banished for his crime.'

'He's trying to get back into the king's good graces. He's been ordered not to come into the city, so he's staying with us, and we have to treat him as a guest. What a travesty. Pierre de Craon is a murderer and a thief.'

'I thought we were rid of him. But at least if he can't come into the city, I won't see him at the palace, God be praised.'

'Are you working at the palace?'

'I'm copying a book for the Duchess of Orléans.'

'Then you will probably see a man named Thibault de Torvaux who comes to plead Pierre's case with the duchess. Stay away from him. He's just as evil as Pierre.'

'Why does he come to the duchess?'

'I suppose it's because she's the most sympathetic person at the court.' Michel sighed and fingered his prayer beads. 'Admirable woman. It is most unjust that she should be the subject of so much slander.'

'I've heard the duke might try to send her away. Do you think that's possible?'

'I do. The slander is so pervasive that as long as the doctors are unable to explain the king's illness, people will believe she has bewitched him, and they will persecute her.' A gust of wind tugged at the monk's cowl, pulling it off his head. His white hair swirled around his tonsure.

'What do you know of those doctors? Do you think they will ever be able to cure him?'

'The first one did bring him back to his right mind for a while, but that was only temporary. Doctor Harsigny was very old, and he went back to his home in Laon to die. The others have been of no use, no use at all. One said the king had to eat alone so he wouldn't be disturbed by conversation. Charles sent that doctor away so swiftly he had no time to pack up all his belongings.' He laughed and pulled his cowl back over his head. 'Then there was the one who decided to drill a hole into Charles's head, to let the evil spirits out. Charles did say he felt a little better afterward, but that didn't last long. Now all we have are charlatans and sorcerers.'

Two courtiers came along, talking loudly. 'The sorceress makes him tear off his clothes and throw his food at his servants. She even gets him to strike the queen,' said a man in a fur-lined *houppelande*.

'That was several months ago,' Michel muttered under his breath. 'And he's never actually attacked the queen.'

'He runs naked around the palace, hitting his head against the walls,' the other man added, taking off his beaver hat and hitting it against his thigh.

'He's not doing that at the moment,' Michel said angrily as he watched the men saunter away. 'And if he does, his retainers have an iron cage to put him in. So he won't hurt himself, you know. Doctor Harsigny had it built for him.' He fingered his prayer beads.

'I saw the king the other day, in the palace gardens,' Christine said. 'He knows the malady will come again, and he's terrified.'

'That is true,' Michel said.

'I imagine you see everything that goes on at the court,' Christine said, thinking of the history of the king's reign he'd been commissioned to write.

'Unfortunately, yes, all of it. At least it gives me a chance to write in my chronicle that this business about Valentina and sorcery is nonsense. I hope you are not getting involved, Christine.'

'I can't help it. I'm sure you know about the murdered woman found in the palace gardens?'

'That has nothing to do with you.'

'Unfortunately, it does. I was the one who found her.'

Michel took a step back and clapped his hand to his forehead. 'God forbid! Not again, Christine!'

'You sound like my mother.'

'I can't believe it!'

'Unfortunately, that's not all,' Christine said, thinking that Michel was the one person at the palace to whom she could tell the whole story. 'The woman left a baby in the garden. The child had been starved, and her face was blackened so superstitious people would think she was the Devil's child, meant to be substituted for the queen's baby. The duke's fools found her. They knew that Valentina would be blamed.'

'These are terrible things you're telling me, Christine! What did the fools do with the baby?'

'They convinced me to take it home to my mother.'

Michel stared at her, open mouthed, his eyes blinking furiously.

'I know what you're thinking, Michel. But she realized right away that it was not the Devil's child. Georgette, on the other hand, tried to drop the baby into the fire.'

'Merciful God!'

'I stopped her.'

'God be praised.' Michel muttered a prayer under his breath. 'Is the baby with Francesca now?'

'Yes. My mother is devoted to her. Georgette, too, now that she knows the truth.'

'And what about the murdered woman? Was she the child's mother?'

'That's what I thought, but I took Marion to the morgue to see if she could identify her, and she told me the woman was a friend of hers, and she'd never had a baby.'

Michel sighed and tucked his hands into the sleeves of his habit. 'So now I suppose you've decided to track down the murderer.'

'First I have to find out where the baby's mother is.'

'How are you going to do that?'

'I'll think of something. I'm convinced all this has to do with the rumors about the Duchess of Orléans.'

'You know very well the rumors come from the Duke and Duchess of Burgundy and their son. They're using Valentina as an excuse to slander the Duke of Orléans himself. They will do anything to thwart him.'

'Murder?'

Michel took his hands out of the sleeves, waved them in her face, and cried, 'You can't go around accusing members of the nobility of murder, Christine!'

'But someone has committed a horrible crime. Do you expect me to ignore it?'

He shook his head and tucked his hands back into his sleeves. 'I know you won't,' he said.

ELEVEN

The leaves, seed, and juice of henbane, taken inwardly, cause an unquiet sleep like unto the sleepe of drunkennesse, which continueth long, and is deadly to the party.

John Gerard, *Herbal*, 1597

Marion couldn't stop asking herself how her friend had come to be lying dead at the morgue. She and Fleur had worked together at the brothel on the rue Tiron, so she decided to go there and see whether any of the other prostitutes knew what had happened to the girl.

She found all the prostitutes huddled together in the common area of the old cottage that housed the brothel.

'Where are the customers?' she asked.

'We sent them away,' said Agnes, a flamboyant girl who, like Marion, wore sparkling beads in her hair and gold belts she usually made no attempt to hide. 'We may be in a lot of trouble.' She drew Marion aside and whispered, 'Oudine entertained a man who associates with a criminal. We shouldn't have let him in.'

'Who was he?'

'A friend of Pierre de Craon, the man who tried to kill the king's constable. Pierre's trying to get the king to pardon him, but he can't come into the city. He has to stay at the abbey of Saint-Denis, so he sends this friend. We don't want to be associated with him.'

'I know one of the monks at the abbey. I'll ask him to help you if you have any problems.' *It would be a good way to get back at Michel,* Marion said to herself, remembering all the times the monk had criticized her.

'You have a friend who's a monk? You really have changed, Marion.'

Marion looked around the room. A fire blazed in a large fireplace and clean rush mats covered the floor. It was a comfortable place, and she'd spent much of her life there. She sighed. 'I haven't changed that much,' she said.

Agnes laughed. 'Are you thinking of coming back?'

'No. I've come to ask you about Fleur.'

'Fleur? I haven't seen her for a while.'

'Then you'll be shocked at what I have to tell you. She's been murdered.'

Agnes put her hands over her eyes and shook her head. 'I thought she was acting strangely lately. She didn't have many clients, and she needed money. She might have done something foolish. But get herself murdered? How is that possible?'

'That's what I want to find out,' Marion said. 'Her body was found in the gardens at the Hôtel Saint-Pol, and she had henbane seed pods clutched in her hand. You know about herbs. Where would she have gotten henbane?'

'Not in the palace gardens, that's for sure. Henbane is deadly. I know, because old Margot told me about it. She used to grow it.'

Marion remembered Margot. The old woman had been strangled because she'd sold one of her poisonous herbs to the wrong person. 'Can you think of anyone else who might sell henbane?'

'There's a woman named Mahaut who deals in magic and poisons. Fleur used to go to her for a special potion to make herself more attractive to her customers.'

'Where can I find her?'

'She lives near the rue des Bourdonnais. I don't know exactly where. You'll have to ask somebody.'

Several of the other prostitutes came over to greet Marion. 'You're lucky to be away from here,' one said. 'We have a big problem.'

'If you mean Pierre de Craon's friend, don't worry,' Marion said. 'Let me know if anyone tries to arrest you and take you to the Châtelet. I know what to do.'

'You always did have ways of getting us out of trouble,' someone said. 'You should visit more often. We miss you.'

'I miss you, too,' Marion said, thinking how lonely she sometimes got with only a parrot for company. *My old way of life wasn't so bad, no matter what Christine and her mother say,* she mused.

She said her goodbyes and walked down to the water trough near the entrance to the Grand Pont. A group of beggars gathered around her, each one looking as though he suffered from some disfiguring illness. She knew they were all fakes, but they were her friends, nevertheless. They laughed when she asked about Mahaut.

'What do you need?' asked a man who'd covered his body with a mixture of flour, plaster, and animal blood. 'Snake powder? Ground-up bones from the corpse of a hanged man? A magic mirror to summon the Devil? The white woman has them all.'

'What do you mean?'

'You'll see,' said a man who'd stuffed his clothes with rags so he seemed to have a large tumor. 'You want a toad to put under someone's doorstep to make him get sick? The blood of a white dove to drive away evil spirits? Mahaut has everything.'

'Tell me where she lives,' Marion said.

'Not far,' said a man who dragged himself along on a little cart because he appeared to be missing a leg. 'Go down to where the rue de la Limace meets the rue des Bourdonnais. There's a cul-de-sac there, and Mahaut carries on her devilish trade in a house at the end of it.'

Marion suspected she would need something valuable to give Mahaut in exchange for information. She decided to go home and see what she could find. As she walked down the rue Saint-Honoré, she came to the crossing of that street and the rue de l'Arbre Sec, saw the corpse hanging from the gallows, and clapped her hand to her head. She'd thought of the perfect offering.

Babil greeted her with loud squawks and flew down from the top of his cage to help her rummage through a chest, pulling out garters, hose, and underclothes and scattering them around the room. Marion found what she was looking for and tucked it into her sleeve. Then she saw what the parrot had done. She started to laugh. 'I'll never say you aren't good company, Babil.' The parrot bounced up and down and flew back to his cage.

Marion walked up the rue Saint-Honoré, turned down the rue des Bourdonnais and came to the place where it met the rue de la Limace. There she searched until she found the entrance to the cul-de-sac, which was so narrow she'd never noticed it before. The shabby houses leaning out over the street on either side shaded everything, making it so hard to see that it was nearly impossible to avoid slipping into the gutter carrying rotten carrots and cabbages, sewage, and a dead rat past her feet. Holding her nose, she walked to the end of the cul-de-sac and found a small door. She opened it and stepped into a dark hallway, and when her eyes had become accustomed to the lack of light, opened another door, and entered a windowless room lit by dozens of candles. She shielded her eyes and saw a phantom leaning against a chair on the other side of the room. The ghostly figure said, 'Come in. I know who you are.'

'Then perhaps you know why I'm here,' Marion said.

'That I do not. But come close and let me look at you.'

Marion crossed the room and stood before a tall woman dressed all in white. Her face was deathly pale and her hair, which hung to her waist in two long braids, was the color of bleached straw. She emerged from the shadows like a specter. The woman said, 'I used to be a prostitute, too.'

'How do you know about me?'

'You'd be surprised at what I know.'

Marion took off her crimson cloak and threw it over her arm. 'It's warm in here,' she said. 'How do you live with no windows?'

Mahaut laughed. 'I like it this way.' She looked at Marion, her eyes shining like small blue stones against her deathly white skin. 'I see that you are not afraid,' she said.

'Why should I be afraid?'

'Have you not heard that I am dangerous, because of what I sell?'

Marion looked around the room. Herbs hung from the ceiling, many of them dry and dusty, and the walls were lined with cabinets. The place looked and smelled like an apothecary shop.

'You'd like to know what's in those cabinets, wouldn't you?' Mahaut said.

'Why don't you tell me?'

Mahaut laughed again. Her voice, which was dark and gruff, belied the whiteness of her skin and hair. 'I have anything you want. Bones of dead men, dried blood of doves, skulls of vultures, ashes of burned ravens, powder of precious stones. Do you want to make a man love you? Drive your enemy mad? Get wealth? I can help you.' She put her hand on a cluster of keys that hung from a cord at the waist of her white gown.

'I don't want any of those things. I want to know about the herbs hanging from the ceiling.'

'Ah. There's elecampane, viper's bugloss, bishop's wort, cleavers. Mix them with goose fat and they will cure any disease. Mandrake and vervain to numb your pain. Rosemary to drive away evil spirits. Artemisia to thwart a sorcerer.' Mahaut lifted the keys and let them drop back. They jangled menacingly at the end of the cord.

'And to kill someone?'

'Do you think I would sell anything like that?'

'Not to me, perhaps. But to someone who pays you well, or who knows your secrets.'

'Are you thinking of anyone in particular?'

'Has anyone been here lately seeking henbane?'

'What do you know about henbane?'

'I know it can be used to cure a toothache. I also know that when its leaves are burned, the smoke numbs the senses. And I know that its seeds can kill.'

'You know so much, why do you ask me?'

'Because I think you've sold henbane lately. To someone who used it for an evil purpose.'

'Do you really think I would tell you about my customers?'

'Perhaps you would if I gave you this.' Marion reached into her sleeve and took out a piece of rope.

Mahaut sneered. 'What would I want with that?'

'You've seen the hanged man on the gallows at the crossing of the rue Saint-Honoré and the rue de l'Arbre Sec?'

'Of course.'

'I found this on the ground there. Part of the rope around his neck had fallen away.'

Mahaut reached out for the rope.

Marion pulled her hand away. 'I want some information first.'

'I need that rope. It will cure someone's headache,' Mahaut said.

'If it's so valuable, tell me who came here to buy henbane. Was it a woman?'

'No woman has been here recently.' Mahaut held her hands behind her back, to keep them from reaching out.

'Who, then?'

'A man. I don't know his name.'

'No one else?'

'Not lately.' She reached down to the floor, picked up a crutch, leaned on it, and reached up to the ceiling. She pulled down some leaves. 'This is henbane. Do you want some? I'll give it to you if you give me that piece of rope.'

'Do you have any henbane seed pods?'

Mahaut hopped to one of the cupboards and opened a drawer. 'I don't have many left. The man who came bought most of them.' She took out a handful of seed pods. Marion held her nose. 'They may smell bad, but they're valuable. You could sell them for a lot of money,' Mahaut said.

'I don't sell things. Tell me about the man who bought them.'

'He may live in one of the houses in this cul-de-sac. I've seen him before. He wears a big black cloak with a hood that covers his face.'

'I guess you can have this.' Marion held out the rope. Mahaut hobbled over and seized it, almost losing her balance in her eagerness. She tucked it securely into the sleeve of her white dress. 'I would have paid you a lot of money for this,' she said. 'You were too stupid to ask.'

Marion laughed. 'And you were too stupid to ask where I got it. How do you know it's really what I said it was? The hanged man on the gallows at the crossing of the rue Saint-Honoré and the rue de l'Arbre Sec has been there for a long time. If that rope had been around his neck, it would be green and moldy by now.'

Mahaut sneered. 'What does it matter? My customers believe anything I tell them.'

'Too bad for them,' Marion said. 'Thanks for the little bit of information you've given me.' She turned and left.

Out in the deserted cul-de-sac, she looked around at the houses. Mahaut had said that the man who'd bought the henbane might live in one of them, so she decided to try all the doors. She crept down the street, avoiding the filthy gutter by flattening herself against the walls, and ran her hands over the rough wood of closed shutters and doors. One of the doors swung open. She stepped through.

She was in a dark hallway with an opening at the end, through which she could see the light of day. Cautiously, she crept along this hallway, coughing as her feet kicked up dust and mold. Finally, she stepped out into the open air. After the dark street and the even darker hallway, the light blinded her, and she stood for a moment with her eyes closed, reveling in the warmth of the sun and the touch of a cool breeze passing over her cheeks. Then she looked around and saw that she was in an abandoned garden. Two sparrows hopped about pecking at the unturned soil, and, except for their soft chirping and the rustle of a few dead leaves, the place was ominously silent.

A path led to an open door on the other side of the garden. She started along this path but was tempted to turn back when she saw the prints of large boots in the mud. A huge black dog bounded out the door and ran toward her. He leapt up, nearly knocking her down, and put his paws on her shoulders, his tail wagging furiously and his pink tongue dripping drool on to her cloak. She put her hands on his paws and pulled him away, whereupon he raced back to the open door, turned, and looked at her, waiting for her to follow. When she hesitated, he galloped back, seized the hem of her gown in his mouth, and tried to draw her along. Since she couldn't free the gown from his strong jaws, she let him lead her to the door and pull her through it.

She was in a narrow hallway, pressed up against the wall by the dog, who stood over something lying on the ground, barking and whining, his tail thrashing against her skirt. She pushed him aside and bent down to see what was making him so excited.

At her feet lay the body of a young woman. Her long blond hair covered her face, and blood stained her gown. She pushed the woman's hair back and saw that there was a deep gash in her throat. She'd been there for some time, for the air was foul and the face had started to decompose. Gagging and trying to avoid the smell by taking shallow breaths, she looked more closely. She let out a cry. It was someone she knew.

TWELVE

Those who wish to live in peace must hear, see, and say nothing.

Latin proverb

Marion stared at the body. She'd known Klara at a time when the girl's husband had disappeared and she'd lived with Christine and her family. She'd liked Klara and tried to help her, even though she'd been difficult. She hadn't seen her for three years, and now she lay dead at her feet. She knew she should run to get the sergeants from the Châtelet; but she was tempted not to tell anyone, to let Klara stay there until someone else found her, someone who wouldn't be able to identify her. Then Martin du Bois would never know his wife had died in such a horrible way.

The black dog tried to push her away from the body, and she didn't resist. He followed her into the garden, panting and drooling, his huge paws sinking into the mud beside the human footprints she'd noticed earlier.

She went out into the cul-de-sac and stood for a long time, her head bowed, remembering all the trouble Klara's petulant ways and deceptive nature had caused. *Had she changed, learned to be a good wife?* she wondered.

The black dog sat at her feet. She laid her hand on his head. 'What should I do?' she asked.

'Go home,' said a voice behind her.

She swung around and found herself facing Henri Le Picart. The dog jumped up and ran away.

'You go away, too, Marion,' Henri said.

'You can't order me around!'

'I can and I will. What are you doing here?'

'None of your business.'

'It *is* my business.' He wore his usual black cape with the ermine collar and long black hood, and the fingers of his black-gloved hands curled around the gilded top of a walking stick with a very sharp point.

She looked at the stick, took a deep breath, and asked, 'Did you kill her?'

Henri laughed. 'Jumping to conclusions. Just like a woman.'

'*Allez au diable!*' she cried, lashing out at him with her fists.

He grabbed her hands. 'You don't know what to do about it, do you?'

'You mean about the body?' She tried to pull her hands free, but he held them tightly.

'I do mean that. Listen to me. *I* know what to do about it. *You* don't.'

'What do you mean?'

He pulled her into a dark doorway, waited until an old woman who came ambling by had gone into one of the houses, then led her out into the narrow street again. 'I mean we aren't going to do anything. Not yet.'

'But we have to tell the sergeants from the Châtelet! Or her husband. We can't just let her lie there!'

'You're right. We have to tell the authorities. But I'm going to do it, not you.'

'Who's going to tell her husband?'

'I'll take care of that. All you have to do is keep out of this.'

'*Crétin!*' she cried, shaking with anger.

'She can stay there for a while,' he said calmly. 'Martin du Bois will be told in due time. Or perhaps you, with your woman's wisdom, think it would be better if he never found out what happened to his wife.'

She remembered thinking exactly that. But she hated herself for thinking such a thing for even a moment. How could she not tell Klara's husband, Martin, who would be sick with worry? And how could she not tell Christine and her mother, who had been so kind to the girl? What did Henri have in mind? She'd never trusted him, and she wasn't about to start trusting him now.

Henri was watching her with a self-satisfied smile on his face. 'I know what you're thinking,' he said. 'But for your own good, you'd better leave things to me.' He let her hands go, turned her around, and gave her a push. 'Go home. Forget about what you've seen.'

As if in a trance, Marion did as she was told, and headed down the street toward her house. But when she got to the rue de l'Arbre Sec, she came to her senses. *How could I let that man tell me what to do?* she asked herself. She thought of everything she knew about

Henri Le Picart: he worked as a scribe, he owned a lot of houses that he rented out, he wrote poetry, and he was even reputed to be an alchemist. *Alchemists are supposed to be sorcerers and magicians,* she thought. She remembered his pointed walking stick. *I've heard that magicians can kill people.*

'Damn the man,' she said out loud.

'Damn you, too,' a beggar standing in the street swore back.

'I didn't mean you,' she said.

'I feel sorry for whoever you did mean.'

The beggar wore a tattered tunic and his shoes had holes in them, but he had a pleasant smile on his face, not the sneer she'd seen on Henri Le Picart's. *I might as well ask him,* she said to herself.

'Should I go home, or should I put myself in danger?'

'Go home.' He sounded just like Henri.

'That's exactly what I'm *not* going to do.'

'I don't know what you're talking about,' the beggar said. He held out a cup and shook it.

She threw a coin into it.

The man stared into the cup. 'Can't you spare more than that?'

'That's for giving me bad advice.' She made up her mind. She would find Christine and tell her about Klara, and they would decide what to do, no matter what Henri Le Picart said. She looked around. The little man in the black cape with the ermine collar was nowhere in sight. But she imagined she heard him laughing.

THIRTEEN

Nature alwaies intendeth and striveth to the perfection of Gold.

Roger Bacon (c. 1214–c. 1292), *The Mirror of Alchimy*

On her way up the rue Saint-Honoré, Marion decided to turn down a side street that led to Henri's house. She'd always hurried past this large mansion, trying not to look at the dragons and serpents carved in the wood of its heavy front door. Now she stopped and stared. One of the dragons bared his knifelike

teeth at her, and another raised a foot with long, spiked claws. A
serpent, coiled and ready to strike, showed his sharp, pointed fangs.

A young man in a ragged brown jerkin and with a patch over
one eye limped to her side. 'Do you know what Henri Le Picart
does in there?' he asked.

'I've heard he practices alchemy,' she said.

'Does that mean he's a magician?'

'That could be.' Suddenly she had an idea. She turned and hurried
back down the rue Saint-Honoré to the old clothes market next to
the wall of the cemetery of the Innocents. She pushed her way
through the crowds – not stopping as she usually did to examine the
fur-lined *houppelandes*, velvet capes with ermine linings, and gold
embroidered gowns in the stalls where the cast-off finery of the
nobility was sold – and made her way to a far less fancy booth.
There she bought a faded brown jacket with a rip down the back,
a pair of filthy black breeches, muddy boots, and a shapeless, much-
worn, blue woolen hood with a very long liripipe that she could
use to cover her face if necessary.

'What do you want with all this old stuff, Marion?' the shopkeeper
asked.

'None of your business. Just get me something to hold these
pants up.'

The man reached up to an overhead hanger and pulled down a
belt. She examined it. 'I need something older.'

He looked at her askance, shook his head, went to a pile of
clothes that had just been delivered, and untied a dirty, frayed belt
that had been used to keep everything together. 'No charge for this,'
he said as he handed it to her.

Marion trudged home, the jacket, breeches, and hood draped over
her arm, the big boots dangling from one hand, and the belt hanging
down from the other, its corroded brass buckle making a tinkling
sound as it scraped over the paving stones.

Babil watched as she took off her crimson cape and embroidered
gown. When she took the glittering beads out of her hair, he picked
them up with his beak, one by one, and carried them to his cage.

'I'll need them back,' she said to the parrot. He bobbed his head
and climbed to the top of the cage.

She put on the jacket, breeches, and boots, fastened the belt
around her waist, and covered her red hair with the hood, wrapping
its long liripipe around her neck. Then she hobbled around the room,

learning how to walk in boots much too large for her. Babil beat his foot against the side of his cage in time with the thumping of the boots on the floor.

She said goodbye to the parrot and went to the water trough at the entrance to the Grand-Pont. Not one of the reprobates recognized her, not even the young man she'd met earlier in front of Henri Le Picart's house.

She stomped up to a rogue who'd covered his tattered clothes with muck and blood from a dead cat and tapped him on the shoulder. 'I need work,' she said in a deep voice. 'I heard you had a job with the man who lives in that big house with the dragons and serpents on the door.'

'You mean Henri Le Picart. He does something with a fire in a brick oven. He paid me to work the bellows to keep it going.'

'So you saw what he has in his house?'

'It's a strange place, at least the room I was in. Glass vials full of colored liquids, books with sinister-looking marks on the covers, roots and dried plants hanging from the ceiling.'

'Do you think he still needs help?'

The man looked her up and down. 'You look like a strong fellow. Go and ask him.'

Marion went back to Henri's house and stood in the street for a long time, waiting to see if he would appear. Then she went to the front door and knocked, wincing as she came near the dragons and serpents and being careful not to touch them.

No one answered. She knocked again, louder this time. Still no answer. Gingerly, she pushed on the door and jumped back when it slowly opened. She hesitated, looked around, and stepped in.

Whatever she'd been afraid of encountering, it was not there. Instead, she found herself in an entrance hall, the likes of which she'd never seen before. High-backed chairs, their arms carved into the forms of mermaids, basilisks, and centaurs, stood against the walls, tapestries embroidered with ancient heroes swayed slightly in the breeze that came in through the open door, and a floor paved with gold and silver tiles glistened at her feet. She closed the door and crossed the hall, cringing as she sensed that the figures in the tapestries were looking down disapprovingly at her big boots clumping over the costly tiles. She came to a small courtyard and stood on a mosaic of red lions with fins, green serpents with wings, blue fish with legs, and purple birds with camel's feet. In the center of this courtyard a fountain gushed water into a small pool, and stacked all around were pots of flowers in full bloom. The smell of daffodils, jasmine, and other blossoms she couldn't identify filled the air. Butterflies fluttered around her head, and birds flew down through an open space in the roof and drank from the fountain.

She crept across the courtyard and entered a room with more tapestries, enchanted scenes of men and women sitting in gardens carpeted with flowers as they listened to minstrels playing lutes and vielles. She imagined she heard the music, and it seemed to lift her off her feet and carry her into another room, where the walls were formed of wooden panels inlaid with geometric designs. Here she found tables covered with games – chess and backgammon sets, dice, and playing cards – and an intricately carved ivory gaming box from which spilled chess pieces decorated with hunters and dogs.

Feeling confident that no one was around, she sat on a chair at one of the tables and opened a large book. She couldn't read, but she knew from the pictures that it contained instructions for playing the games she saw scattered about. She thought she heard someone whisper in her ear, 'Not for you.' She jumped up and went on to the next room, which was full of musical instruments. She ran her hands over the strings of a harp and blew into a strangely shaped horn, making a blast of sound so loud she was sure someone would come running. But no one appeared. Next she came to a study with book-lined shelves and a huge wooden desk covered with sheets of parchment, inkhorns, and quill pens. Someone had been there recently, writing a letter. She longed to be able to read it.

She climbed a wide staircase and came to a large bedroom where light filtering in through windows of colored glass made the embroidered coverlet on the bed shimmer red, blue, and green. She peered through a window and saw even more glimmering colors.

She went back downstairs, passed through the central hallway, and wandered out into an exterior courtyard with a garden and a building that housed the kitchen. *Where are all the gardeners, cooks, and other servants Henri needs to care for this grand place?* she asked herself. *But then, if he makes gold, he probably doesn't want anyone to see what he's doing.*

She went back to the main part of the house and looked around again. This time she found a room with a locked door. She suspected this was the room she was looking for, the one the rogue had described. All the answers to her questions about Henri were surely there. But there was no way she could get in to see.

Small tiles with mysterious markings on them framed the doorway, and her big boot touched one that had fallen away. *Perhaps it has to do with what's in that room. Christine will know,* she thought as she picked it up and stuffed it into the sleeve of her beggar's costume. Then she decided it was time to leave.

As she clumped up the street away from his house, she saw Henri Le Picart coming toward her. She lowered her head as he passed. She was sure he didn't recognize her.

FOURTEEN

For healing morphews: Just before you go to sleep, hold as many fava beans as you can in your hand and say: 'You, Sun, high and precious lord, make this morphew vanish from wherever it may be on my body.' Then throw the beans behind your shoulder, one by one, repeating these words with each throw, until all the beans are gone. Do this for seven nights in a row, when the moon is waning.

Picatrix, ninth-century Arabic book on magic,
translated into Spanish and Latin in 1256

'Where is that girl?' Francesca asked as she sat at the kitchen table cutting up carrots and turnips for soup, something Georgette was supposed to do. Beside her, Christine stood holding the baby, gazing at her and thinking how much better the child looked now that so much care had been lavished on her by Georgette and her mother. 'The sores on her head are healing,' she said.

'It is the fava beans,' Francesca said.

'What are you talking about?'

'Do you not know? If you throw fava beans over your shoulder at night, blisters and sores will disappear.'

'What nonsense. Did you actually do it?'

'Of course. You should not make fun of my remedies. Do you know how many times I cured your warts with chickpeas, when you were a child?'

'I don't know, and I don't want to.'

'I will tell you how it works. You put a warm chickpea on a wart and then you throw out the chickpea, and it takes the wart away with it.'

'How absurd.'

'Ask Georgette about the fava beans. She saw me throwing them, so when she sees how well the baby's head has healed, she will believe my remedies work.' Francesca jabbed her knife into a turnip. 'She should be here. I need her.'

'She'll be back soon, I'm sure,' Christine said. 'She never goes far from this child if she can help it.'

'She is getting too attached to her,' Francesca said. She got up from the table, stood beside Christine, and smiled at the child in her arms.

'Who's getting too attached?' Christine asked.

The children came into the kitchen, followed by Goblin. The baby reached out for the dog. 'Here, baby,' Jean said as he lifted Goblin so she could pat him.

'Why does everyone make such a fuss over babies?' Thomas asked, turning his back on the others.

'You'll understand someday when you're married and have children of your own,' Christine said, tousling his curly brown hair.

'I'm never getting married. Women are bad. They leave their children around.'

'Just because one woman abandons a child, that doesn't mean they all do,' Christine said.

'Do you think I'm like that, Thomas?' Marie asked.

'You don't count,' Thomas said. 'You're never going to get married.'

'Thomas!' Christine cried.

'I don't mind,' Marie said. 'I don't want to get married.'

'I know why Thomas talks like that,' Jean said as he set Goblin on the floor. 'He's heard what people say about women, how they're just like Eve, who did what the snake said and took a bite of the apple. I don't pay any attention to all that.' He brushed a strand of his straight brown hair away from his face, and Christine felt a wave of sadness pass over her. He looked exactly like his father.

'Help me with the soup, *Cristina*,' Francesca said. 'If we do not get these vegetables ready, there will be nothing for dinner.'

Christine handed the baby to Jean, sat down at the table beside her mother, picked up a knife, and started to cut up some carrots.

'Those pieces are too large,' Francesca said.

Christine threw down the knife. 'I never seem to do anything right in the kitchen.'

'You spend too much time reading and writing.'

'That's what I do best, Mama. Have you ever considered what would have happened if Papa hadn't taught me to read and write? How would we live, now that he and Étienne are gone?'

'I do not know, *Cristina*. But you should have learned more about cooking and sewing.'

'How many times do I have to tell you, I don't care about cooking and sewing!'

'So you use your great learning to get work at the palace, where the king is mad, the duchess is a sorceress, and evil infects everyone. Then you start bringing strange people home and finding dead bodies and putting yourself and the rest of your family in danger!' Francesca started to cry, which frightened the baby so much that she started to cry, too.

Francesca jumped up, ran to Jean, lifted the child from his arms, and held her under the laurel branch, sniffling and patting the baby's cheeks, making both of them cry even harder. The children crowded around, whispering and making silly faces.

'There, there, baby. It's all right,' Marie said.

'Here, baby, here's your dog,' Jean said, lifting Goblin so she could pat him again.

Thomas shouted, 'Stop crying, baby!'

'Baby is making me sad,' Lisabetta wailed.

'We have to stop calling her "baby,"' Christine said. 'We have to give her a name.'

'She already has a name,' said a deep voice from the doorway.

FIFTEEN

No matter whether he be noble or not, a man can have no better treasure than a virtuous and wise woman.

From a book of moral and practical advice for a young wife,
Paris, 1393

Everyone whirled around to see Martin du Bois standing at the door, with Georgette beside him. Francesca nearly dropped the baby, who stopped crying and reached out her arms. 'Papa,' she lisped.

'She can talk!' Marie exclaimed.

'Is that her father?' Thomas asked.

'It can't be!' Jean cried.

'*Impossibile!*' Francesca gasped.

Christine just stood in shock, not able to utter a word, while Lisabetta, not understanding what was going on, went to Martin and said, 'You took Klara away. Have you brought her back?'

'No,' Martin said. 'But this is her child. Her name is Bonne.' He strode to Francesca, took the baby, and cradled her in his arms, laughing and crying at the same time.

'Klara!' Francesca cried. 'Her baby! Where is Klara?'

'I don't know.'

'But how can that be?' asked Christine, who finally found her voice. 'This child was left in the palace gardens. She'd been half-starved and she had black grease on her face!'

'I know,' Martin said. 'Georgette told me.'

They'd forgotten Georgette, who still stood in the doorway, grinning from ear to ear.

'How did you know this was Martin's baby?' Francesca asked.

'It was the preserve you were making,' Georgette said. 'You got the recipe from what he wrote for Klara. When we were talking about it, I remembered Colin telling me the other day that Klara had disappeared, along with her baby.'

Colin always knows everything, Christine thought, remembering her past experiences with Georgette's brother, who was a snoop.

'Is that true?' Christine asked Martin.

'I'm afraid it is. She was very unhappy, and she left me. I've been looking for her.'

'But to take her baby and abandon it. How could she!' Francesca exclaimed.

'I told you. Women are no good,' Thomas said.

'He has a point,' Jean said. He sat at the table with his head in his hands. 'I think I agree with Thomas. I don't want to get married. I'd be afraid my wife would run away.'

Christine sat beside her son and put her arms around him, speechless with wonder and sadness. Lisabetta went to them and stroked Christine's hand. 'Don't be sad,' she said. 'The baby's father has been found.'

'So he has,' Christine said, jumping up and going to Martin. 'Tell us about Klara.'

'You know what she's like,' he said. 'After all, you and your family put up with her when I had to go away so she'd be safe. She's told me all about her stay here. She wasn't as unhappy as you think. But I know she'd rather be with the queen. I'm sorry you took her to the palace.'

Christine had to smile, remembering how Klara had tried to charm the queen by pretending to be a good little wife. She wondered whether she should tell Martin about that, and decided it would be unkind. Instead, she asked, 'Has Klara ever gotten used to being a housewife?'

'That's just it. She hasn't. She doesn't like any of it, even though I've hired several girls to help her. She aspires to royalty. By taking her to the palace, you gave her enough of a taste of it to make her long for something she can never have.'

'And the baby? Doesn't having a baby help?'

'At first I thought it would, but I soon realized it only makes things worse. She resents the baby.' He held Bonne close.

'But why did she take her away?' Francesca asked.

'I don't know. She just walked out of the house with her, and she hasn't come back.' He held the child even closer.

Bonne smiled at him and said again, 'Papa!'

'We have to find her!' Francesca cried. She finished cutting up the turnips and carrots, put them in a pot with water and spices, and hung the pot over the fire. 'Stir it, and do not let the pot burn,' she called out to Georgette as she rushed out of the kitchen. Soon she came back, carrying a mirror. 'I have heard that if you look into certain mirrors, you will see a person who is lost. Let us see if this is one of those mirrors,' she said.

'What superstitious nonsense!' Christine said.

'It is not nonsense,' Francesca said as she gazed into the mirror.

'What do you see?' Georgette asked.

'Just myself,' Francesca said with a sigh. She held the mirror out to Martin. 'Here, you try.'

Martin shook his head. 'Christine is right. It's just superstition.'

'I'll try,' Georgette said, reaching for the mirror.

'No, you won't,' Christine said. 'Please take that back upstairs, Mama. It can't help us.'

'I suppose you are right,' Francesca said. She turned to go upstairs again.

'While you are up there, bring the pages Martin wrote for Klara. They're on my desk. He should have them back now,' Christine said.

'Don't bother,' Martin called out. 'Even if Klara returns to me, she won't read what I wrote.' He looked around and smiled sadly. 'It's been a long time since I've been with a real family.'

Christine remembered the passages in his manuscript that spoke of the joy of having a good wife and a happy marriage. As if he'd read her thoughts, Martin said, 'Klara is incapable of being a good wife.'

'Perhaps she wasn't meant to be,' Christine said. She thought back to the days when Klara had lived with her family. The girl had been rude and haughty, and she'd made the children very unhappy. But she'd had some good qualities. She'd befriended Loyse, the deaf lion-keeper's assistant. And after Christine had convinced the queen to take Loyse into her entourage, Klara had offered to take her place with the lions, and she'd done well with the job. In many ways, Christine sympathized with her, recognizing her as a kindred spirit who resented being treated as a mere woman, good for nothing but housekeeping and caring for her husband. As much as she liked Martin du Bois, she realized that he thought, as Francesca did, that women were not meant to have lives separate from their husbands.

'I want to know more about how you found my child,' Martin said. 'Tell me about the woman who left her in the palace gardens.'

'She was a prostitute, and someone killed her. That's all I know.'

'How is it possible that she had my little girl? And why did she do those terrible things to her?'

'Perhaps she stole her from Klara. She may not have known what she was doing. I think she'd been drugged by a poisonous plant.'

'What plant?'

'Henbane,' said Francesca, who'd come back.

Martin nodded. 'I know about that plant. I'd never grow it in my garden.'

'Neither would I,' Francesca said. 'Especially if there are children around.' She looked at Bonne, who rested happily in Martin's arms, reaching up every now and then to touch his face.

'I think the woman who left Bonne in the garden did it for someone else, someone who wanted to hurt the Duchess of Orléans,' Christine said. 'Someone who knew that superstitious people would think a disfigured child was a child of the Devil.'

'And kill her,' Martin said, his voice shaking.

Christine winced, remembering that Georgette had almost thrown the baby into the fire. She looked over at Georgette, who stood by the fire talking to Francesca, and was relieved to see that the girl hadn't heard.

'The duke's fools found her,' she said. 'They were afraid of what might happen to her, so they gave her to me.'

'And your mother agreed to take her into her home,' Martin said, looking at Francesca stirring the pot of soup. 'She's a good woman.'

'She does have her superstitions,' Christine said.

'Like most women.'

'Not all, Martin. But we won't talk about that now. We have to find Klara. And we have to find the person who killed the woman who left your daughter in the palace gardens.'

Martin gazed at Bonne with tears in his eyes. He cradled her in the crook of one arm, and with his free hand he grasped the handle of a small dagger that hung from his belt.

'Yes, that is exactly what we have to do,' he said.

SIXTEEN

Make a candle inscribed with the names of ten demons, light it, and as it burns, declare that all the power and knowledge of your victim shall turn to madness.

From a fifteenth-century manual of demonic magic,
Bayerische Staatsbibliothek, Munich, Clm 849

On the rue Saint-Antoine the angry talk swelled to a roar. It had rained heavily during the night, and black clouds threatened another storm. But news of the murdered woman in the palace gardens had spread through the city, and bad weather couldn't keep people from coming out to condemn the Duchess of Orléans. On her way to the palace, Christine joined a group of angry old men who were trying to outshout each other.

'Of course she did it!' one cried.

'But why?' another demanded to know.

'She murders people, just like her father,' a third barked. 'She should go back to Italy, back to her bloodthirsty family!' He forgot to lean on his crutch and nearly fell over in his excitement.

'Let the Viper of Milan come here and get her,' bellowed the first, waving his hands about so furiously that he nearly toppled over, too.

Christine longed to reprimand them, but she held her tongue and moved on. In her haste to get away, she bumped into an old woman with a basket of vegetables.

'*Stupide comme un chou!*' the woman hissed as she bent down to pick up some onions that had fallen into the mud. Christine bent down too, so she could help, but the woman shooed her away angrily.

Two noblemen with short jackets and tight-fitting hose stopped to watch, smirking. A strong gust of wind blew their feathered hats off their heads, and they raced after them, jumping over puddles and tripping on the long points of their *poulaines*. Christine silently cheered each time the hats flew out of their reach just as they were about to catch them. The woman with the onions stood wiping her muddy hands on her apron and glaring at her. 'It's all your fault,' she said.

Christine didn't know whether to laugh or cry, she was so exasperated with everyone.

At the palace, she hoped to have a chance to talk to Valentina, but as she passed the chamber where the duchess received petitioners in the morning, she looked in and saw that the duchess already had a guest, a slender man dressed in a short green velvet jacket with padded shoulders and tight silver hose. He'd been on his knees, and he was struggling trying to rise, finding it difficult because the long points of his *poulaines* kept getting in the way. Valentina, who seemed to be trying not to smile, wore a simple blue *houppelande*, decorated with only a gold belt and a lace collar. The simple elegance of her costume made a sharp contrast with the ostentatious attire of her visitor.

Christine longed to know what the man was saying but was prevented from going closer by one of the duchess's ladies, who stood by the door and gestured her away.

She went up the stairs to the library to retrieve the Aesop's fables and found Gilles Malet sitting at his desk, mumbling to himself as he turned the pages of a book. All of a sudden he closed the book and slammed it down. One of the fur-lined sleeves of his *houppelande* caught on the edge of the desk, and he pulled it away so abruptly that it ripped. His bushy eyebrows quivered.

'That's no way for a librarian to treat books!' Christine said. 'Or his clothes!'

'Don't reprimand me!' Gilles shot back.

Christine had never seen him so agitated. 'What's wrong, Gilles?' she asked softly.

'Did you see that man with the duchess?'

'Who could miss him, the way he's dressed?'

'Like a peacock. And those shoes! I hope he falls over them.'

'Is he someone important?'

'Dangerous is a better word. His name is Thibault de Torvaux, and he comes to plead with the duchess for Pierre de Craon, the fiend who tried to kill the king's constable.'

Christine remembered what Brother Michel had said about Thibault, and she shuddered. 'What does this have to do with the duchess?' she asked.

'Thibault is trying to persuade Valentina to take Pierre under her wing so he can come back to the court. He's telling her that she should be grateful to Pierre because he told her about her husband's affair with another woman.'

'Surely Valentina won't be swayed by pretty words.'

'Don't be so certain. Pierre de Craon and his friend have fooled many people in the past, and they will do so again.' Gilles stood up and began pacing around the room, paying so little attention to where he was going that he collided with a man who had just come through the door. 'Out of my way!' he cried as he pushed the man aside.

'Nobody talks to me like that!' the man shouted.

Christine walked over and put her hand on the man's sleeve. The duke was having his library refurbished, and this was his painter, Colart de Laon, who was covering the walls between the cabinets with frescoes. Colart didn't take slights lightly. She'd heard him shouting at one of the duke's *huissiers* because he'd made a disparaging comment about a design he'd painted on one of the duchess's carriages. 'There's no place for that here in France,' the *huissier* had declared, pointing to Valentina's coat of arms, the Visconti emblem of a viper swallowing a child. 'I'll paint what I like,' Colart had shouted. He'd raised his fist and would have hit the *huissier* if the man hadn't walked away.

'Gilles didn't mean it, Colart,' Christine said.

The painter pulled his arm away and started out the door.

'Come back!' Gilles called out.

Colart continued down the hall.

Gilles ran after him. 'Wait, Colart!' he cried. 'I didn't mean to insult you.'

Christine had to smile when they came back, Colart muttering to himself and waving a paint brush about, and Gilles following sheepishly behind him.

'They're beautiful,' she said, pointing to the nearly finished figures of Ovid, Vergil, Horace, Terence, and Juvenal on the wall, ancient writers whose works the duke had collected. The illustrious men stood tall and proud in brightly colored robes, their names lettered neatly beneath their feet.

Colart stomped to a ladder, climbed it, and started to work, mumbling angrily all the while. Gilles sat down at his desk, picked up the book he'd been reading, and bent over it, his bushy eyebrows bouncing up and down. Then he remembered Christine and shoved the book under a pile of manuscripts.

'Why are you hiding that?' Christine asked.

Gilles looked over at the painter and covered the manuscripts with his hand.

Colart's assistant came to the door and called him away. When he'd gone, Gilles still kept his hand on the manuscripts. 'This is not for your eyes, Christine.'

'Will you never stop treating me as though I'm too frail or foolish to know what's going on?' She pushed his hand away, reached under the manuscripts, and pulled out a book in a leather jacket covered with mysterious symbols.

'Is this something the duke acquired recently?' she asked.

'The duke never bought this book. Someone left it at the door to the library this morning. It shouldn't be here. You shouldn't be touching it. It's evil.'

'I'll decide that,' Christine said. She opened the book, glanced at its contents, and exclaimed, 'This is a book of demonic magic!'

'I know that. That's why you shouldn't be touching it.'

'I'd rather read it. See here. It tells how to drive someone mad by burning a candle with the names of demons inscribed on it.'

Gilles grabbed the book and threw it to the floor.

Christine bent down and retrieved it. 'Are you afraid I'll try to follow some of the instructions?' She turned the pages until she came to a section on mirrors. 'The scribe who did this made beautiful letters,' she said, 'but the text is ridiculous. It tells how to conjure demons in mirrors so they'll tell you how to find things you've lost. My mother believes that.'

Gilles took the book and plunked it down on the desk.

Christine opened it to the section on mirrors again. 'You know, Gilles, people are spreading a rumor that the duchess has a steel mirror she looks into when she wants to conjure the Devil.'

Gilles shook his head. 'More slander. She may have a mirror, but she uses it to look at herself.'

Christine closed the book. 'You say this was left at the door? Do you have any idea who left it there?'

'None at all. But I know *why* it was left. People are meant to think it's something Valentina uses for spells. That's why I have to hide it.'

'From me? You don't think *I* believe such things, do you?'

'I'm sure you don't. But I don't trust you not to try to find out who does. You're always getting into trouble.'

Christine laughed. 'That's what my mother says.'

'You should listen to her. Stay home with your cooking and sewing.'

'You know I'll never do that.' She pushed the book away. 'Hide this well, Gilles.'

He slid the book under the pile of manuscripts again, rose, went to a cabinet, and returned with the Aesop's fables. She took it and started out the door, then turned and looked at Colart, who was now back on his ladder. She watched him pick up his brush and begin to add bright red paint to Ovid's robe before she went out and climbed the stairs to the room where she did her copying.

SEVENTEEN

Make a mirror in the name of Floron. Have it made of pure steel, luminous and shiny as a sword, the size of one palm, with a handle. Around the unpolished part of the rim have the names of ten demons, with the name of Floron in the center. In a secret place anoint it with pure and lustrous balsam, and fumigate it with aloes, ambergris, myrrh, and frankincense.

From a fifteenth-century manual of demonic magic,
Bayerische Staatsbibliothek, Munich, Clm 849

The fools were waiting for her. Blondel lay on the floor in front of her desk, and the others stood around him, every now and then poking him with their feet. Hanotin held one of his arms over his chest, hiding something in the wide sleeve of his jacket. The monkey, who sat on his shoulder chattering with excitement, reached down and tried to draw the object out. Hanotin shifted his arm to keep it hidden.

Blondel sat up and said to Christine. 'Tell us about the baby.'

'She's well,' Christine said. 'We found her father, and she's with him now.'

Blondel jumped up, slapped his thighs, and began to laugh. Coquinet and Giliot started to laugh, too, and they ran around the room, whooping and bouncing off the walls, bumping against Hanotin, who held the monkey by his feet, turned him upside down, and swung him at Fripon just as he tossed some small balls into the air. All the balls fell to the floor, and so did the fools. Christine tried to keep a straight face, but it was impossible; soon she was laughing so hard, tears ran down her face.

'Why are you crying?' Blondel asked.

'I'm not crying.'

'Your face is all wet. You look terrible. You'd better not look at yourself in a mirror.'

Giliot stood up, shook his thick mane of hair, and announced, 'Tell your mother not to let the baby look at herself in a mirror, either.'

'So she won't grow up to be a thief,' said Coquinet, who rolled over and stood on his elbows.

'Or get ugly like him,' Hanotin said as he rose to his feet, grabbed the monkey, and stared into its face. The object he had in his sleeve started to fall out, and he pushed it back.

'That's one of my mother's superstitions,' Christine said. Francesca wouldn't look into a mirror at night because she believed she might wake up the next day and find she'd grown ugly. 'What other superstitions do you know about?' she asked, thinking of what she'd read in the book of demonic magic on Gilles's desk.

'There are a great many,' Giliot said. 'For example, I'll bet your mother wears a necklace of olive pits.'

Christine laughed. Francesca had indeed taken some olive pits, put holes in them, strung them on a black silk thread, and made them into a necklace, believing it would ward off any evil that might befall her, especially when she went out at night.

'Or perhaps a bracelet of fava beans,' Hanotin said. 'The smell drives demons away.'

'It's the stalk, not the beans,' said Coquinet. 'How can you wear that?'

'My mother could probably devise a way,' Christine said.

'If she's so smart, does she know who left the baby in the garden?' Fripon asked, looking at her slyly.

'My mother doesn't know everything.' She went to the desk and started to unpack her writing materials.

'Do you?' Fripon asked.

'No. But I know you fools have some thoughts about it. Why don't you tell me?' *And why doesn't Hanotin tell me what he's hiding in his sleeve?* she asked herself.

The fools all started to talk at once, and in the confusion of words, Christine heard again and again, 'Valentina.'

'The duchess didn't put the baby in the garden!' she exclaimed.

The fools shook their heads vigorously. 'Of course she didn't!' Giliot cried. 'It was put there so people would *think* she put it there.'

'But we found it first,' Coquinet said. 'And you took it to your mother. So no one knows.'

'But people think Valentina murdered the dead woman in the garden,' Giliot said.

The fools sat down on the floor and hung their heads.

'Poor Valentina,' Giliot blubbered, wiping his nose with the back of his hand.

Coquinet slid over and put his long arms around him, Fripon stared at his feet, and Hanotin kept one arm over his chest and ran the fingers of the other through his hair, making the tufts over his ears stick up. The monkey, sitting on his shoulders, put his paws on his own head and scratched it. Blondel stretched out and cried so hard Christine thought she felt the floor shaking.

She felt like crying herself. She'd come to like and respect the Duchess of Orléans, admiring her dignity in the face of all the terrible things people said about her. She knew that Valentina had other sorrows, too. Her husband was unfaithful, and if what Jacopo the dwarf had said was true, she couldn't even be sure Louis would defend her in the face of all the slander. He might even send her away.

Suddenly the fools stood up. The monkey lost his balance and almost fell from Hanotin's shoulder. Coquinet twisted his body into a knot, Fripon ran around tossing balls into the air, and Blondel bumped against Christine's desk, nearly upsetting her inkhorn.

'We have to help Valentina!' Hanotin cried.

'But how?' Christine asked, thinking it was foolish to ask a group of fools to have a solution to any problem, let alone that one.

'We know what you're thinking,' Coquinet said. '"Poor fools. They don't know anything."'

'Or perhaps you're thinking there's not much difference between a fool and a madman,' Blondel said, sliding down the side of the desk and hitting the floor with a thud.

'You really should be thinking there's not much difference between a fool and a *wise* man,' Hanotin said. He reached into his sleeve and removed a piece of rolled-up parchment. Just as he was about to hand it to Christine, the monkey reached down, seized it, jumped off his shoulder, and ran around the room, chattering to himself. Blondel stuck out his foot and tripped him. The monkey howled and ran back to Hanotin, who grabbed the parchment, unrolled it, and handed it to Christine.

The parchment was wrinkled and torn, but she could see that it was covered with the same symbols and words she'd seen in the book of demonic magic that Gilles had tried to hide from her in the library. She shuddered. 'Where did you get this?'

'Behind the duchess's chair,' Hanotin said.

'Do you know who put it there?'

'It must have been the peacock.'

Christine had to think for a moment. Then she remembered what Gilles had said about Valentina's visitor, Thibault de Torvaux. She laughed. 'He really does look like a peacock.'

'Except for his feet,' Giliot said.

'What's wrong with his feet? Other than the fact that the points of his *poulaines* are so long, he can hardly stand up.'

'That's just it,' Giliot said. 'That man thinks he's beautiful. But his feet are ugly, and he screams when he looks at them. That's what peacocks do, you know.'

'I didn't know. But now I'll think of it every time I see that man.'

'And you'll laugh,' Giliot said. 'Good for you.'

Hanotin pointed to the parchment. 'The peacock put that behind the duchess's chair.'

'Did the duchess see it?' Christine asked.

'No!'

'Do you know what's written here?'

'You tell us.'

'It's best that I don't.'

'I'll bet you don't know,' Fripon said.

Christine laughed. 'I'll tell you this much. People would think the duchess could use this to make the king lose his mind.'

'Then it must be spells,' Hanotin said. He picked up the monkey, who'd been sitting at his feet, and shook him. 'Why don't you teach me how to read?' he shouted.

The monkey bared his teeth. 'He's going to bite you,' Blondel cried.

'No, he's not,' Hanotin said. 'He's telling me he's sorry I can't read.'

'You don't need to know how to read, Hanotin,' Christine said. 'You knew enough to take this piece of parchment away so no one else would find it.'

Hanotin grinned and hugged the monkey.

Coquinet knelt in front of Christine. 'Does it have anything to do with the baby?' he asked.

'Does it tell you how to find out who put the baby in the garden?' Giliot asked.

'And who killed the woman in the garden?' Blondel asked.

'Maybe it tells you to get a mirror, like the one the duchess uses to summon demons,' Fripon said.

'That's not funny,' Giliot said.

'Giliot is right,' Christine said. 'When people make jokes like that, they cause trouble for the duchess.'

'It wasn't a joke,' Fripon said. 'The duchess does have a mirror.'

'Everyone has a mirror!' the other fools cried.

'What do they see when they look into them?' Fripon asked.

'Themselves,' Hanotin said.

'Lost people, too, according to what I've heard,' Fripon said. 'People say the duchess found a boy who'd drowned. His body was under a mill wheel, and she saw it in her mirror.'

Christine went to the door of the room and shut it. 'We shouldn't be talking about such things.' She held up the piece of parchment. 'We should be trying to find out who put this behind the duchess's chair.'

'I told you,' Hanotin said. 'It was the peacock.'

Christine put her writing materials back into her pouch. 'I'm going to talk to that man,' she said.

'We'll come with you,' Fripon said.

'No, you won't. Why don't you all go and amuse the duchess? She probably needs cheering up.'

The fools ran out of the room, and Christine walked down the stairs to the library. Gilles was watching Colart, who stood on the ladder, bracing himself against the rungs, his long, thin face set in concentration and strands of his thinning brown hair hanging about his face as he leaned over to apply orange paint to Juvenal's robe. She placed the book of fables on the desk and left before Gilles could see her.

She hadn't decided how she was going to meet Thibault de Torvaux, but the problem was solved when she found him coming out of Valentina's reception room. He saw her, made a deep bow, and stood before her looking as innocent as Thomas when he'd been caught with his hand on his grandmother's honey wafers.

'Ah. The lady who copies manuscripts for the duchess,' Thibault said. 'Such an interesting job for a woman.' His silver hose was very tight, and his green jacket was so short it didn't cover his buttocks. The points of his *poulaines* were the longest she'd ever seen, and she wondered how he could walk in them.

'How do you know who I am?'

'Your reputation precedes you.' He smiled, causing a big scar on his cheek to wrinkle.

She resisted the temptation to slap him, instead saying, 'I presume you are here to see the duchess.'

'Yes, indeed. Such a wonderful woman. Who could resist the opportunity to visit her? And her estimable husband, the duke, of course.'

'I'm sure you have many things to talk about.'

'My friend and I have had so many fascinating experiences on our travels. The duchess is eager to hear all about them.'

'Your friend?'

'Surely you know Pierre de Craon. He is staying at the abbey of Saint-Denis for the moment. Soon he will come here himself to visit the duke and duchess.'

I think not, Christine said to herself.

'And you, how does your work progress?'

'Very well, thank you.'

'Perhaps I could see some of the manuscripts you're copying.'

She wondered how he knew about her work, and she felt her skin crawl, but she managed to answer civilly. 'That would be most pleasant, but there is much to be done, and I have no time for visitors at the moment.'

'Then I shall wait patiently until the time is right,' he simpered.

I can't take any more of this, she thought. She picked up her skirt and attempted to walk away, but he stepped in front of her.

'I'm sure we'll meet again.' He smirked, and the scar on his cheek turned bright red.

EIGHTEEN

I should be the king of ugliness.

Eustache Deschamps (c. 1340–1404), *Ballade 774*

T he next morning as she walked past the duchess's receiving room, Christine looked in through the door, afraid she would see Thibault de Torvaux. Instead she saw the king, slouched in a high-backed chair, playing chess with Valentina. He'd pulled his bright blue *houppelande* up over his knees, and he tugged at his thinning blond hair. When he reached out a long, bony hand to move a pawn, she was horrified to see that his fingers were bleeding; he'd bitten his nails down to the quick.

Valentina, dressed in a plain rose-colored gown and a simple white headdress, sat quietly, leaning carefully over the table whenever it was her move. Her two Italian maids, Julia and Elena, were at her side, and every now and then she reached out and drew one or the other of them close. The sisters wore simple gowns and headdresses much like Valentina's, and they looked fresh and innocent in comparison with the duchess's ladies-in-waiting, older woman who clustered around her in crimson, purple, and green brocaded *houppelandes*, gold belts, and jeweled necklaces. The ladies fidgeted and shrank back every time the king shifted in his chair, the long, fur-lined sleeves of their *houppelandes* rippling and swaying as they lifted their hands, covered their mouths, and whispered uneasily to each other. One of the ladies twisted a long pearl necklace through her fingers and looked around as though she expected the demons who plagued the king to come through the door at any moment. Another clutched her jeweled rosary so tightly her knuckles showed white. Madame de Maucouvent held Valentina's little son, Charles, in her arms and tapped her foot on the floor. The child stared at the chess players, turning his face away and burying it in her ample breast whenever the king squirmed in his chair.

One lady seemed unconcerned with the king. She strode around the room in a crimson *houppelande* decorated with a gaudy pattern of birds and stars and cut so low at the neck that nearly all the flesh of her ample breasts was exposed. The duke, in a purple jacket and silver hose that showed off his shapely legs, leaned against a wall, his arms crossed over his chest, and never took his eyes off her. Christine realized with a start that this was the woman with the bare breasts about whom Jacopo the dwarf had told her.

The duke's fools sat on the floor at his feet, nodding and nudging each other. The king's fool, Hennequin, leaned against the wall with his arms crossed over his chest in imitation of the duke. Next to him Jacopo stared off into the distance, pretending not to notice what the fools were doing.

The room was quiet except for the rustle of the king's *houppelande* as he slid around on his chair. In an instant the silence was shattered. The king jumped up, stretched out his arm, and swept everything off the chess table on to the floor. The sound of splintering wood rang out as he stomped on the chess board. Then he lurched against a sideboard, sending silver pitchers and ewers flying and a large ceremonial glass platter crashing against the wall where it splintered into a thousand pieces. 'The swords are pricking me again!' he cried.

The duke dashed to his brother's side, grasped him by the shoulders, and tried to enfold him in his arms, but Charles wriggled out of his grasp. Valentina rose from her chair, stepped around the debris on the floor, laid her hand on the king's arm, and led him to a day bed, where she sat beside him. She put her hand on his forehead.

Christine heard two of the king's sergeants-at-arms whispering together. 'She's put something on his head,' one said. 'That's how she calms him.'

'No one else can do it,' the other said. 'It has to be sorcery.'

Christine strained to see whether it was true that the duchess had put something on the king's head, but her view was blocked by the voluminous gowns of several ladies-in-waiting. She sensed someone behind her and turned to find a hunched man who said, 'It has nothing to do with sorcery.' He frowned and shook his fist at the two sergeants-at-arms.

'I know,' she said. 'I think it might be the coolness of her hand that soothes him. My mother eases the pain of my headaches that way.'

'You have a wise mother,' said Eustache Deschamps, the duke's *maître d'hôtel* and the unofficial court poet. Dark, stooped, and ungainly, with a short torso and long arms, he described himself in one of his poems as looking like a monkey, and Christine had to agree. But his looks meant nothing; he was one of the most intelligent people at the court. She was not surprised to see him, for she knew that Valentina was fond of him, and he of her. He'd even written several poems in her honor, poems the duchess delighted in reading to her guests.

'The king has not been himself today,' Eustache said. 'But he seems better now.'

What the poet said was true. The king sat quietly, slumped against the duchess, his eyes closed and his hands hanging limply at his side.

'It's a marvel that Valentina can sooth him,' Christine said.

'It's good for the king, but bad for her. Her influence on him has gained her many enemies.'

'I know you are not one of them,' Christine said.

'Someone has to stand up for her.'

A lady standing in front of them turned, and Christine recognized Symonne du Mesnil. The young woman stared at Christine for a moment, turned, and walked away.

'Do you know why she's here?' Christine asked Eustache.

'She comes here often. The duchess is pleased to have her because she hopes Symonne will go back and report to the queen that nothing inappropriate is going on between her and the king. This is important, you know, because the Duchess of Burgundy tells the queen lies about Valentina.'

'The Duchess of Burgundy seems to have a sack full of lies about Valentina.'

'People believe those lies. They have made so many enemies for Valentina, it's a wonder she trusts anyone. And with all the strange things going on here, I think she's beginning to be afraid.'

Christine wondered what strange things Eustache Deschamps was referring to. *Does he know about the baby abandoned in the palace gardens?* she asked herself. It was no secret that the body of a woman had been found in the gardens, but so far as she could tell, the fools were the only ones at the court who knew about the baby. At least, that was what she hoped.

'On the other hand,' Eustache continued, 'Valentina has friends. Including the duke's fools.'

'Why does the duke need so many fools?'

'He has a melancholy side, you know. He needs a lot of cheering up. Once he even hired a man to do nothing but make funny faces for him.'

'It seems to me the fools could do that just as well. But why doesn't Valentina have any fools of her own?'

'She did have a fool when she left Italy. But he came to a bad end.'

'What happened?'

'When she was on her way here, her favorite necklace disappeared, and someone said they'd seen her fool steal it. I don't think Valentina really believed he'd taken it, but that villain, Pierre de Craon, who was with the party the duke sent to meet her, convinced her to question him. The fool was frightened. He ran away, fell from a bridge, and drowned. Valentina loved that fool, and she vowed never to have another one.'

'Do the duke's fools know this story?'

'They do. They're sorry for her, and they make it their business to try to cheer her up. They also want to protect her from all the slanderers.'

'Do you think they can help her? After all, they're only fools.'

'You, of all people, must realize there are many kinds of fools. You have to decide which ones are worth paying attention to.'

He turned away abruptly, and Christine thought he might be angry with her. But then he turned around and asked, 'Have you brought me anything?'

It took a moment for her to realize what he was talking about. She'd forgotten that in a moment of weakness she'd told him she'd tried her hand at writing poems, and he'd said he'd like to read them.

'Do you really want to see them?'

'You mustn't be shy about it,' Eustache said. 'Everyone has to start somewhere.'

'I'll bring them soon,' she promised.

'Good,' the poet said, rubbing his hands together. 'We need some new talent at the court.' He stepped close to her and said in a low voice, 'Talent not just for writing poetry. I think you can help the duchess. She is in grave danger.'

'What can I do?'

'Listen to the fools. You know which ones I mean.'

NINETEEN

If you give someone a concoction of equal parts of darnel seeds, crocus, frankincense, and wine lees, he will sleep, lose the power of speech because his tongue will be so dry, and not be able to stand up. If you add mandrake, wild lettuce seed, black pepper, and henbane seed, he will be drunk, lose his senses, and be completely out of his mind. This recipe should be kept secret from any wicked person.

Picatrix, ninth-century Arabic book on magic,
translated into Spanish and Latin in 1256

C hristine climbed the stairs to the library, but before she got there, she heard shouting and cursing. She peered into the room and saw Colart the painter brandishing a paintbrush and yelling at the top of his voice. Gilles was trying to calm him, but without success.

'What happened?' she called out to Gilles.

'Someone tampered with Ovid. Come in and take a look.'

Christine went to the painting and saw that names of plants had been scratched into the hem of the poet's red robe. She was familiar with some of them – crocus, mandrake, and henbane. Darnel and wild lettuce she would have to ask her mother about. But the meaning was clear: it was a formula for some kind of potion.

Colart danced around in a fury. 'It's an outrage!' He threw his brushes on to the floor.

'Why would anyone do this?' Christine asked.

'To slander the duchess,' Gilles said. 'We're meant to think these are plants she uses to bewitch the king.'

Colart jumped up and down. 'That beautiful red! Do you know how long it took to make that beautiful red paint?' He glared at Gilles. 'No, I don't expect you do.'

'Calm down,' Gilles said. 'I'll help you repair the damage.'

'No, you won't!' Colart shouted. 'You think painting is easy. You don't know a thing about it!' He stomped out of the room.

Gilles shook his head. 'Colart is a fine painter. I hope he doesn't decide to leave us.'

Colart stomped back into the room and bellowed, 'Someone is doing this to me because they know I'm friends with the duchess!' He stormed out again.

Eustache Deschamps wandered in. 'What's wrong with Colart?'

'Take a look at Ovid,' Gilles said.

Eustache went to the painting and examined the writing on the robe. 'No wonder he's upset,' he said. 'We must keep this from the duchess.'

'She may know already,' Gilles said. 'She was here earlier this morning.'

'One more thing to distress her,' Eustache said. 'And that scoundrel, Thibault de Torvaux, keeps coming here to annoy her.'

'I don't know why the duchess listens to him pleading for that criminal at the abbey,' Gilles said.

'She can't help being gracious to everyone, even a dog like Thibault.' Eustache slammed his hand down on Gilles's desk.

'Do you think the duchess will actually forgive Pierre?' Christine asked Eustache.

'Perhaps. But she shouldn't. Pierre will never forgive *her*.'

'For what? She was the one who was wronged!'

'That's not what Pierre thinks. He told her about her husband's affair with Mariette d'Enghien, and instead of being grateful to him, she went to the duke and confronted him with the information about Louis's infidelity.'

Gilles shook his head. 'Such a stupid thing for Pierre to do. All he got for his trouble was banishment from the court.'

'I presume Mariette d'Enghien is the lady-in-waiting parading around the duchess's room in the low-necked gown,' Christine said.

'She certainly is,' Eustache said.

'She doesn't make a secret of her affair with the duke,' Gilles said.

Eustache grinned. 'She wasn't always so brazen. Do you want to hear some gossip?'

Gilles held up his hand. 'No!'

Eustache stared at Gilles with wide-eyed innocence. *He really does look like a monkey,* Christine thought.

Gilles went to the door and shut it.

'I knew you'd want to hear it,' Eustache said.

Or a fox, Christine thought.

Gilles sat down at his desk. 'Are you planning to write a poem about it, Eustache?'

'Perhaps. Shall I tell you?'

'I'm sure you will, no matter what I say.'

'And I'm sure you're only pretending you don't want to hear.'

Christine stamped her foot. 'Get on with it, Eustache.'

'Three years ago, Louis offered Mariette a thousand gold crowns if she'd share his bed.'

'We know that,' Gilles said. 'She refused.'

'But she shares his bed now,' Eustache said. 'How do you suppose that happened?'

'I thought it was Louis's persistence. And his charm,' Gilles said.

'There's a story going around that he needed another kind of charm,' Eustache said. 'A love charm. And he got someone to make him one.'

'Who?'

'A monk who left the church and became a sorcerer. He smeared the branch of a cherry tree with the blood of a chicken and told Louis that if he touched Mariette with this branch, he could have her.'

'That's ridiculous,' Gilles said.

'It worked, didn't it?'

'Do you believe it, Eustache?' Christine asked.

'I don't know. But I do know that Mariette gave in. Then Pierre de Craon told the duchess, the duchess confronted Louis, Louis told the king what Pierre had done, and the king banished Pierre from the court because he'd betrayed the secret.'

'So now that you've told us the latest gossip, Eustache, let's talk about something else,' Gilles said.

'But there's more.'

Gilles sighed and put his head in his hands.

'You know that Mariette is married to the duke's chamberlain, Aubert de Canny,' Eustache said.

'Of course,' Gilles said. 'Go away and let me do my work.'

Eustache put his elbows on the desk, rested his chin in his hands, and stared at Gilles. 'But do you know why Aubert stays married to Mariette?'

'What do you mean?'

'Aubert stays with Mariette because someone decided that would be a good way to make everyone think she's a proper little wife, not Louis's concubine.'

'Who told you that?'

'I have my sources. But the thing is this: everyone thinks Aubert is angry with Louis because he's stolen his wife. But Aubert isn't angry at Louis. He's angry at Valentina.'

'Why?' Christine asked.

'Because it was *her* idea to make him stay with Mariette. Aubert hates Valentina for that. He may even be one of the people who goes around spreading rumors about her.'

TWENTY

Badly fed and badly clothed, they feed on the wind and build castles in Spain, thinking how well they will live when they know how to make gold and how they will spend it.

Christine de Pizan, *Le Livre de l'advision Cristine*, 1405

Christine decided to go home. After all that had happened at the palace, she knew she'd never be able to concentrate on her work. On the rue Saint-Antoine she slipped in a puddle left by a morning storm and fell into the arms of a tall beggar in baggy pants, and ill-fitting boots. He set her on her feet, made a little bow, and followed her down the street. She stopped and threw him a coin. 'Now go away,' she said.

The beggar made another a little bow. 'That's no way to treat a friend!'

She knew the voice. 'Good God! What are you doing in that costume, Marion?'

'I fooled you, didn't I?'

'You look ridiculous.'

'Ridiculous enough to fool Henri Le Picart. I put my disguise on again to see if I could fool you, too.'

'What are you talking about?'

'It's a long story. First, I have to tell you something. Klara is dead.'

'Klara? How is that possible? How do you know?'

'I wanted to find out who sold henbane to Fleur's killer. Agnes at my old brothel told me to go to a woman named Mahaut who sells poisons in a cul-de-sac near the rue des Bourdonnais. People call her the "white woman" because she dresses all in white and looks like a ghost. She told me that a man who may live in the cul-de-sac bought some henbane. I went looking for him. I wandered around until I found an open door. Naturally, I went in.'

'Naturally.'

'But I didn't find the man who'd bought the henbane. I found Klara, with a big gash in her throat.'

Christine caught her breath as the full impact of what Marion was saying hit her. 'That's terrible!'

'It is. You should have seen her, all covered with blood.'

'I'm glad I didn't. Klara caused havoc in my family, but I'm sorry she's dead, especially if she's been murdered.'

'I know,' Marion said. 'She wasn't all bad. I thought she might be reconciled to marriage, the night Martin du Bois came to take her home.'

'It turns out she wasn't reconciled at all. I have news for you, too, Marion. Walk home with me, and I'll tell you.'

'Aren't you embarrassed to be seen with such a disreputable person?'

'Not at all. I can't wait to see my mother's face.'

'You don't give her enough credit. She'll probably know right away who I am. But what do you have to tell me?'

'Georgette found the father of the baby I brought home.'

Marion stopped in the middle of the street so abruptly that a man carrying a large sack of flour bumped into her and dropped the sack into the street. The sack broke, and flour poured out. The man shook his fist at Marion. 'You thought you could steal it, didn't you? All you beggars should be arrested. I'm going to call the sergeants from the Châtelet.'

'There's no need for that,' Christine said. She reached into her pouch and drew out some coins. 'This should cover the cost,' she said as she handed them to the man.

'What's a respectable woman like you doing with this good-for-nothing?' he asked as he pocketed the money.

Marion stared at Christine. 'What were you saying before?'

'Gerogette found the father. He's Martin du Bois.'

Marion stood with her mouth open, for once not able to utter a word. Finally, Christine shook her arm. 'Wake up, Marion. Don't you want to hear about it?'

Marion nodded dumbly.

'Georgette heard that Klara and her child had disappeared, so she found Martin and brought him to our house. He told us Klara had never been happy as a wife and she was even unhappier as a mother, so one day she took the baby and left.'

'What did she intend to do with the baby?'

'We don't know.'

'And she's been murdered. Why?'

'Tell me about the place where you found her.'

'There's nothing special about it. Just a house in a cul-de-sac. But here's what I haven't told you yet. When I went out into the street, planning to go and get the sergeants from the Châtelet, I met Henri Le Picart standing in front of the house where Klara was killed. He told me to forget about what I'd seen. He told me he'd take care of everything.'

'What did you say to him?'

'He had a walking stick with a sharp point. It looked like it could have been used to cut her throat. I asked him if he'd killed her.'

Christine took a step back and stared at Marion in disbelief.

'He must have been there for a reason,' Marion said calmly.

'You're lucky he didn't cut *your* throat! What did he say?'

'He just laughed. He told me to go home. I didn't know what else to do, and I was beginning to be a little afraid of him, so I walked away. But then I remembered hearing that he experiments with alchemy. People say alchemists are magicians. They can kill people. I decided to go to his house and see what I could find out about him.'

Christine shook her head. 'How did you think you were going to get away with that?'

'These clothes. I decided to disguise myself and get him to give me a job. I know someone he hires to keep a fire going for his experiments, so I thought I could do the same. But when I got to his house, no one was home. I tried the door and it was open, so I went in and looked around.'

'You are a fool!'

'You should see his house! He must have barrels of money.'

'You put yourself in great danger, Marion.'

'But you see how well I've disguised myself. If he'd come home, I'd have pretended to be a half-wit who had just wandered in.'

'Did you find what you were looking for?'

'No. But I brought something away.' She reached into the sleeve of her tattered jacket and took out the little tile with the mysterious markings. 'There's a locked room in Henri's house. I found this on the floor in front of the door.' She handed the tile to Christine. 'Do you know what it says?'

'I do,' Christine said. 'My father told me. It's the seal of the demon Berith, who's supposed to help alchemists turn things into gold.'

'What things?'

'Anything they can get their hands on. I've even heard about a man who tried to do it by burning old shoes. His neighbors chased him away because of the stench.'

'But maybe Henri really can make gold!'

'Alchemy is ridiculous. Men have made themselves paupers because of it. But they keep trying.' Christine handed the tile back to Marion. 'Don't show this to anyone else. You could get into trouble. And don't go to Henri's house again. Your visit may not turn out so well the next time.'

'I'm sure he wouldn't recognize me in these clothes. After I left, I met him coming down the street and he passed right by me. I really had him fooled.'

'I wouldn't be so sure,' Christine said.

Christine and Marion stood at the door to the kitchen and watched Francesca, who sat at the table cutting up a chicken. 'I thought Georgette was supposed to do that,' Christine called out to her mother.

'She went to the market. She took the children with her,' Francesca said without looking up.

'I've brought someone home for dinner, Mama.'

Francesca raised her head and let out a cry. '*Mio Dio!* What have you done now, *Cristina*?'

'Don't you recognize Marion?'

Francesca jumped up, went to Marion, unwound the liripipe from her neck, nearly choking her as she did so, and yanked the hood off her head. 'This is outrageous,' she said. She dragged Christine out into the hall. 'I have had enough of that girl.'

'Don't be so hard on her, Mama. She put on those clothes for a good reason. You'll understand when she tells you about it.'

Francesca stomped back into the kitchen. Marion sat at the table cutting up the chicken. Goblin sat at her feet, sniffing her muddy breeches.

'You had better tell me the meaning of this,' Francesca said, grabbing the knife out of Marion's hand.

'And *you'd* better sit while I tell you,' Marion said, pulling Francesca down on to the bench.

Francesca look at her apprehensively.

'I know you've learned who the father of the baby is,' Marion said. 'That's good, because the child's mother is dead.'

'Klara? It cannot be!' Francesca cried, jumping up from the bench. 'That poor man. And the child!'

'I know,' Marion said. 'And it's especially sad the way she died.'

'How?'

'She was murdered.'

'*Madonna!*' Francesca folded her hands in prayer. 'Klara had her faults, but she did not deserve that.'

She certainly did have her faults, Christine thought. She remembered Klara's rudeness and her disdain for her husband. But most of all, she remembered how when she'd taken her to the queen, the girl had tried to deceive Isabeau by telling her how much she loved Martin and how she missed him.

'How do you know this?' Francesca asked.

'The woman Christine found murdered in the palace gardens was a friend of mine. I wanted to find out who killed her. Fleur had henbane in her hand, so I decided to find out how it got there.'

'Horrible plant,' Francesca said. She went to a chest, took out the henbane seed pods Christine had found in Bonne's rags, looked at them, and shut them up in the chest again.

'Why have you kept those?' Christine asked.

'To remind me of the evil person who took a baby and tried to make it seem that she was the Devil's child. And now to remind me that there is no end to the evil.' She turned to Marion. 'So what did you find out?'

'Only that someone bought henbane from a woman who sells such things. That person must have killed Fleur, but I have no idea who it is.'

'And now it looks like that person killed Klara, too,' Christine said.

Francesca sank down on to the bench. 'I do not understand what is going on.'

'It's all because of superstition and the rumors that the Duchess of Orléans is a sorceress,' Christine said. 'Someone knows foolish people assume a disfigured baby is the child of the Devil. That person, certain that Valentina would be blamed, must have persuaded Marion's friend Fleur to bring a disfigured baby to the palace gardens, take the queen's baby, and leave the other child in its place.'

'Agnes told me Fleur needed money. That must be why she did it,' Marion said.

'But Fleur didn't take the queen's baby,' Christine said. 'She just left the disfigured baby and ran away.'

'Maybe she realized what a terrible thing she was doing. Or perhaps she got frightened. It didn't matter; she got herself killed,' Marion said.

'Of course she was killed. The person who drew her into the plot couldn't let her live to tell anyone else about it.'

'And Klara?' Francesca asked.

'We know the baby was hers. Now we have to find out why *she* was murdered.'

'Do you think it's possible Klara sold the baby to someone?' Marion asked.

'What a dreadful thought!' Francesca said.

'She ran away from her husband. She probably didn't have any money with her,' Christine said.

Francesca shook her head. 'I just cannot believe Klara was that bad.'

'She was deceitful, Mama. I even caught her lying to the queen,' Christine said. Nevertheless, she remembered Klara's good qualities, especially her kindness to Loyse, the deaf lion-keeper's assistant. The thought of the girl lying in a strange house with her throat cut grieved her.

Francesca turned to Marion. 'Did you call the sergeants from the Châtelet? Surely you did not leave poor Klara lying there. And what are you doing in those awful clothes?'

'Do you remember Henri Le Picart?'

'He was a friend of my husband's. I never liked him.'

'He seems to like Christine. He's always involved in whatever she's doing.'

'That's enough, Marion,' Christine said. 'But it's true, Mama. Henri is involved in this. He didn't want me to try to find out who the dead woman in the palace gardens was, and—'

'I'll tell her,' Marion said. 'He was in the street in front of the house where I found Klara. He told me to go away and not tell anyone. He said he'd take care of calling the guards.'

'Why did he not want you to tell anyone? Do you think he killed her?' Francesca asked.

'That's what I wanted to know,' Marion said. 'That's why I'm wearing these clothes. I disguised myself so I could get into Henri's house and find out what he's all about.'

Francesca put her hand over her heart. '*Pazza!* What a dangerous thing to do!'

Marion started to get up from the table, but Francesca pulled her down again. 'Tell me, what did you learn?'

'His house is incredible: gold and silver floor tiles; a courtyard with fountain and flowers; rooms full of games and musical instruments; beautiful tapestries; stained-glass windows – I could go on and on.'

'But did you find anything to prove that he killed poor Klara?'

'No. I think he might have done it, but so far all I can tell you about him is this: he's really rich.'

TWENTY-ONE

Some alchemists are great charlatans who deceive the lords.

Christine de Pizan, *Le Livre de l'advision Cristine,* 1405

At the duke's residence the next morning, Christine passed the room where Valentina greeted her visitors and looked in to see the duke and his chamberlain, Aubert de Canny, standing to one side while the duchess talked with her ladies. The duke had his eyes fixed on Mariette d'Enghien, who was dressed in a purple velvet *houppelande* cut very low at the neck and embroidered down the front with large gold and silver dragons. She returned the duke's gaze boldly.

Valentina, graceful and elegant in a simple blue gown, looked wan and pale as she watched the duke and Mariette. Her two Italian maids stood next to her, wearing similarly plain gowns. Christine couldn't help noticing that Julia had lowered the neck of hers so that the tops of her breasts were exposed.

Aubert de Canny, a very large, rough-looking man with a square face and a pug nose, seemed indifferent to what was going on between the duke and Mariette. He ran his hand through his unkempt blond hair and stared at the duchess with a frown on his face.

Christine turned from the doorway and found Eustache Deschamps standing behind her, gazing at Mariette. 'Why does the duke insist on bedding that woman?' he asked. 'Valentina is magnificent, and yet he fancies himself in love with a strumpet. His desire for her has caused a lot of trouble.'

'Her husband doesn't seem concerned.'

'I told you before, Aubert only stays married to Mariette because Valentina wants him to.'

'Do you think he would do anything to harm Valentina?'

'All I know is that Aubert is an unhappy man.'

Christine pondered this as she went to the library to get the fables of Aesop. Colart, who seemed to have forgotten he was angry with Gilles, stood on his ladder, reaching out with a brush to touch up the green on Terence's robe. Gilles sat at his desk, searching for something in a large book. When he saw Christine, he closed the book with a bang.

'What's wrong today, Gilles?'

He pointed to Colart and put his finger to his lips. 'He repaired Ovid's robe, but it's been damaged again. Someone scratched a strange seal into it. I tried to cover it with some red paint. Colart hasn't discovered it yet.'

'I'm sure he will.'

'I copied the seal, and I'm trying to find out what it means.'

Christine leaned over to see what was on a piece of paper he held in his hand, but he pulled it away. 'It's nothing you should concern yourself with, Christine.'

'Because I'm a woman and shouldn't know about anything unsavory?'

'That's right. Why don't you take the Aesop fables and get on with your work?'

Christine grabbed the paper. On it was the seal of the demon Berith, the same seal as on the tile Marion had taken from Henri's house. She handed the paper back to Gilles and hurried back down to the duchess's receiving room. Eustache was still there. She stood at the door, and when he looked her way, she motioned for him to come out.

'Is something wrong?'

'Do you know Henri Le Picart?'

'Of course. He comes here often because he's a friend of the duke's. He loans him money. Louis never seems to have enough, no matter how much the king gives him.'

'Have you heard that Henri dabbles in alchemy?'

Eustache laughed. 'I've heard. The duke does, too. He and his astrologer do their experiments in a little room next to where you do your work. Sometimes Henri joins them. Why do you ask?'

'I was just wondering about Henri.'

Christine went back to the library, preoccupied with thoughts of Henri Le Picart, his pointed walking stick, and the locked room Marion had found in his house. Henri practiced alchemy, he had tiles with a demon's seal on them, the same seal that had been scratched into the robe of one of the figures on the wall of the duke's library. She didn't really want to believe that Henri was a murderer, but she couldn't put the thought out of her mind.

She retrieved the Aesop's fables, and climbed the stairs to her room. Before she went in, she looked around. Colart the painter had a studio opposite hers, and she'd seen his assistant, Baudet, going in and out, getting materials to bring for the work in the library. As for the room Eustache had mentioned, the door was always shut, and she would never have suspected that Louis and his astrologer and Henri were experimenting with alchemy there.

She went into her own room, sat at her desk, and was immediately interrupted by the fools. Blondel ran in, lay down on the floor at her feet and buried his face in his hands; Coquinet twisted himself into a tight little ball; and Hanotin stroked the monkey, which was unusually quiet. Fipon stood to one side, juggling some large buttons, watching the others. Giliot shook his mane of brown hair and said, 'The duchess's heart is pierced with grief.'

'I've seen it,' Christine said.

'Friends should help her,' Giliot said.

'We must find out who is tormenting her,' Hanotin said.

'Then tell me, who at the court wants to make people think the duchess is a sorceress?' Christine asked.

'Maybe people who want to hurt the duke, not the duchess,' Giliot said.

Coquinet and Blondel stood up and chanted together, 'Aim at the duchess, hit the duke.'

Christine thought about this. The fools stared at her.

Finally she said, 'So if the duke is the target, who is the archer?' *Great God! I'm beginning to think like they do.*

The fools bobbed their heads up and down. They looked so funny, Christine started to laugh. The fools laughed, too.

'Good! You've got it,' Giliot said, and the fools joined hands and danced around the room.

'Now let's think who the archer is,' Giliot said.

'It has to be Aubert the cuckold,' proclaimed Fripon.

'No, it's the peacock,' said Hanotin.

'He's right,' Giliot said. 'It has to be the peacock.'

Fripon started to laugh. Blondel looked at him and started to laugh, too – violent laughter that went on for so long, Christine was afraid he'd burst. Coquinet clasped him in his long arms, which made him hiccup. Hanotin slapped him on the back, which made the hiccups worse.

'Powdered crocus!' Fripon said. 'Someone must have put powdered crocus in his wine.'

'He'll die if he doesn't stop,' Hanotin said.

'No, I won't,' Blondel said, abruptly getting control of himself and lying down on the floor.

Christine wondered why Fripon thought powdered crocus had anything to do with Blondel's uncontrollable laughter. *Perhaps Mama knows,* she thought. But more than anything, she was annoyed. 'Why are you acting so foolishly?' she asked the fools, then realized what a stupid question that was.

'Don't you know?' Giliot asked. 'We have to act that way. If we stop being foolish, nobody pays any attention to us.'

The fools were staring at her. 'What's the matter?' she asked.

'Aren't you going to catch the villain?'

'Don't worry,' she answered. 'I'll do it.'

'When?'

'Soon, I hope. But I have a question for you. Do you know anything about what the duke does in that room with the door that's always shut?'

The fools looked at the floor.

'We're not supposed to go in there,' Fripon said.

That doesn't mean they don't, Christine thought.

TWENTY-TWO

He who asks what he should not, hears what he would not.

Old proverb

Christine left the Duke of Orléans's residence thinking of her discussion with the fools. They were amusing, and their ideas, though expressed foolishly, weren't always foolish. But she needed more than that, and she was pleased to see Marion, dressed in her crimson cape, her red hair studded with a great quantity of silver beads, outside the queen's residence.

'I'm glad you've discarded those horrible beggar's clothes,' she said.

'Not for long. Now that I know I can fool people by dressing that way, I intend to use them again. But today I had to look proper. I've been to see the queen. She ordered some embroidered belts for her ladies.'

'You're going to get into trouble if you put on those awful clothes again and sneak into people's houses.'

'You're going to get into trouble, too, Lady Christine.'

'What do you mean?'

'You're up to something.' She clapped her hands. 'I know what it is. You're going to find out who killed Klara and Fleur.'

'I don't have a plan yet. I need your help.'

'Of course I'll help. I feel terrible about Klara and Fleur.'

'Then come home with me so we can decide what to do.'

Marion whirled around, attracting a group of noblemen in big beaver hats who stopped to stare.

Christine took her arm and hurried her away. 'Why are you acting like that?'

'I'm happy because we're going to catch the murderer. Are we going to tell your mother?'

'Absolutely not. You know how frightened she'd be.'

'Tell me what you've discovered so far.'

'The duke's fools have given me some ideas.'

'The fools! They can't help. They're too foolish.' Marion laughed at her own joke.

'Don't be so sure. They know everything that goes on with the Duke of Orléans and his wife.'

They arrived at Christine's house. Francesca sat in the kitchen with the children and Georgette. Goblin jumped up and wagged his tail. 'He, at least, is glad to see me,' Marion said as she took off her crimson cloak.

'You should hide that gold belt,' Francesca said.

'You forget, I have a different profession now, so I can wear what I like.' Marion reached into a sack she was carrying, drew out a belt embroidered with flowers, birds, and winged cherubs, and handed it to Francesca. 'This is for you. I sold one just like it to the queen.'

'The queen! What do you have to do with the queen? She has dozens of embroiderers and seamstresses to keep her dressed properly.'

Marion went to the fireplace and stared into the flames. Christine put her arm around her mother and whispered in her ear, 'Why do you talk to her like that? You always wanted her to give up being a prostitute, and now that she has and is making her living respectably, you keep insulting her.'

The children came in and crowded around to see Francesca's gift. She held up the belt and said, 'It is just like one she made for the queen.'

'What did the queen say about it?' Marie wanted to know.

'She liked it,' Marion said. 'But it didn't cheer her up as much as I'd hoped. She's very unhappy these days.'

'I know,' Thomas said. 'The king keeps losing his mind.'

'Hush, Thomas,' Francesca said. 'We must not say that. We should just say that he is very ill.'

'I know what they say at the court,' Jean said. 'When he goes out of his mind, they say he's having one of his absences.'

'He won't even talk to the queen when he's having one of his absences,' Thomas said. He snickered. 'He talks to the Duchess of Orléans.'

'There's nothing wrong with that,' Christine said. 'The duchess is kind and gentle. That calms him.'

'Isn't the queen kind and gentle?' Marie asked.

It was a fair question, and Christine considered it. It seemed to her that Isabeau had changed. She'd worn herself out with grief, and the red, tear-stained face she presented to her husband made an unbecoming contrast to the peaceful countenance he saw when he looked at Valentina, who had her own grief and was better at hiding it. She said, 'The queen is a kind person, but life has become too hard for her. Can you imagine what it must be like to have a husband who loses his mind and rejects you whenever you come near him?'

'They say that he runs around the palace throwing things and shouting bad words,' Jean said.

'Someone put a spell on him,' Lisabetta piped up.

'No, Lisabetta, no one can do that,' Christine said.

'Yes, they can!' Thomas cried. 'The Duchess of Orléans can.'

'The Duchess of Orléans does no such thing.'

'Perhaps it's the duke,' Georgette said. 'I've heard all kinds of stories about the duke.'

'Some of those stories are true,' said Marion, who'd been standing quietly by the fire. 'Do you want to hear about it?'

The children clustered around her. 'Tell us!'

'Perhaps she shouldn't,' Christine said.

'Yes, she should!' Thomas cried.

'You may not be happy you heard it,' Marion said.

'We'll decide that,' Jean said.

Marion went to the bench by the table. 'Sit here.'

Jean and Marie sat down beside her. Thomas went to the other side of the table, leaned on his elbows, and looked at her intently with his chin in his hands. Georgette stood behind him, her eyes wide with anticipation. Lisabetta stationed herself beside Francesca and clung to the hem of her apron. Christine sighed.

'There's a story going around about the duke,' Marion began. 'He made friends with a monk who'd renounced his religion.'

'If he's given up his religion, he's an apostate,' Thomas said. 'An a-pos-tate. We learned that word in school.'

'Now that you've told us how smart you are, Thomas, are you going to let me finish the story?'

Thomas nodded.

'This monk probably never had religion in the first place,' Marion continued. 'He was a very cunning man, and he had three friends who were just as cunning as he was. They knew the Duke of Orléans wanted some magic done so he could get a certain woman into bed with him. They went to the duke and told him they could do the magic.'

'If you are going to tell us about the tree branch with the chicken blood on it, I have already heard that story at the market,' Francesca said.

'Do you know the rest of it?'

'There is more?'

'You seem to know all about it. Why don't you tell it?'

'No, no. You go on. I am sure you can tell us more about it than I can – you have so many friends who are privy to such things.'

'More than you know,' Marion said under her breath. She leaned across the table and pinched Thomas's cheek. 'Anyway, the monk and his friends got Louis to give them his sword and his dagger and his ring, and they went to a place out in the countryside and did some evil things.'

Christine looked at the children. 'I don't think they really want to hear this.'

'Yes, we do,' the children cried in one voice.

'Oh, let them hear,' Georgette said.

'Perhaps they'll learn not to ask to hear things they shouldn't know about,' Christine said. She looked at Marie. 'Are you sure you want Marion to go on?'

Marie nodded.

Marion grinned. 'The apostate monk took the sword and made a circle on the ground and took off all his clothes and got down on his knees inside the circle. He consecrated the sword and the dagger and the ring in the name of a demon, and then he stuck the sword and dagger into the ground beside him and put the ring there, too. Two demons appeared. They were all dressed in green.'

'Was he scared?' Thomas asked.

'I don't know. I would have been. They took the ring, disappeared for a while, and then one of them came back with the ring, and it had turned fiery red.'

'They must have put it in fire,' Francesca said.

'Obviously,' Marion said. 'Let me go on with the story because what followed was worse. The demon told the apostate monk that he and his friends should go to the Montfaucon gibbet, take down one of the bodies hanging there, put the ring in the dead man's mouth, thrust the sword and the dagger up his—'

'That's enough,' Christine said.

'The apostate monk and his friends did something else with the body of the hanged man,' Marion went on. 'They took some of his bones, ground them up, added some pubic hair and . . .'

Marie put her hands over her ears, Jean looked away, and Thomas gagged. Lisabetta didn't understand, but she knew she'd heard something bad and she started to cry.

'That's enough, Marion!' Christine cried.

'She's right. Perhaps you shouldn't tell the rest of it,' Georgette said.

'Just a bit more,' Marion said. 'They put the bones and the hair into a little pouch, gave it to the duke, told him to wear it under his clothes and the woman would love him.'

'But the duke is married,' Marie cried. 'What about the poor duchess?'

'The woman was married, too,' Marion said. 'But that didn't make any difference.'

'I don't believe this,' Jean said. 'You're making it up.'

'I am not,' Marion said. 'I'll tell you a secret to prove it. But it's just between us. You must never tell anyone.'

'Only if there are no more dead bodies in it,' Jean said.

'There aren't.' She looked at Francesca. 'This has to do with the story you heard at the market, about the tree branch with the blood on it. I have a friend who knows it's true because she was there.'

'How could that be?' Thomas asked.

'Because she was the apostate monk's girlfriend.'

'Monks don't have girlfriends,' Thomas sneered.

'I told you, this monk had renounced his religion. He could do anything he wanted.'

'Because he was an apostate,' Jean said, looking at Thomas.

'Did his girlfriend see him call up the demons?' Thomas asked.

'Not exactly. He took her up into a tower. He had a lot of books there, and he read out loud something she didn't understand. There was a noise, like thunder, and he told her to wait for him there and he went out. When he came back, he told her about the demons. He also told her that he'd made another love charm for Louis. That was the branch of a certain kind of cherry tree consecrated with the blood of a cock and a hen.'

'Ugh!' Thomas said. 'I hope that's the end of your story.'

'You wanted to hear it.'

'I think we've heard enough,' Jean said.

'I agree,' Marie said. 'I'm sorry we asked.'

'I said you would be.'

'Did the duke really wear the pouch with the bones and the hair under his clothes?' Thomas wanted to know.

'He did. One of the king's courtiers found out about it and reached under his jacket and pulled it out to show everyone the duke was practicing sorcery.'

'I had not heard that,' Francesca said. 'Who was the courtier?'

'The man who got banished from court for telling the Duchess of Orléans about Louis's love affair with the woman he used the magic on.'

'Really, Marion,' Francesca said. 'You are not making sense. The man who told her was her husband's good friend, Pierre de Craon.'

'That's who I'm talking about.'

'Why would Pierre have told everyone the duke was practicing sorcery?'

'Who knows? Pierre's a devious character,' Marion said. 'It's even possible that he's the one who put the apostate monk up to his evil scheme.'

That could be, Christine thought. *Pierre is older than Louis, and he's always had a lot of influence over him. It's almost as though he could bewitch him. No matter what he's up to, his motives are surely evil.*

Francesca looked at Christine. 'Praise God, you do not have to worry about meeting Pierre de Craon at the court. The king banished him.'

'I'm afraid he's come back,' Marion said.

'*Madonna benedetta!* You must stay away from the palace, *Cristina!*' Francesca cried.

'She won't meet him,' Marion said. 'He's been ordered to stay at the abbey of Saint-Denis and not go anywhere near the court.'

Francesca breathed a sigh of relief.

'He has a friend, though, and he sends him. This man can go wherever he wants, even to my old brothel. Everyone there was frightened when they found out who they'd been entertaining.'

Francesca started to pray.

'They should be frightened,' Christine said. 'He seems to be just as evil as Pierre.'

'Do you think Thibault de Torvaux may have something to do with the murders?' Marion asked.

'The duke's fools think so,' Christine said.

'They can't do anything about it.'

'But we can. I have an idea, Marion. Meet me outside the palace stables tomorrow morning.'

TWENTY-THREE

If you put a mare's tooth on the head of a madman, he will soon be delivered from his frenzy.

The Book of Secrets of Albertus Magnus, thirteenth century

'What are you up to now, *Cristina*?' Francesca asked.

'Don't worry, Mama. I just want to show Marion the duchess's new carriage.'

Francesca went to the fireplace and jabbed at the ashes with the poker. 'I do not believe a word of it.' She threw down the poker and stomped up the stairs.

'Why do you want to meet me at the stables?' Marion asked.

'Georgette's brother Colin is a stable boy there. Since you know everyone who works at the palace, I'm sure you know the stable master. Perhaps you can convince him to let Colin take some time off so he can help us.'

'Do you think we can trust the boy?'

'The queen doesn't. A murderer who was planning to kill the king got into the palace because of Colin's big mouth. That's why he's stable boy now, rather than a messenger. But I'm going to give him a chance to prove that he can do something right.'

Francesca stomped back down the stairs. 'I'd better leave,' Marion said.

Supper was a quiet affair, with Francesca fretting about what Christine was planning to do the next day and the children still upset about what Marion had told them. Things were no better the next morning. Christine grabbed her cloak and left the house before her mother could deliver one of her lectures on the evils at the palace.

Outside the stables, she found Marion standing beside a brightly colored carriage, talking to Colart de Laon. 'He did this!' she said. 'For the duchess. Isn't it beautiful?'

Christine looked at the decorations on the carriage: a snake, a fleur-de-lis, a turtle dove on a bramble branch, and a banner inscribed with Valentina's motto, '*à bon droit*'. All of this set against a glittering gold background inscribed with the initials of the Duke and Duchess of Orléans. The carriage was so ostentatious she couldn't picture Valentina riding in it. *If I know her, she'd rather ride her favorite horse*, she thought.

'The duchess will love it,' Marion said to Colart.

'You must come and see what else I'm painting for the duke and duchess.'

'And I'd like to show you the embroidery I do for the queen,' Marion said.

Christine ducked her head so they wouldn't see her smiling.

Colart went off to the palace, whistling. 'Nice man,' Marion said.

They went into the stables and were greeted with the rich, heavy smell of hay and manure and the sounds of neighing and snorting. A groom who was brushing a big black horse called out, 'Hello there, Marion. I see you've brought a friend.' A small boy combing the horse's tail looked up.

'That's his son,' Marion said as she went to the boy and tousled his hair. The horse turned his head and tried to nibble her beads.

A farrier holding the hoof of a dappled pony between his knees while he trimmed it looked up and waved, and a trainer leading a big chestnut destrier smiled and nodded.

'I come here and play dice with them,' Marion said.

Colin, a lanky boy of seventeen, appeared, carrying a pail that slopped water on to his feet. 'Have you come to see the horses? There're all kinds – gray, dappled, white, black, chestnut. There's even a golden one. Come and see,' he said, and he loped past walls hung with bridles, crops, blankets, and saddles to an enclosure where a pale yellow destrier stood. He set the pail down, and the horse dipped his head into it and drank noisily.

'What's that red stuff on his leg?' Marion asked when she and Christine caught up with him.

'He's got a sore,' Colin said. 'It's dragon's blood, to make it better.'

'Not really!'

'It is. When an elephant kills a dragon, the dragon bleeds all over the ground and someone collects his blood and we use it to cover the horses' sores so they'll heal.'

Marion reached down and touched the red patch. 'Don't believe everything you hear, Colin. This is some kind of resin.'

Colin looked at the floor and kicked a piece of dung. 'Do you want to see the other horses?'

They followed him to a stall where a grey courser circled round and round, tossing his head and snorting. 'His name is Beauregard,' he said. 'He's really a man's horse, but he belongs to the duchess. She rides him very well, even though she's a lady. He's her favorite because the duke gave him to her.'

Next to the courser stood a small white palfrey. 'She's *my* favorite,' Colin said. 'I have to take good care of her because she's missing a tooth.'

'How'd she lose a tooth?' Marion asked.

'Someone pulled it out so they could put it on the king's head and cure him of his madness.'

'We pulled the tooth because it was rotten, you stupid cur,' said a deep voice behind them. They turned to find the stable master, a stout man with a large mustache who had a riding whip in his hand and looked angry enough to strike Colin with it.

He slapped his thigh with the whip. 'Stop repeating that foolish superstition.'

'It might work,' the boy said. 'You should have kept it so someone could try.'

'Imbecile.'

'Hello, Yves,' Marion said. 'I've brought someone who wants to ask a favor.'

'It's not often a lady comes in here,' Yves said, bowing slightly to Christine. 'It must be important.'

'It is. I'd like to borrow Colin.'

'I can't imagine why you'd want him.' He waved the whip in Colin's direction.

I'm not sure I do either, after listening to all his foolish talk, Christine thought. But she had to finish what she'd started.

'I need his help,' she said.

'I suppose I can let him go for a little while. He's not much use around here anyway.'

'That's not true!' Colin cried. 'I feed the horses and brush them and shovel up after them.'

'I suppose you do,' Yves said. 'But you talk too much.'

Once they were outside, Christine said to the boy, 'We have a secret mission for you.'

Colin drew himself up to his full height and put on his boldest face.

'There's a man who comes to visit the Duke and Duchess of Orléans. His name is Thibault de Torvaux. He has a big scar on one cheek and he wears fancy jackets with padded shoulders, very tight hose, and long, pointed shoes.'

'I've seen him,' Colin said. 'He leaves his horse here while he goes into the palace. He's rude to us stable boys, but he puts on a big smile and bows all over the place when someone important comes along.'

'That's Thibault all right,' Christine said. 'Can you follow him around without being seen and find out what he's doing in the city?'

'He comes to see the duke and duchess. He's with them right now. I can't go in there.'

'Wait until he comes out.'

'And then follow him where?'

'Anywhere he goes, ninny,' Marion said.

'There's someone else you could watch out for,' Christine said. 'Would you recognize Pierre de Craon?'

'Of course. He's the one who tried to kill the constable. The king sent him away.'

'He's back now. He's not supposed to be in the city, so if you see him, tell the palace guards right away.'

'I can't keep track of both of them if they're in different places!'

Christine laughed. 'Of course not. But do the best you can.'

Colin thrust out his chest. 'You can count on me.' He sprinted away.

'I hope you've done the right thing,' Marion said.

'So do I,' Christine said.

TWENTY-FOUR

Take as many frogs as you can get and hang them upside down on spits driven from their mouths to their anuses. Have a lead vessel for collecting the oil that comes out of their mouths. Save this oil, because it is a deadly poison that harms and kills.

Picatrix, ninth-century Arabic book on magic, translated into Spanish and Latin in 1256

M arion left, and Christine went into the duke's residence to continue her work. As she passed the chamber where Valentina received visitors, she heard music and looked in to see the duke and duchess and their courtiers listening to a minstrel. Valentina motioned for her to come in.

The duchess, dressed in her customary plain, unadorned gown, sat on a high-backed chair, looking like a delicate lily next to her ladies-in-waiting in their elaborate *houppelandes* and huge padded headdresses glittering with rubies and emeralds. Her two maids, Julia and Elena, looked similarly unassuming, except for Julia's open-necked gown.

The duke leaned against a wall, twirling a walking stick and watching Mariette. She kept her head down, but Christine could tell she was aware of Louis's every move. Eustache Deschamps, standing beside the duke, looked at Mariette's gold-trimmed red and blue *houppelande* with its tight waist and revealing neckline, and frowned. He wore a beaver hat so large that it covered his head almost down to his eyes. Christine knew he was embarrassed about going bald and had special permission to keep his hat on in the duke's presence. She wondered whether the duke himself felt any embarrassment about the fact that he was also losing his hair.

The duke's fools loitered in the background – Hanotin cradling his sleeping monkey in his arms, Blondel lying on the floor with Coquinet and Giliot standing over him, tapping his stomach gently with their feet in time to the music, and Fripon standing nearby with his arms folded across his chest and a smirk on his face as he watched the duke and Mariette.

There were many musicians at the Orléans court, but this one, whom Christine hadn't seen before, was especially colorful. He wore an olive-green knee-length surcoat and bright red leggings, and had a tall yellow hat that he'd set on the floor at his feet. His long fingers flew over the strings of his lute as he sang a *lai* about a nobleman and his mistress, his high, sweet voice seeming to float around the room. Every time he came to a passage about the pleasures of love, Mariette raised her eyes and smiled slyly at Louis, and Eustache's frown became more pronounced. Madame de Maucouvent held Valentina's little son Charles and turned his head so he couldn't see what his father was doing, and the duchess's other ladies shuffled their feet and shook their heads disapprovingly. The queen's lady-in-waiting, Symonne du Mesnil, was there, too, and she watched the duke with a mocking smile on her face.

When he wasn't frowning at the duke and Mariette, Eustache hummed along with the music and nodded to the minstrel, who seemed to be a friend of his. Christine looked around the room. Colored light streaming in through large stained-glass windows danced on the floor and set the jewels in the ladies' headdresses sparkling. Gold and silver vessels on a sideboard glistened, and gold threads shimmered in the robes of the ancient heroes and heroines in the tapestries covering the walls. The legendary figures seemed to be looking at the minstrel and his audience, and Christine felt that an Amazon queen – holding a sword with a golden hilt and wearing a coat of golden chain mail and a golden helmet – was staring directly at her.

She looked around and saw Henri Le Picart standing at the back of the room, resplendent in an emerald-green jacket with ermine trim and a wide gold belt, seemingly listening to the music but actually scrutinizing everyone. She tried to hide behind Aubert de Canny, who had just come in and stood glowering at the duchess.

Valentina was looking at Louis, a sad smile on her lips. Christine knew how much the duchess cared for her husband, no matter what he did. She thought of Queen Isabeau, who also had pain to bear, not because her husband was unfaithful, but because he had been taken away from her by his illness. She looked at the Amazon queen and vowed never to let any man cause her such sorrow.

There was a disturbance at the door: a page had brought in Thibault de Torvaux. The duke motioned to some courtiers who stood nearby and left the room. Valentina, however, nodded politely to Thibault.

Christine decided she'd had enough, and she turned to go, only to find Henri Le Picart at her side.

'I know you see what is going on with the duke and his wife,' Henri said. 'I also know you are thinking of interfering. I advise you not to.'

'You can't tell me what to do.'

'I'm telling you what *not* to do. The tragedy unfolding here is too great for anyone to stop, especially a woman.'

'Perhaps it's just the thing for a woman.' She turned and went out the door.

She climbed the stairs to the library, her anger increasing with every step. She brushed past two housemaids, and stopped when she heard them whispering together.

'She saved a woman from burning at the stake,' one said.

'She's braver than me,' said the other.

She knew they were referring to her, and her mood lightened. But then she saw something black and greasy dangling from the latch of the door to the library. It was a dead frog, its body run through with a stake, hanging upside down, its mouth open. The stench was horrible. She shrank back and bumped into Henri, who'd followed her up the stairs.

'You see? You should go home and attend to your cooking and sewing.'

Christine resisted the temptation to lash out at him with her fists. 'What makes you think I'm afraid?'

'You were about to run away.'

'I was not. I only wanted to get away from the smell!'

Henri went to the door and took down the frog, which was fastened to the latch with a bit of frayed rope. 'I'll wager this rope was taken from the neck of a hanged man,' he said.

'Why do you say that?'

'To frighten you.'

'I'm not so easily frightened.'

'You might be, when I tell you what this frog signifies.'

Christine moved closer. There seemed to be something dripping from the frog's mouth. She looked at Henri.

'That oil is deadly poison,' he said. 'Or at least that's what sorcerers say. I suppose you believe them. Women always do. Ask your mother.'

'You don't know anything about my mother.'

'You forget, I was a friend of your father's. I know your mother doesn't like me.'

'I can't say I blame her.'

Henri laughed. 'Not many people like me.' He made the frog dance up and down in front of her eyes.

'Get rid of that before anyone else finds it,' Christine said. 'It was obviously put here to throw more suspicion on Valentina.'

'Like the baby you found in the palace gardens.'

Christine backed away. 'How do you know about that?'

'I know almost everything. That's why I'm telling you to go home and forget about any plans you have to interfere with the terrible things going on here.'

'I'll do as I please.' She went into the library, retrieved the fables of Aesop from Gilles's desk, brushed past Henri, who tried to block the doorway, and went up the stairs to her workroom, relieved to find that the despicable little man hadn't followed her.

She sat at her desk, wondering about Henri. Why had he followed her up to the library? Perhaps it was because he knew what she would find hanging on the door latch. Perhaps he'd hung the frog there himself, expecting some superstitious person to find it and blame Valentina. If that were so, he'd put up a good front when his plan was thwarted.

She opened the book and came immediately to the fable of the two fighting bulls and the frogs. She'd had enough of frogs for one day; she could almost smell them. She closed the book, went to the open window, and looked down at the street, where she saw the Duke of Orléans talking with his cousin, Jean of Nevers, both of them looking very angry. *How different they are,* she thought, comparing Louis's fair, boyish countenance to Jean's dark, pinched face with its long, sharp nose, and sour expression.

Jean sneered at Louis and turned away, his hatred palpable. The sight was frightening. *Just like the fable,* she said to herself, remembering that the vanquished bull ran into a marsh and trampled on the frogs, proving that when the great do battle, the weak suffer. *All of France suffers because of the enmity of those two powerful cousins,* she reflected.

Then another person came out of the duke's residence – Thibault de Torvaux. He passed Louis and Jean, nodded to them, and swaggered down the street. As he turned the corner, a fourth person appeared. Colin, his cap pulled down over his eyes and walking on his toes as though that would make him invisible, was following him.

TWENTY-FIVE

The difference in character made itself felt in all their opinions. According to what I have been told by people at the court, anything one decided to do was angrily condemned by the other. This rivalry ended by enflaming between them an implacable hatred.

The Monk of Saint-Denis, *Chronique du Religieux de Saint-Denis, contenant le règne de Charles VI de 1380 à 1422*

Christine walked slowly out into the street, glad to get away from the palace. Brother Michel came toward her, took one look at her face, and asked, 'What happened, Christine?'

'I saw the Duke of Orléans and the Duke of Burgundy's son Jean talking together. I thought they would come to blows. How is it possible for two cousins to hate each other so much?'

'Surely you can see it, Christine. Louis has all the advantages. As regent, he has more power, and as a person he has all the desirable attributes that Jean lacks. Jean, on the other hand, is a very unattractive person, and he has no manners, no manners at all. It's unfortunate that even his own father doesn't seem to care much for him. Whenever Jean has an idea, Philip dismisses it.'

'Jean always looks so angry.'

'He is. And fearful, too. He wears a coat of chain mail under his clothes because he knows there are many people who would like to do him harm.'

'That must be uncomfortable!' Christine exclaimed.

'It certainly doesn't make him any more presentable at the court.'

'I've never seen him at the Orléans residence.'

'He won't go there. Haven't you heard? He found his wife dancing with Louis, and he immediately concluded that they were lovers.'

'Were they?'

'Who knows? But Jean thinks so, and that only increases his hatred of Louis. Louis returns the animosity. Have you noticed Louis's knotted walking stick?'

Christine shook her head.

'There's a motto on it, a motto used in dice games: "I challenge you." Jean has a similar stick, only his has the motto "accepted" and an image of a carpenter's plane.'

'To plane the knots off Louis's stick?'

'Exactly.'

Christine almost laughed, but the seriousness of the cousins' feud was too frightening. Instead, she asked, 'Where are you going, Michel? Why don't you come home and have supper with us? My mother would be glad to see you.'

'I'd like to see her, too. Perhaps she has some new superstitions to tell me about.'

Christine smiled. Michel loved talking with her mother about her superstitions almost as much as he loved her cooking.

Francesca was in the kitchen with the children, Georgette, and Martin du Bois, who was holding Bonne.

'Look, *Cristina*, Martin has come back to visit, and he has brought Bonne!' Francesca cried. Her cheeks were red, and she was smoothing her flour-dusted apron.

Christine was surprised to see Martin and Michel greet each other warmly, until she remembered that Martin had once been one of the Duke of Berry's secretaries and would have known many people at the court.

Francesca threw up her hands and protested, as she always did when she saw Michel, that they weren't having anything special for supper, but he had to stay anyway. He said, as he always did, that anything she prepared would be better than what he'd get at the abbey. Then he said to Martin, 'Henri Le Picart told me about your wife. I am sorry.'

Martin shifted Bonne from one arm to the other and wiped his eyes. 'I went to get her at the morgue, and I saw what had been done to her.'

'Have the officials at the Châtelet been able to find out who murdered her?'

'No. They've questioned many people in the neighborhood where she was killed, but they haven't learned a thing.'

Have they questioned Henri? Christine wondered.

Francesca, who was making soup, called out, '*Cristina* found the recipe for this simple soup in what you wrote for Klara, Martin.'

'It won't be as good as any of your soups, *grand-maman*,' Thomas said.

'It's not polite to say that,' Jean said, looking at Martin.

Martin laughed. 'It's just leftover meat, egg yolks, a little white wine, and some verjuice. *Old* verjuice, Francesca. *New* verjuice will make it turn.' He tousled Thomas's curly hair. 'It's nice because it can be made quickly. Doesn't that sound like a good idea, Thomas?'

'I suppose so,' Thomas said. He went to the other side of the room and began to play with Lisabetta, who wasn't interested in recipes for soup, either.

'Where is your wife buried?' Michel asked Martin.

'In the cemetery at Saint-Gervaise. The priest there is a friend of mine, and he was her confessor.'

Christine remembered what Martin had written for Klara about the correct way to confess. She wondered how closely Klara had followed his instructions.

Georgette set up the trestle table, put out bread and cheese, and everyone sat down. While Georgette ladled the soup into bowls, Thomas and Lisabetta began to poke each other and giggle.

'*Basta*,' Francesca said. 'We have guests. And you will set a bad example for Bonne.'

Bonne, who had wiggled out of Martin's arms and sat on the floor playing with Goblin, looked at her and laughed as though she understood. Martin was deep in conversation with Michel.

'I've heard you have an unusual guest at the abbey,' Martin said.

'You mean Pierre de Craon,' Michel said. 'Yes, it is an unusual situation, very unusual. He's supposed to stay far away from the king. Unfortunately, he has an emissary, a man named Thibault de Torvaux, who visits the duchess and pleads his cause.'

Martin jumped up, nearly overturning the table.

'You know Thibault!' Michel exclaimed.

'I certainly do! I didn't know he was here. He's a dangerous man.'

'Is he going to kill someone?' Thomas asked.

'Really, Thomas!' Marie said.

'He's a conniver, just like Pierre, charming and treacherous,' Martin said. He slapped his hand on the table, making the dishes rattle. Bonne started to cry.

Martin picked his daughter up. 'You see! He causes trouble even from a distance.'

He sat down and said in a calmer voice, 'Do you remember when the Duke of Anjou went to Italy to claim the Kingdom of Naples? It must have been fourteen years ago. The duke ran out of money to pay for his campaign, so he sent Pierre de Craon to Milan to borrow some from Gian Galeazzo, the Lord of Milan.'

'Valentina's father,' Christine said.

'That's right. Pierre stole the money and came back to Paris in great state, as though nothing had happened. Thibault was with him. I was working for the Duke of Berry at the time, and I was there when he accused Pierre of being a traitor. No one did anything about it because Pierre is related to the Duchess of Burgundy. Instead of being punished, Pierre became the Duke of Orléans's close friend and confidant. That miscreant can get away with anything, and Thibault is just like him.'

'I remember seeing Louis and Pierre together,' Christine said. 'They were so enamored of each other, they even dressed alike.'

'That is so. Pierre is much older than Louis, and his influence over him was great.'

'What has Thibault to do with this?' Christine asked.

'Thibault claims he was with Pierre when he went to Milan to get the money. I heard him gloating about it one day. When he realized I was listening, he threatened me. He told me I was only a secretary and he could have me dismissed. I said Pierre's treachery had caused the Duke of Anjou's death, and Thibault became so angry he would have killed me on the spot, had not the Duke of Berry appeared at that moment. Shortly after that I retired from the duke's service, and I never saw Thibault again. But he's a scoundrel, and I would believe anything of him. He may very well be the one who is tormenting Valentina.'

'I've seen Thibault,' Christine said. 'The duchess treats him kindly, but I don't think she's deceived. Gilles Malet certainly doesn't like him. Neither do the duke's fools.' *And neither do I*, she thought.

'Thibault is Pierre's friend. That alone should tell you he's up to no good,' Martin said.

'He comes to the abbey and confers with Pierre,' Michel said. 'Whatever they're discussing, it's sure to be bad for the country.'

'Why?' Thomas asked.

'You children need to know a bit of history.'

'Ugh. A history lesson. We get that in school,' Thomas said. Francesca gave him a slap and told him to sit up straight.

'It all has to do with this man we're talking about, Pierre de Craon. Do you do remember the first time the king went mad?' Michel asked.

'Of course,' Jean said.

'That's when all the trouble started. Pierre de Craon tried to kill the constable, and then he ran away to Brittany. The king went after him, but before he got to Brittany, he went mad.'

'He killed four of his own men,' Thomas said.

'Is killing all you're interested in?' Marie asked her brother.

'Because the king had gone mad, his uncles took over,' Jean said. 'They dismissed all the king's advisers. They hated them because they were commoners. They said they looked like those funny little figures on the capitals of columns and piers in churches.'

'The uncles hate the king's brother, too. Why don't they dismiss *him*?' Thomas asked.

'They can't. After the king recovered from his first attack, he made Louis regent,' Michel said. 'That means Louis can take over whenever the king has one of his absences. The king's uncles don't like that at all.'

'Especially the Duke of Burgundy,' Martin said. 'The Duke of Berry is really only interested in his castles and his jewels and his illuminated manuscripts. But the Duke of Burgundy wants power, and he fumes because he doesn't have as much of it as Louis.'

'Philip's wife is even more power hungry than he is,' Michel said. 'She goads him on.'

Thomas was squirming. 'I want to know about the bad man, Pierre de Craon,' he said.

'He wants the king and his brother to pardon him for trying to kill the constable,' Michel said.

'Will we see him?' Thomas asked. 'Is he as bad as the *loup-garou* *grand-maman* is always so worried about?'

'There's no such thing as a *loup-garou*,' Christine said.

'There is. It looks like a wolf, and it eats children,' Thomas said. 'It drinks their blood, too.'

'Some things are worse than imaginary beasts,' Michel said. 'There is much evil around.'

'I know,' Francesca said. 'If that man, Pierre de Craon, is at the palace, *Cristina*, you should not be going there.'

'I told you before, it's not Pierre who visits Valentina. It's his friend, and he's not there for me, so there's nothing to fear.'

'You *should* be afraid,' Martin said. 'Thibault is just as evil as Pierre.'

TWENTY-SIX

He who overestimates his own strength is a fool.

Old proverb

Colin followed Thibault down the rue Saint-Antoine. The man wore a big black cloak, which meant he could easily get lost in the crowds, but at least he'd left his horse at the palace and Colin could keep up with him. The boy set his cap at a jaunty angle and strolled along confidently, proud that he'd been given this mission and sure he would accomplish it and make up for his past mistakes.

Thibault elbowed his way through groups of old ladies who stood in the street gossiping, jumped out of the way as a man galloped by on a black destrier, and shook his fist at a crowd of ruffians who brushed up against him. A cabbage fell from a market basket and rolled on the ground to his feet. He picked it up and hurled it at the boys. Colin crept after him, every now and then hiding behind men hawking pork pies and cheese pastries. He threw a coin at a vender, grabbed a pie, and munched it as he wove in and out of the crowd.

Thibault turned down the rue Tiron. This street was not crowded, and Colin had to hang back and duck into doorways to keep from being seen. Thibault stepped along steadily, swinging a walking stick and whistling to himself until he got to the brothel. Without missing a step, he went to the door, pushed it open, and disappeared inside.

Colin was familiar with the brothel, and he wished he could go in, too. But instead, he had to find a place to hide until Thibault came out, so he went into a deserted shack in a garden behind the cottage. An old woman who grew and sold herbs had been murdered there, and the thought made him shiver, but he told himself he was not frightened, just cold. He kicked aside some dried leaves and broken glass, made a place for himself on the floor where he could look out at the door of the brothel, and sat down to wait.

He waited so long that he fell asleep. A strange sound coming from the other side of the room awakened him. He jumped up and started for the door, told himself he was a coward, looked back, and realized that the sound was only the creaking of an old leather curtain that had been hung across one end of the room. *There might be someone hiding there,* he thought. *But I'm going to be brave.* He crept to the curtain and pulled it back. There was nothing behind it but an old crutch, which he picked up and tucked under his arm, thinking it might be useful, in case Thibault realized he was being followed and confronted him.

'That doesn't belong to you,' said a voice from the doorway.

Colin jumped, swung the crutch, and nearly struck a girl dressed in a bright red gown with a jewel-studded gold belt. She put her hands over her face and cried, 'What are you doing here?'

Colin dropped the crutch. 'Don't tell anyone, Agnes. I'm on an important mission.'

Agnes laughed. 'You?'

'You think I'm just a boy, but I'm going to prove otherwise. I'm going to find out what one of your guests is doing.'

'You mean Thibault? He comes here all the time. You know what he's doing.'

'There are other things, Agnes. Things you don't know about. I've been chosen to discover what they are.'

Agnes laughed and stepped closer to Colin. 'There's something better you could be doing.' She lifted her skirt above her knees and pressed against him. Colin put his arms around her and nearly forgot to watch the door of the brothel until out of the corner of his eye he saw something move. He pushed Agnes away and rushed out of the shack, nearly falling over the doorstep and catching his jacket on brambles as he raced after Thibault.

If Thibault heard any of the noise Colin was making, he didn't show it. He strode down the rue de la Verrerie until he came to the rue Saint-Martin and the church of Saint-Merry, a place Colin usually avoided because he'd heard that a famous murderer and brigand was buried there. Small brothels were constructed along the wall of the church, and several prostitutes came out and beckoned to him. But he continued on after Thibault, charging through a cemetery and out into a street that was very dark because it was in the shadow of the church, and so narrow that he had to jump in and out of the gutter running down the middle, getting his shoes wet and slimy with offal and garbage. A stray dog ran along beside him, and he fervently hoped it wouldn't bark and cause Thibault to turn around. It didn't, and Thibault walked on, whistling to himself. He crossed the rue Saint-Martin, continued on to Les Halles, turned down the rue des Bourdonnais, and came to the place where that street met the rue de la Limace. Then he disappeared into a cul-de-sac. As Colin tried to follow him, he slipped and fell against the side of one of the houses. The rough stones caught his jacket and held him. He looked down so he could pull the jacket away without tearing it, and when he looked up again, Thibault was gone.

Swearing to himself, he walked on. He was nearly at the end of the cul-de-sac when he felt an arm go around his neck and pull him through an open door. Then he felt nothing at all.

TWENTY-SEVEN

Making ultramarine blue is an art for pretty girls rather than men because girls stay at home and have steadier, more delicate hands. But beware of old women.

Cennino Cennini,
Il libro dell'Arte o Trattato della Pittura, c. 1400

Despite her fears, Christine went back to the palace the next day, hoping Thibault wouldn't be there. But he was, looking more like a peacock than ever in a close-fitting blue-green jacket, shiny silver tights, and red *poulaines* with the longest points she'd ever seen. She marveled that Valentina could listen to him so patiently.

Gilles was not so composed; he paced around the library, mumbling about Thibault and his villainous friend Pierre de Craon. She spoke to him softly, but he just glared, went to his desk, picked up the book of fables and thrust it at her.

'Take it, and get on with your work,' he said. 'If you find some remedy in there for the evils that beset this place, tell me about it. Otherwise, let me be.'

Colart climbed down from his ladder, followed Christine out the door, and clumped up the stairs behind her.

'It's impossible to work when he's stomping around like that,' he fumed. He paused at the door to his studio. 'I'm making a painting of the duke and duchess. Would you like to see it?'

'I would indeed,' Christine said, flattered that he'd asked.

Colart's studio was just what she expected – pots of paint, brushes, mixing bowls, and dirty rags scattered everywhere. She smelled plaster and glue and heard the sound of something being ground in a mortar. In the center of the room, the painting rested on an easel.

Colart had depicted Louis and Valentina kneeling before the Virgin Mary, Valentina wearing a brocaded emerald-green gown and Louis in a rose-red *houppelande* with fur-lined sleeves. The Blessed Mother wore a robe of rich blue and sat on a golden throne, holding the Child, who stretched out his arms to two saints: Agnes, in a saffron-yellow gown clutching a tiny lamb, and Dorothy, clad in violet and carrying a basket of red roses. Above them, two angels dressed in white floated in a deep blue sky and held a crown over Mary's head. The vibrant colors, especially the blue of the Virgin's robe, took Christine's breath away.

'That blue is more expensive than gold,' Colart said. He pointed to his assistant, who sat at a table crushing some blue stones. 'Baudet is making it from lapis lazuli. Not many people know how.'

Baudet looked up. 'Some people say only pretty girls can do it.'

'And never old women,' Colart added slyly. 'But Baudet does it best.'

Christine wished she could learn the process, but she supposed that even though she was only in her early thirties, they might consider her too old.

'How do you like the way I've depicted the duke?' Colart asked.

'It's very like him,' Christine said, noting that he'd captured the sensitivity of Louis's boyish, unshaven face with its delicate nose and sensuous mouth. He had also depicted him as partly bald.

'But why haven't you tried to disguise the fact that he's losing his hair?'

'Louis won't be upset,' said a voice behind her. Eustache Deschamps stepped into the room. 'I've tried to get him to cover up the bald spot, or at least wear a hat. But he says he doesn't care.'

'He's beautiful, with or without his hair,' Colart said.

Christine had to agree. Louis, blond and fair, resembled the angels in the sky. Valentina, dark and rather austere looking, with a long face and aquiline nose, had a different kind of beauty: she was elegant.

'You've depicted Valentina perfectly,' Eustache said. 'Perhaps when Louis looks at this painting, he'll be reminded that his wife is far lovelier than that harlot he chases after.'

'I hope no one ever asks me to do a painting of *her*,' Colart said. 'Louis may find her pretty, but I think she's repulsive.'

'So do I,' said Baudet, waving his arm around and nearly over-turning his mortar.

Eustache gasped. 'Don't spill any of that expensive stone!'

'Don't worry,' Colart said. 'The duke buys a lot of it. Gold, too. I have everything I need for my painting. More than I ever had at home in Laon.'

'You're using it well,' Christine said. 'The painting is exquisite.'

'It will be the most admired painting in Louis's collection,' Colart said. 'That and the frescoes I'm doing in the duke's library. I must go down and try to finish them.' He gave some instructions to Baudet and started out the door. Then he remembered something and turned.

'The silver seal I always wear on my wrist has been stolen. Do you think you could help me get it back, Eustache?'

'You don't know that it was stolen,' Baudet said. 'It may have fallen on to the floor somewhere.'

'I know it was stolen! People are always stealing things from me.'

'Why would they do that?' Christine asked.

'They're jealous. Last week the Duke of Burgundy's misshapen son snuck up on me at the palace stables and took some of the brushes I used to decorate Valentina's carriage. When I tried to stop him, he walked away, mocking my decorations. He said the banner with Valentina's motto should be used to strangle her. He probably thinks that by taking my brushes he can make me stop painting. But he's wrong.'

'Who do you think stole your silver seal?' Eustache asked.

'Someone who's envious because I'm Valentina's friend. She gave me that seal because she appreciates my talent. It has my name on it, and a *coq*.'

'Appropriate. Something that crows,' Eustache said.

The painter sneered and left the room.

'Someday your arrogance is going to get you into trouble, Colart,' Eustache called after him.

TWENTY-EIGHT

So many people I see today are in pain and distress. I've looked for good government, but I can't find it anywhere. God's work and true religion are eclipsed. Division, covetousness, pride, and avarice have been born among the people. Everything is in disorder.

Eustache Deschamps (c. 1340–1404), *Ballade 1246*

'I wonder whether Colart knew Doctor Harsigny,' Christine asked Eustache when they'd left the studio. 'They both came from Laon.'

'It's possible. But I don't think Doctor Harsigny would have liked him. Harsigny was a humble man.'

'Did you know him well?'

'We had many conversations while he was here. He was very learned, and he'd grown weary of the world. When he left, he told everyone the king was getting well and would continue to do so if he were given time to rest from affairs of state. But he knew it was not true. He told me the case was hopeless.'

'It must have been a great disappointment for him,' Christine said.

'He'd successfully treated many people all over the world, but Charles's case confounded him. He died not long after he got back to Laon, and he'd ordered a most unusual funeral effigy: it shows him naked and emaciated. I think it was his way of admitting defeat. All our hopes wither.'

'Did he know about the rumors of sorcery?' Christine asked.

'He did, and he knew that the Duke and Duchess of Burgundy were spreading them, frightening everyone and causing people to

act in senseless ways – joining mindless processions, falling on their
faces in churches, chanting futile prayers. He was uncomfortable at
the court because he realized what was going on and he could do
nothing about it.'

'I'm sure you feel the same way, Eustache.'

'I do. I've learned it's best to have one foot in and one foot
out of the court. But I pride myself on being an honest man and,
as such, I can't keep quiet about the evils I see. I don't think
anyone takes me seriously now that I'm old. Some even mock
me.' He laughed. 'I'll get back at them. I'll write about what it's
like to get old, so they'll know what they're in for: rotting teeth,
thinning hair, no more hearing, gout, chills, trembling . . . Shall
I go on?'

'I'd rather you didn't.'

'Then let's talk about Valentina. I know you're determined to
find out who is leaving signs of sorcery here in the duke's residence.
I hope you realize that even if you do, you won't be able to stop
the slander.'

'I know that. But whoever is leaving these vile things around is
a murderer.'

'You think he killed the woman in the palace gardens?'

'I'm sure of it. This person has to be caught before someone else
dies.'

'Have you any idea who it is?'

'Not yet. But I took your advice: I've been listening to the duke's
fools. They think it could be Aubert de Canny or the Duchess of
Burgundy or Thibault de Torvaux. Thibault is their main suspect.'

'Do they think it has anything to do with the queen? The Duchess
of Burgundy has told her so many lies about Valentina, she's starting
to believe them.'

'The fools don't mention Isabeau. I'm sure she isn't the one
causing all this trouble.'

'I'm sure of that, too. She's distressed at the way the king treats
her, but she still cares for him and tries to help him. She realizes that
one of the reasons he acts as he does is that he can't always understand what's said to him, even when he isn't having one of his
absences. So she's asked one of his secretaries to make memory
images for him – pictures that will suggest things he is supposed
to remember – to help concentrate his mind.'

'Of course, these pictures will be of things that *other* people, like

the Duke and Duchess of Burgundy, want him to remember.'
Christine laughed. 'I'm beginning to sound like you, Eustache.'

'You've been around the court too long. You'd do better to stay away.'

She thought of all the other people who wanted her to stay away from the court. Gilles Malet, whose high morals dictated that women should attend to their housework and shun anything that might be dangerous; Henri Le Picart, who thought women were too weak and foolish to understand; Brother Michel, who was truly concerned for her safety; her mother, who feared evil spirits. Francesca knew little of the *real* evils, the evils resulting from the king's illness and affecting all of France, not just the court. Those were the evils Eustache was concerned about.

'Everything is in disorder here, Christine,' he said.

She nodded and watched him go slowly down the stairs.

TWENTY-NINE

The mice held a marvelous conference to discuss how they could defeat their enemies, the cats. The advice they got won't be carried out because one has to ask, 'Who's going to bell the cat?'

Eustache Deschamps (c. 1340–1404), *Ballade 58*

Christine hadn't been working on the fables long before the fools appeared. Coquinet, Hanotin, Giliot, and Fripon raced through the door, followed by Blondel who rolled to her feet. Hanotin had a little sack in his hand, and he placed it on the desk.

'Open it,' he said. The monkey stood on his shoulder chattering and baring his teeth.

The sack was so dirty, and the string that held it shut so old and frayed, she hesitated to touch it. Hanotin shoved it toward her. 'Please open it!' Cautiously, she untied the string, looked in, and saw a small tail, a clump of hair, pieces of skin, and nail clippings.

There was an unpleasant odor. 'Nasty bad things for working spells,' Hanotin said, his round, unblinking eyes fixed on her.

'Do you see the tail?' Coquinet asked.

'All too clearly,' she replied. 'Where did this come from?'

'A rat, of course,' Blondel said.

'I mean the sack.'

'In the room where the duchess talks to her guests,' Giliot said, shaking his mane of hair from side to side.

'Do you know who put it there?'

'We want you to find out,' Hanotin said.

'I haven't even been able to discover who put the baby in the garden.'

They sighed, sat down, and put their foreheads to the floor.

'I know you all have thoughts about what's going on around here,' Christine said. 'Have you told anyone else about them?'

'Of course not,' Giliot said. 'We're fools, and we're expected to be fools. If we tried to be something else, we'd be considered absurd.'

'That's why we can speak the truth without getting our heads cut off,' Hanotin said. 'No one knows it's the truth.'

'What *is* the truth?'

'The peacock did it,' Hanotin said.

'Yes, the peacock,' said Blondel, Coquinet, and Giliot together.

Christine felt a chill. She'd asked Colin to follow Thibault, and he hadn't come back to her with any news.

'It's Aubert the cuckold,' Fripon said. He tossed some nuts into the air. 'I'm sure it's Aubert. See how he looks at the duchess. He hates her.'

'But he's Louis's chamberlain,' Christine said.

'That doesn't mean he won't do anything to hurt the duchess,' Fripon said. 'I'll watch him. I'll follow him around the palace and catch him leaving something that makes her look bad.'

'How are you going to do that?' Hanotin said. 'Aubert doesn't like you. He kicks you aside when you talk to the duke.'

'I have a plan.'

'What is it?' Christine asked.

'That's for me to know and you to find out,' Fripon said, and he raced out of the room.

'Do you know what he's going to do?' Christine asked the others.

'Better not to know,' Hanotin said. He shook his head so vigorously that the monkey bounced off his shoulder on to the floor.

'Leave him alone and he'll decide. If it's something foolish, he'll soon find out. Like any fool, he must be taught by experience,' Giliot said. 'And anyway, how do you know Fripon is a fool? Even wise men act like fools sometimes.' He scratched his head. 'Or the other way around. In the right clothes, even a fool can pass for a wise man. All he has to do is hold his tongue. If he does that, people will think he is a philosopher.'

'There isn't much difference between a fool and a madman anyway,' said Hanotin.

'You look worried,' Coquinet said to Christine.

'Not so much worried as confused, because of all your babbling.'

'You need to laugh,' Hanotin said. He grabbed one of the monkey's paws, Blondel grabbed the other paw, and they joined hands with Coquinet and Giliot and danced around her.

Christine laughed and told them to go away so she could get back to her copying. But she couldn't concentrate. She was worried about Fripon. Aubert de Canny was a large man who looked capable of violence. The jaunty little fool with the curly black hair seemed to think he knew what he was going to do, but she doubted he had any idea of the danger.

THIRTY

What can be more evil and unpleasant or cause more suffering for an innocent person than to hear herself unjustly defamed?

Christine de Pizan, *Le Livre de l'advision Cristine,* 1405

Christine returned home to find that Martin and Bonne had come to visit again, much to the delight of Francesca and Georgette, who hovered over the baby, cooing and making witless sounds that sent the other children into gales of laughter.

'Aren't they ridiculous?' Thomas asked his mother. 'What's so special about a baby?'

'You'll know someday,' Christine said.

Francesca held Bonne, and Martin stood close to her. *Mama is still a handsome woman,* Christine reflected. Lately, Francesca had been more attentive than usual to her appearance, arranging her hair – which was black with only a few streaks of white – under a starched cap she usually kept for special occasions, dressing in a freshly washed and ironed *cotte* decorated with an embroidered collar Marion had given her, and making sure her long white apron was clean and neatly tied. Martin was older, but he was still a good-looking man. Her mother had gained weight, but she didn't seem old. Christine smiled to herself.

Francesca handed the baby to Georgette and went to the fire, where she was cooking one of her Italian dishes: chicken with verjuice. Martin followed her and peered into the pot. 'That can also be made with veal,' he said.

'How much wine do you use?' Francesca asked, and the two of them began a lively discussion that fascinated Georgette, who sat at the table holding Bonne and listening intently. *She will soon be married,* Christine thought. *That's why she's suddenly become so interested in cooking.*

Francesca noticed Georgette watching and said to Christine, 'You could learn from what Martin has to say, too.'

'You know I have no interest in cooking. I have other things to do.'

Martin laughed. 'She's right.'

'I want her to stay home!' Francesca cried. 'I do not want her to go to the palace. There is nothing but evil there. She is lucky she is still alive.'

'Don't say things like that, *grand-maman,*' Thomas wailed.

'Stop frightening the children, Mama,' Christine said.

Bonne held out her arms and called, 'Papa!'

Martin took his daughter from Georgette and asked Christine, 'Have you made any progress in your search for the killer of the woman who stole my child?'

'None. But signs of sorcery keep turning up at the palace, and I'm sure they have something to do with the murder.'

'Is Marion coming to tell us more stories about sorcerers and monks with girlfriends?' Thomas asked.

'We have heard enough about that!' Francesca cried. She was beating verjuice and egg yolks in a small pan over the fire, and Martin looked on anxiously.

'Are you sure those yolks won't curdle?' he asked.

Francesca shook her head. 'I found a spider on my dress this morning, so nothing bad will happen to me today.'

'Do you really believe those things?' Martin asked.

'She does,' Christine said.

'I have some news for you,' Martin said to Christine. 'I went to the abbey of Saint-Denis to see what I could find out about Pierre de Craon and Thibault de Torvaux. I spoke with some of the monks. They told me Pierre and Thibault are telling everyone that Louis played a nasty trick on Mariette's husband. They say the duke brought Aubert to his bedroom where a naked woman lay on the bed, her face covered by a sheet. He asked Aubert if he knew who the woman was, which he didn't, because he couldn't see her face. Then Louis pulled the sheet away so Aubert could see it was his own wife.'

'*Scandaloso!*' Francesca cried.

'Pierre and Thibault say he was furious,' Martin said.

If he stays married to Mariette because Valentina forces him to, he must be only pretending to be angry, Christine thought. *He doesn't want people to know that it's Valentina he hates, not Mariette.*

'It is a disgrace!' Francesca said. 'Women should stay home where they belong and tend to their cooking and sewing.'

'I'm not sure I understand what that has to do with the prank,' Christine said.

'Nevertheless, your mother is right,' Martin said.

He's perfect for her, she thought.

'Did you talk to Thibault at the abbey?' she asked him.

'I did. He's as nasty as ever, at least to me. With the monks, he's a toad, all smiles and false piety. Brother Michel told me he spends most of his time in the city, a lot of it at the palace. Do you see him there?'

'I do.'

'He's a dangerous man, Christine. You should stay far away from him.'

Francesca let out a cry of anguish.

'There have been two murders, Mama. Someone has to find out who the killer is.'

'But not you! You are a woman.'

'We always have this argument,' Christine said to Martin. 'Don't pay any attention to her.'

'But don't you see how concerned she is? You're making things difficult for her.'

Jean put his arm around his mother. 'I'm proud of you,' he said.

She hugged him and said to Martin, 'Whatever you think about women, Martin, I need your help. What's happening to the Duchess of Orléans is terrible. Someone is inflaming people's resentment of her. How could anyone do that to an innocent woman? She tries not to show it, but she suffers greatly.'

'Pierre de Craon must be behind it,' Martin said.

'But it's Thibault de Torvaux who goes to the palace.'

'Because Pierre can't go there himself. Perhaps Thibault has some grudge of his own against Valentina. Who understands the motives of either of those two? They're capable of anything. They're dangerous, Christine.'

Francesca crossed herself.

'Aubert de Canny has a motive,' Christine said. 'I've been told that he hates the duchess because she forces him to stay with Mariette, to keep up the pretense that Mariette is a proper wife, not Louis's concubine.'

'Perhaps it's the Duke and Duchess of Burgundy,' Jean said. 'They hate the Duke of Orléans because he has all the power.'

'You said yourself, the Duchess of Burgundy spreads the rumors about the Duchess of Orléans,' Marie said. 'And I've heard the queen cries all the time because the king pays more attention to the Duchess of Orléans than to her. Who wouldn't want to do bad things to someone who takes her husband away from her?'

Francesca sat down on the bench by the table and started to cry. 'What's wrong?' Martin asked.

'Now my daughter is going to denounce the queen. *Cristina* will be thrown into prison!'

'No. It's the Duchess of Burgundy who's going to be put in prison. Mama's going to put her there,' Thomas said.

Christine sat down beside her mother. 'You must stop worrying, Mama. I'm not the only one who knows the Duchess of Burgundy is spreading lies. People gossip about it all the time. So far, no one has been put in prison.'

But, she reflected, *someone is spreading more than lies: dead frogs, sacks with rats' tails, pieces of parchment with incantations to summon demons. It could be Thibault de Torvaux or Aubert de Canny, but certainly not the queen or the Duchess of Burgundy. Unless . . .* She decided it was time to pay a visit to the queen.

THIRTY-ONE

I don't know how to tell how profound was the sadness the august Queen Isabeau experienced because of the king's state.

The Monk of Saint-Denis, *Chronique du Religieux de Saint-Denis, contenant le règne de Charles VI de 1380 à 1422*

As Christine walked to the palace the next morning, she could hardly stay on her feet, the wind was so strong. She hurried past swaying trees, recoiled when a broken branch fell to the ground beside her, and covered her face with her cloak as a black destrier carrying a man in a windblown mantle galloped past, his hooves kicking up stones. Men gripped their hats and women clutched their market baskets, but even the cruelest wind couldn't keep the people indoors or drown out the chorus of complaints about the Duchess of Orléans that rose above its howls and shrieks. She arrived at the palace and breathed a sigh of relief as she entered the silent courtyard of the queen's residence. Simon, the burly *portier* who had been her friend for years, waved to her, and she dashed to the entrance, with the wind at her heels. Simon opened the door and ushered her in. 'I haven't seen you for a while,' he said.

'Do you think the queen will receive me?'

'A visit from you would do her good.' He sent a page to announce her, and while they waited for him to come back, she told him she'd talked to Renaut at the lion's stockade. 'He seems so happy as the lion-keeper's assistant,' she said.

'He wants to take the old keeper's place when he retires,' Simon said.

'I miss seeing him here,' she said, remembering the first time she'd met the boy, when he'd been running around the fountain in the courtyard.

The page came back. Alips was with him.

'I'm glad you're here,' the dwarf said to Christine. 'The queen needs to talk to someone like you.'

They wound their way through galleries, passages, and courtyards, followed by gusts of wind that blew in through open doorways and shook the tapestries lining the walls. They climbed a winding staircase, went along a hallway, and came to the queen's apartments, where they found Isabeau sitting on her ceremonial day bed with her head in her hands. Her long black hair hung loose around her face, she wore a faded green dressing gown, her feet were bare, and no jewels sparkled at her neck or on her head. Perched on big cushions at her side were several ladies-in-waiting, far fewer than she'd once had, and Christine knew why: the Duchess of Burgundy, determined to be the only one to have influence with the queen, had sent most of Isabeau's entourage away.

Everyone seemed as dispirited as the queen. Old Jean de la Tour held her hands in her lap to stop them from shaking, little Catherine de Villiers quivered like a nervous bird, and large, bossy Marguerite de Germonville admonished everyone to cheer up. Symonne du Mesnil sat apart, a small, slender woman in a simple white headdress and a rather plain *houppelande* who frowned as she watched the others.

A sudden blast of wind rattled the window, and the queen's white greyhound, who'd been lying at her feet with his head on his paws, barked and jumped up. Isabeau's monkey leapt onto the window seat and pawed the glass, chattering to himself. 'He'll break it!' Marguerite de Germonville cried as she rose from her cushion. The monkey screeched and ran to the other side of the room, startling the queen's minstrel, Gracieuse Allegre, who grasped her lute and raised it over her head so the monkey couldn't touch it. The deaf girl, Loyse, who stood next to the queen's mute, Collette, looked over, saw Christine, and came toward her, her arms outstretched. She pointed to the queen, and tears came to her eyes.

The queen's fools, Guillaume and Jeannine, had been sitting quietly in a corner, but when they saw Christine they bounded over to her. Guillaume bowed and said, 'Welcome, fair scribe.' Then he went to the queen and did a little jig. She paid no attention to him. Guillaume took Jeannine's hand and led her back to their corner, where they sat with their heads bowed.

Christine knelt by the queen's side. Isabeau barely raised her head. 'There is nothing with which you can help me this time,' she said in her thick German accent. 'You have saved the king once, but now all is lost.'

'You must not despair, *Madame*.'

The queen held in her hand a bracelet studded with rubies and emeralds. She held it up. 'This the king gave to me, when he loved me.' Tears ran down her face.

'I am sure he still loves you,' Christine said. 'It is his illness that causes him to act so strangely.'

'Strange indeed,' said Madame de Malicorne as she came into the room carrying the queen's little daughter, born just over a year ago. *This is the child who would have been stolen, except for the good sense of the duke's fools,* Christine said to herself.

The queen took her little daughter in her arms and gazed at her sadly. The child reached out and touched her cheek, and the queen started to smile but then burst into tears. The baby started to cry, too, and Madame de Malicorne lifted her from her mother's arms and carried her away.

The queen held her face in her hands again. Guillaume pranced up and began to jump up and down.

'Do be still!' Isabeau cried.

Guillaume sat down on the floor and started to cry.

Alips tugged on Christine's sleeve. Christine bent down, and the dwarf whispered, 'She tried to see the king this morning, but he told his chamberlain to send her away. She loves him so much, and he used to love her. Now he responds to the Duchess of Orléans instead. You can't imagine how much this hurts her.'

'Surely she doesn't think Valentina is trying to seduce the king!' Christine said.

'That is what some people think. If not seduce, bewitch. The Duchess of Burgundy started those rumors, you know.'

'I do know. It was a terrible thing to do.'

'The Duchess of Burgundy has a soul of mud,' Alips said. She looked at the queen sadly. 'I remember so well how much Charles loved her when they were first married. You know how they found each other, don't you?'

'Of course. She was brought all the way from Bavaria to meet the king. He fell in love with her at first sight. Unfortunately, the marriage was accomplished through a deception.'

'I know,' Alips said. 'It was all politics. But she always loved her husband. I remember how when they were first married she would dress in her most elegant clothes and flirt with him all the time. Everyone at the court saw how she aroused his desire, and they snickered when they saw them going to the royal bedchamber, the queen looking very small and childlike as she skipped along beside her husband, trying to keep up with his loping gait. They made an entertaining couple, the little dark-haired queen and her big, blond, boisterous husband. She still dresses up for him and tries to induce him to love her. Sometimes he does, you know. Sometimes they sleep together. But the doctors say that that's not good for him. He often has one of his attacks after he's spent the night with her.'

Christine watched Isabeau sit slumped on the ceremonial bed, bleary-eyed from weeping.

'The king is fairly calm at the moment,' Alips said. 'When he's in the throes of a bad attack, he threatens her. The palace guards have to pin his arms behind his back and drag him away.'

There was a sound at the door, and the greyhound started to growl as the Duchess of Burgundy swept in. She was dressed all in black, and her diamond necklaces jingled as she marched up to the queen. The ladies stood and curtsied, but Guillaume danced away. The duchess called out to him, 'Come back, fool, and make the proper obeisance.'

Guillaume stepped up to her, made a mock bow, and raced to the other side of the room where Jeannine stood shaking with laughter.

The duchess looked down her long nose at Alips. 'You are too short to curtsy. You would fall on your face.'

Alips curtsied anyway. The duchess turned away in disgust, pretended she didn't see Christine, and said to the queen, 'I know you tried to speak with the king this morning. I know he sent you away. Do you know why? That Italian woman told him to. She has bewitched him.'

Isabeau sat up and looked the duchess in the eye. 'Why do people say that? I do not believe it.'

'What other reason could there be for the king's behavior? He goes to see her every day. She can calm him, something you cannot do.'

'I do not believe she bewitches him.'

'She puts spells on your husband. She uses a mirror to summon evil spirits that tell her how to do it. Why don't you get a mirror like that? Or an apple to poison her child, the way she tried to poison yours?'

'I do not believe that Valentina did that.'

'You really are a fool. Just like that one over there,' the duchess said, pointing to Guillaume.

Guillaume raced over and stood as tall as he could before the duchess. 'An enraged fool is a most dangerous beast, *Madame*.'

The duchess started to slap him but stopped when Isabeau leapt up from the bed and stayed her hand. 'You will not hurt him,' she said. 'I am queen, not you.'

Symonne du Mesnil giggled, but instead of admonishing her, the duchess smiled. Christine whispered to Alips, 'There is something strange about that young woman. What can you tell me about her?'

The dwarf drew her aside and whispered, 'The Duchess of Burgundy brought her here. No one knows who she is or where she came from, but she does the duchess's will. I know this much about her: she drinks too much wine. That's why she giggles.'

'Do you think the duchess sends her to Valentina?'

'I'm sure she does. Jacopo told me he heard Symonne arguing with one of the duke's guards, telling him she had every right to be there because the Duchess of Burgundy had sent her.'

'Do you talk to Jacopo often?' Christine asked.

'We've become good friends.'

Christine looked away so the dwarf wouldn't realize she'd noticed her blushing. She said, 'Someone brings books of magic and vile objects to Valentina's residence and leaves them around to be found by people who think they prove she's a sorceress. Could you ask Jacopo whether he thinks it's Symonne?'

'I'll ask him,' Alips said. 'But I can tell you this. Anything malicious is possible with the Duchess of Burgundy.'

THIRTY-TWO

The prize for chattering goes to the women of Paris; say what you like about the Italians, no one prattles like a Parisian.

François Villon (1431–1463), *Ballade*

Colin woke up in a dark cellar, bound by ropes around his wrists and ankles. Above him he could hear women talking. Sometimes they whispered, sometimes they raised their voices, sometimes they laughed, but they never stopped their chatter. He strained to hear and shivered when he realized that they were telling each other how to make potions containing revolting ingredients like crushed serpents, the saliva of dead frogs, and the blood of executed criminals. The women went on and on, becoming more and more excited. Colin strained against the ropes, as anxious to get away from the awful prattling as to get free. He started yelling, sure the crones would hear him.

But the women were so involved in their appalling conversation, they heard nothing else. Colin lay back against the wall and tried to think. But he couldn't think because of the chattering. He tried to see what was around him, but the cellar was completely dark except for a thin ray of light that straggled in through a high, narrow window. He moved his bound hands along the wall, feeling for an opening. Then he got to his knees and inched along the floor to the other side of the cellar, but that didn't do any good either. He was trapped, and he cursed his arrogance. He had been so sure he could follow Thibault without the man's knowing he was there. 'What a fool I was,' he said out loud.

'Yes, you were,' someone said.

Colin screamed, and a hand went over his mouth.

'You're shaking like a scared rabbit,' the man said.

Colin went limp, sure he was going to die.

'That's better,' the man said. He started to untie the ropes that bound the boy's wrists and ankles. 'I suppose you think I'm going to kill you.' He laughed. 'Don't worry. You'll get home to your mother sometime.' He picked Colin up and carried him to the window. Just enough light came in for the boy to see who held him. It was Thibault de Torvaux.

'That will teach you not to follow people who are minding their own business. What did you want with me, anyway?'

Colin didn't know what to say. He'd failed again. Everyone he cared for would despise him. Especially Marion, and that thought hurt the most; he respected her almost as much as he did Christine, in spite of the fact that she'd been a prostitute. And what if his sister found out? And the queen, who had once liked him well enough to entrust him with errands?

Thibault grabbed his ear. 'You'd better tell me, you young puppy.'

'I won't tell you anything,' Colin whimpered.

'I know who put you up to this. That woman scribe who works for the duchess.'

Horrified, Colin said to himself, *Now everyone is in danger because I let myself get caught.* He regained his courage. 'Why don't you tell me what you're up to?'

'Wouldn't *you* like to know. Why don't you follow someone else? The Duke of Burgundy and his sniveling son, Jean of Nevers, for example.'

'Why them?'

'Don't tell me you don't know what they're after. They had a stroke of luck when the king lost his mind. Now all they have to do is get rid of the king's brother, and they get all the power.'

Is someone trying to kill the Duke of Orléans? Colin wondered. This, at least, was a valuable piece of information he could give Christine. Maybe that would save him from looking like a complete fool.

'Are you planning to kill the Duke of Orléans?' he asked.

Thibault laughed and loosened his grip on his ear. 'All I can say is if the king and his brother would take Pierre de Craon back into their good graces, he could help them a lot.'

'Help them with what?'

'Why, getting rid of the Duke of Burgundy and his odious son, of course.'

Colin could hear the women talking above them. On and on they went with their babble. 'What are you going to do with me?'

'Leave you here for a while so you can think things over,' Thibault said. He untied the ropes that bound Colin's wrists and ankles. 'You won't need these,' he said. 'In order to get out, you'd have to go through the room where those women are talking, and they won't let you escape. I've made sure of that.' He started out the door. Then he turned and said, 'When I come back, perhaps I'll teach you how to follow someone and not get caught.'

Colin sighed. The talk above him went on and on.

THIRTY-THREE

Take a white cock, wring its neck or smother it. Turn it over and take out its balls. Burn them and make them into a powder and put the powder into a feather pillow and have your lover sleep on it. Or put the powder into the meat and wine your lover eats or drinks. If you do this, your lover will have greater passion for you than ever before.

A sorcerer's formula,
Register criminal du Châtelet de Paris de 1389 à 1392

Marion was pleased with her beggar's costume, and she wanted to use it again, so she decided to put it on and wander around the district where she'd found Klara's body. Perhaps she'd even sneak into Henri Le Picart's house a second time and see whether she could learn more about him. She wasn't convinced it hadn't been Henri who'd killed Klara. Maybe he'd killed Fleur, too. *Your imagination is running away with you,* she thought. *Or perhaps it isn't.*

She remembered Mahaut, the woman in white who sold henbane. *If Henri is a sorcerer, perhaps he buys the things he needs for his devilish work from her,* she thought. *I'll start there.* She looked at the faded brown jacket with the rip down the back, the filthy black breeches, the muddy boots, and the blue hood with the long liripipe. *It won't do to look so disreputable this time,* she said to herself. Babil watched from the top of his cage as she got out her needle and thread and mended the jacket, scraped the mud off the boots and polished them until they looked almost new, and cleaned the black breeches. She tossed the frayed belt aside, rummaged around in a chest, and found another belt, wide leather with a shiny silver buckle that fascinated Babil, who flew down and pecked at it.

But she'd need something to take as an offering for Mahaut.

I know what to get her, she said to herself. She put on the cleaned and mended clothes, said goodbye to Babil, and rushed to the water trough near the Grand Pont. There she searched through the crowd of beggars until she found her friend who specialized in smearing himself with the blood of dead cats.

'I need your help, Poncet,' she said.

He looked at her. 'I don't know you.'

'Yes, you do.' She took off the hood so he could see her flaming red hair.

The beggar started to laugh. 'You sure had me fooled, Marion. What do you want?'

'A bone.'

'That's easy.' He led her into an alleyway where there were many lifeless cats, some of them recently dead and others in advanced stages of decomposition.

'Does it matter whether it's a leg or a thigh?'

'Not really.'

He picked a large bone out of a pile and handed it to her. 'Anything else you need, just come to me.'

'That will depend on what I'm looking for,' Marion said. 'You don't have *everything* I need.'

Poncet laughed. 'Don't be so sure of that.'

She gave him the fool's finger, put on the hood, and walked down the rue Saint-Germain-l'Auxerrois to the rue des Bourdonnais. At the meeting of that street and the rue de la Limace, she turned into the cul-de-sac where Mahaut had her shop.

In the candlelit room, the spectral woman balanced on her crutch and hung herbs from the ceiling. When she saw Marion, she made an obsequious bow.

'What can I do for the gentleman?' she asked, a sly grin on her ghostly face.

'I need something special,' Marion said in a deep voice. 'In exchange, here's a bone from a hanged man.'

'You wouldn't try to fool me, would you?'

'Of course not. I've been to the gibbet at Montfaucon. Some of those men have been dangling there for so long, their bones have fallen to the ground.'

Mahaut laughed. 'I wish I could go there myself, but I can't walk that far.' She took the bone, hopped to a shelf, and put it next to lot of other disgusting-looking objects. Marion stepped closer to look.

'What do you need? I've got pigs' brains, the eyes of a black cat, a mandrake, the tongue of a white dove, the liver of a hoopoe. A hoopoe liver is very hard to obtain, you know.'

'I didn't know.'

Mahaut picked up two particularly repellent pink objects. 'These are rooster's balls. You can burn them and grind them into a powder to put in your lover's drink to make her more passionate.'

Marion shuddered. 'I've heard two women have been burned as witches for doing that,' she said.

'Well, that shouldn't concern you. You're a man, aren't you?'

Marion gagged. She'd almost forgotten her disguise. 'They were women, using sorcery on a man,' she said. 'Does it work on women, too?'

'Of course. Do you want to try it?'

'Not today. What I need is information. Who comes to buy these things from you?'

Mahaut laughed. 'Do you think I'd tell on my customers? It's dangerous to use the things I sell. I would never use them myself. I could be hanged as a sorceress.'

'I'm just wondering whether a little man with a black beard who wears a black cape with an ermine collar has been here.'

'He may have. But I don't remember all my customers. Why do you want to know?'

Marion remembered that Henri had ways of getting prostitutes out of prison when they'd been arrested for wearing gold belts. 'You might want to know this man,' she said. 'He could help you if you ever get arrested for selling things like this.'

Mahaut fixed her icy blue eyes on her and said, 'I know who you are. You used to be a prostitute. What do you do now? Does it have something to do with that disguise?'

'What I do is none of your business.'

'We could work together, you know. I make good money selling these things.'

Marion knew it was time to leave. 'Keep the bone,' she said as she hurried to the door and out into the street.

I didn't do very well with that, she said to herself as she stood breathing heavily to clear her head of the smell of the dusty herbs hanging from the ceiling in Mahaut's room.

The cul-de-sac was deserted, but she heard laughter and chattering coming from one of the houses. The door was open, and she peered in. A group of old women sat by a fireplace talking loudly. They were discussing ways to get rich.

'You do it by blessing the sun, moon, and stars,' said a white-haired crone in a large blue apron.

A biddy with long grey braids said, 'You have to be careful not to look at the moon when you have nothing in your purse. If you do, you'll be short of money for a month.' She tightened her grip on a little purse she'd attached to the waist of her red kirtle.

'On the other hand,' said a granny in a blue shift, 'bow to the moon when your purse is full, and you'll get even more money.'

'There's a better way,' said a fat hag with her hair in a big knot at the back of her head. 'Put a mandrake in your bed and feed it well.'

Then the conversation turned to other ways to get what they wanted by using potions made of toads' tongues, rats' tails, wolves' blood, and the fat of white rabbits. Marion stood laughing to herself. *What a lot of nonsense,* she thought. *I should bring Christine's mother here.*

She heard a noise coming from a narrow cellar window by her feet. The window had bars, and when she stooped down and peered through them, she saw someone inside perched on a big barrel. 'Get me out of here!' he shouted.

'What are you doing in there, Colin?'

'Oh, God, Marion. I failed.' Colin started to cry.

'You're letting a gaggle of old women keep you prisoner?'

'Thibault told them not to let me go,' he blubbered.

'You let him catch you? Can't you do anything right?'

'I suppose not. But please get me out of here.'

How am I going to do that? Marion asked herself. The women who were chattering so loudly might be old, but they didn't look feeble. *If I go in there, I could end up in the cellar, too,* she thought. Then she remembered she was dressed like a man. Stepping boldly up to the door, she shouted to the women to be quiet because she had a message from the man who'd put the boy in the cellar. 'It's time to let him out,' she said.

The woman in the red kirtle nodded, took down a key hanging on a nail in the wall, and went out of the room. When she came back, she was leading Colin. He tried to look brave as he followed Marion out the door. When they were in the street, he started to laugh. 'What are you doing in those old clothes? You look ridiculous.'

'Never mind how I look. How long have you been in there?'

'I don't know. I lost track of time, what with all that chattering going on. I thought they'd never stop.'

'How did Thibault catch you?'

'I guess I don't know how to follow someone.'

'You certainly don't.'

'Thibault did say that when he came back he'd teach me how to do it.'

'How foolish can you be?' Marion took Colin's arm and steered him up the street toward the palace.

THIRTY-FOUR

A fool often falls short of his intentions.

Old proverb

When the stable master saw Colin, he shouted, 'I thought you were coming right back!'

'Something happened,' Colin stammered.

'Something happened, indeed. You don't work here anymore, boy.'

Colin looked at Marion in dismay. She put her arm around his shoulder. 'Don't worry. We'll think of something else for you to do.'

Christine came down the street. 'Why are you wearing those old clothes again, Marion?' she asked. Then she saw Colin, who was trying to make himself very small in Marion's shadow.

Christine sighed. 'I see our scheme didn't work.'

Colin hung his head.

'Thibault caught him and locked him up – with a group of gossiping old ladies.'

'How did he get away?'

'I found him. It was a good thing I was wearing these clothes. They thought I was a man. So when I told them to let him go, they did.'

'Where is Thibault now, Colin?'

'I don't know.'

'You'd better take him home to my mother, Marion,' Christine said as she turned to go into the palace.

Thibault was sitting in the duchess's receiving room. He looked up and gave her an unctuous smile. She hurried up the stairs to the library, retrieved the fables of Aesop from Gilles's desk, and went up to her workroom.

The fools appeared. Coquinet stood on his head and asked, 'What's fancy and has more eyes than a hundred men?' When she didn't answer, Hanotin lifted the monkey from his shoulder and dangled it in front of her eyes. 'It has ugly feet, like these,' he said.

Christine laughed. 'I know. The peacock. I saw him with the duchess.'

'The peacock is dangerous,' Giliot said. 'We must do something.'

'I hope you aren't thinking of following him around to see what he's up to,' Christine said, remembering that Fripon had decided to do just that with Aubert de Canny. 'Where is Fripon?'

The fools sat dumbly. 'He's going to get into trouble,' Hanotin said.

Christine felt a chill go up her spine. As soon as the fools left she went back down to the library. Gilles was pacing the floor, muttering to himself.

'He's here again. I don't know why the duchess receives him. Surely she must know that anyone who comes as an emissary from Pierre de Craon is up to no good.'

'Do you know Pierre, Gilles?'

'I do. He used to be with the duke all the time. The king is a fool to let him come even as close as the abbey of Saint-Denis. Thibault is here doing his dirty work for him. That man is dangerous.'

Colin is lucky he got away, Christine thought.

Eustache Deschamps came in, and she asked, 'Has either of you seen Fripon the fool?'

'No,' Gilles said.

'I haven't either,' said Eustache. 'But that devil, Thibault, is here again. Anyone who lets himself be taken in by that man is a fool.'

'The duke's fools aren't fooled,' Christine said.

'I told you, you have to decide who is a fool and who is not, Christine,' Eustache said.

She went back to her room and resumed her copying. But she was uneasy. She went to the window and looked down at the street. Thibault was walking away from the palace. Then Aubert de Canny

appeared, strolling along nonchalantly. And behind Aubert came
Fripon, ducking behind people so he wouldn't be seen.

As he walked down the street with Marion, Colin realized he'd
forgotten to tell Christine that Thibault knew he'd been followed
at her request. He started to tell Marion this, but then forgot about
it again when he felt a hand on his shoulder. It was Henri Le
Picart.

'I hear you need a new job,' Henri said. 'Can't you find him one,
Marion?'

Marion stepped back and looked at him, open-mouthed. 'How
do you know who I am?'

'You're not much better at disguising yourself than Colin is at
following someone. The next time you want to see my house, just
ask me.' He looked at Colin. 'Come home with me. I can use an
assistant. You can come, too, Marion, since you're so anxious to
see where I do my experiments.'

'You mean where you make gold?'

'Call it that if you like.'

'Can you really make gold?' Colin asked.

'Perhaps. You can come and keep the fire going.'

Marion looked at Colin and frowned. 'You're supposed to be
coming with me to Christine's house,' she said.

Henri laughed. 'He'll be all right with me. Maybe he'll even
learn something. He's not as stupid as you think.'

'I never said he was stupid. Just foolish.'

'There are many kinds of fools. Be careful when you call someone
that.' Henri took Colin's arm and marched him down the street.

Then Marion became frightened. There was no way she could
keep Colin from going where he wanted. He was old enough to
make up his own mind. But what was Henri up to? She hurried to
Christine's house.

'Why are you in those clothes again?' Francesca wanted to know.
'You and my daughter are doing something dangerous. I know it.'

'I need your help,' Marion said. 'Colin has gone off with Henri
Le Picart. Henri said he'd take him to his house and teach him how
to make gold.'

'I do not believe Henri knows how to make gold. He and my
husband tried, but they did not succeed.'

'How do you know they didn't?'

'I just know it. Henri is a fake. I never liked him.'

Georgette, who had been to the market, stood listening at the door. 'What were you saying about my brother?'

'Henri Le Picart has given him a job,' Marion said.

'Henri Le Picart? Isn't he that man no one likes?'

'Colin is old enough to take care of himself,' Francesca said.

Georgette set her market basket on the table. 'Old enough, but not wise enough. I know my brother.'

'Nothing will happen to him,' Francesca said. 'Although now that I think of it, I saw a white monk this morning. That is a bad sign.'

'And my left ear has been itching. Another bad sign,' Georgette said.

Marion wanted to laugh at them, but she wasn't so sure there wasn't something in what they said. She felt very afraid for Colin.

'We have to do something,' Georgette said. 'Where does Henri live?'

'I do not know,' Francesca said. 'I never wanted to know.'

Christine and I were foolish to let Colin follow Thibault, Marion thought. *Now it would be foolish to let him be with Henri Le Picart.*

'I know where he lives,' she said. 'I'll take you there.'

THIRTY-FIVE

Dogs must know everything, for they make it their business to go everywhere . . . They go into dining rooms, hide under the table, and fight over the scraps; they sleep in beds of state; they tear up the tapestries; and they go into the market to look for cheese.

Eustache Deschamps (c. 1340–1404), *Ballade 1432*

They made a little procession through the streets of Paris. Marion led the way, still dressed in her beggar's costume, but without the hat. Her red hair swirled around her face and everyone recognized her. Francesca trailed behind, trying not to look as though she was with her. Georgette walked quickly, frantic to know her brother was safe.

If Francesca hoped no one would see her walking on the rue Saint-Antoine with Marion, she was mistaken. All her friends were out doing their marketing. A woman in a brown kirtle spotted her and dropped the basket she was carrying. Two live chickens flew out. Georgette tried to catch them, but they were about to get away when another of Francesca's friends dropped her own basket, reached out, and caught one. Onions and carrots rolled along the ground into the path of a third friend, who tripped and nearly fell. Marion started to laugh, which sent them all into a rage. But they forgot about Francesca when a man carrying a bowl of wine approached, inviting everyone to sample the latest offering from one of the wine boats that was docked at the Grève. The women crowded around him.

Georgette pulled on Marion's sleeve, trying to hurry her along. But Marion had stopped to talk to a friend of her own, a prostitute wearing a bright green cape that flew open to reveal a large gold belt.

Francesca pointed to the belt. 'Cover that up before the sergeants from the Châtelet see it!' she cried.

'You're not trying to help a prostitute evade the law, are you Francesca?' Marion asked.

Francesca turned away and marched down the street with her nose in the air.

'Never mind all this,' Georgette said. 'We have to save Colin.'

They came to the rue de la Verrerie, and went down to the rue des Lombards, where Francesca stopped to listen to the conversation of a group of Italian bankers.

'There's no time for that,' Georgette cried, standing behind Francesca and giving her a push.

On the rue Saint-Martin, the crowds were so thick that they lost their way and ended up at the Châtelet. They hurried to escape from the stench of slaughterhouses and butchers' shops and found themselves at the water trough by the Grand Pont, where Francesca's worst nightmares came true when she found herself surrounded by Marion's reprobate friends. She tried to fend off the beggars and other wretches by waving her arms about, but they only came closer, threatening her with their crutches and bandaged arms. A man with blood-stained rags knelt in front of her and folded his hands in a begging motion. She stepped around him and nearly fell over a man who rolled himself along with one leg on a little trolley. Finally, Marion took pity on her and dragged her away through the crowd. When they got to the church of Saint-Jacques-la-Boucherie, Francesca stopped.

'Let me go in for a moment. I want to ask Saint Christopher to protect us.'

'We could use his help,' Georgette said.

Perhaps they're right, Marion thought as she followed them into the dim interior of the church. When they emerged into the sunlight again, she had to admit to herself, she did feel more confident.

They went down a side street and suddenly Henri's house loomed in front of them. When Francesca saw the heavy wooden door with its dragons and serpents, she recoiled in horror and said a prayer to Saint George.

'Are we really going to go in there?' she asked Marion.

'It's beautiful inside. But he's doing something he doesn't want anyone to know about, and we have to find out what it is.'

'We have to save Colin!' Georgette wailed.

'But we cannot just walk in!' Francesca cried.

'You're right,' Marion said.

'Let's just knock on the door and tell him why we're here,' Georgette said.

Marion laughed. 'You don't know Henri. He'd sneer and slam the door in our faces.'

'Let's look in the window, then,' Georgette said.

The house faced the street, but there was an alleyway running along one side. The three women tiptoed over and crept along it until they came to a window too high for them to see through, even when Marion put her hands together so Georgette could stand on them.

On the other side of the alley there was a house that looked deserted. They crept back out into the street and went to the door. Marion pushed against it, and it opened. She motioned to her companions, and they followed her into an empty room.

'We should not be here,' Francesca said. She crossed herself and prayed to all the saints she could think of.

Georgette had no such scruples. She charged across the room and looked through an open window at Henri's house. When she didn't see anything, she dashed up a staircase to the next floor and looked through another window. Before Marion and Francesca got to the top of the stairs, they heard her exclaim, 'They're in there!' They all looked and saw Henri sitting at a table, reading from a large book, and Colin perched on a stool in front of a fire, working a small bellows under a gourd-shaped vessel. All around were oddly shaped jars, flasks, beakers, phials, strainers, and other strange-looking utensils.

Francesca looked at a large mortar and pestle and said, 'I could use that in my kitchen.'

'I don't think it's for mashing garlic,' Marion said.

'Neither is that large ladle leaning against the wall,' Georgette said. 'But the most important thing is that Henri hasn't done anything bad to Colin. My brother looks fine.'

'In fact, he appears to be right at home with all that junk,' Marion said.

'It is not junk,' Francesca said. 'Alchemy is an expensive hobby. You should hear what *Cristina* has to say about it.'

'You wouldn't think it was junk if they actually succeeded in using it to make gold,' Georgette said. 'I hope they do. Maybe Colin will give me some.'

There was a sound downstairs, as though someone had just come in, and they looked around for a place to hide. But there wasn't any place; the house had been emptied out. Marion stood in front of Francesca and Georgette. 'Let me handle this,' she said. 'I'm dressed as a man, so perhaps they'll believe me if I tell them . . . Don't worry. I'll think of something.'

A huge black dog pounded up the stairs and into the room. 'Help me, Saint Christopher!' Francesca screamed. The dog lay down at her feet and rolled over on to his back.

Marion laughed. 'I've seen this dog before. He must be a stray. Why don't you take him home, Francesca? He'd be a good companion for Goblin.'

'Never!' Francesca tried to shoo the dog away, but he just looked at her adoringly.

'Let's get out of here before someone really does come,' Marion said. She and Georgette went down the stairs. Francesca started to follow them, but the dog lying at her feet blocked her way. 'Wait for me!' she cried out, but the others were already gone. She tried to make the dog get up by pushing him gingerly with the tip of her shoe, but he wouldn't budge. She looked around in despair, heaved a great sigh, picked up her skirt, stepped over him, and hurried to the stairs. The dog got up and followed her out into the street.

As they started up the rue de la Verrerie, Georgette stopped and clapped her hand to her head. 'I forgot the cheese!'

'I told you to buy it this morning!' Francesca said.

'We can go down to Les Halles and get some,' Marion said.

'No! I want to go home!' Francesca wailed.

'We'll go soon,' Marion said as she took her hand and led her down the street to the market. The black dog trotted along behind them.

'Who's your friend?' a cheese-seller greeted Francesca, looking at the dog.

'He is not mine,' Francesca replied. 'Take him outside, Georgette.'

Francesca bought some brie, ignoring the comments of the cheese-seller, who assured her it would be the best she'd ever tasted, looked around for Marion, and saw her at the stall of someone selling old clothes. 'You do not need any more of those!' she called out. 'We are going home now.'

Outside, they found Georgette holding the dog by the scruff of his neck and talking to Colin. 'Look who's here,' Georgette said, winking at Marion and Francesca.

'The last time I saw you, you were going home with Henri Le Picart,' Marion said. 'How did that work out?'

'Great,' Colin said.

'What did you do at his house?'

'That's a secret. He told me not to discuss it.'

Francesca sniffed and said under her breath, 'I never liked that man.'

'At least he didn't hurt him,' Georgette said. 'You're all right, aren't you, Colin?'

'What are you worried about? Henri's a fine man. You should see the inside of his house!'

'We have to get home,' Francesca said. She hurried up the street, followed by Georgette, Marion, Colin, and the black dog.

THIRTY-SIX

Many marvels are made from the human body.

Picatrix, ninth-century Arabic book on magic,
translated into Spanish and Latin in 1256

C hristine was surprised to find that her mother and Georgette
weren't home.
'They weren't here when we came in either,' Marie
said.

Christine wasn't worried about the children being home alone;
they were old enough to take care of themselves. But she started to
worry about her mother and Georgette. Then they came through the
door, followed by Marion, Colin, and a big black dog. Thomas ran
to the dog, which leapt up and nearly knocked him over.

'Do not let that beast in!' Francesca cried. Thomas took the dog
by the scruff of his neck and pulled him out of the house.

'Where have you all been?' Christine asked.

'Just to the market to buy some cheese for supper,' Francesca
said.

'I've got a new job!' Colin cried. 'I'm going back tomorrow.'

'Back where?' Christine asked. She turned to Marion. 'I thought
you were going to bring him here so Thibault wouldn't find him.'

'Something better came along,' Marion said. 'He went home with
Henri Le Picart.'

Christine had to sit down on the bench by the fire. 'Did I hear
you correctly?'

'You did. Henri said he could use him for some work. Tell her
what you did, Colin.'

'I helped him keep a fire going. I blew on it with a bellows.'

Christine caught her breath. 'What was the fire for?'

'I don't know. Or at least, I can't tell you. It's a secret.'

'I'm sure it is,' Christine said. 'Everything Henri does is a secret.
At least he didn't harm you.'

'Why would he do that? I like Henri. He knows lots of things, and he says he'll teach me.'

'Don't be so sure,' Christine said.

There was a knock at the door. Georgette answered it and came back into the kitchen with Martin du Bois and Bonne.

Everyone rushed to the baby, who gurgled and laughed. 'Look!' Georgette exclaimed. 'Her hair is growing back. I think it's going to be blond.' Her eyes filled with tears. 'Stop crying,' Christine whispered to her. 'You didn't do it.'

'What's wrong with her?' Colin asked.

Georgette sniffled, wiped her eyes, and said to Martin, 'This is my brother.'

Martin looked at Colin. 'I've seen you before. At the palace stables.'

'I don't work there anymore,' Colin said. 'Now I work for Henri Le Picart.'

'I know him. He's an interesting man.'

'I don't find him interesting,' Christine said.

Martin laughed. 'I'm sure you don't like his ideas about women.'

'I certainly don't.'

'I share some of those ideas. I included them in what I wrote for Klara.'

'Perhaps Klara needed some of your teaching. But not all women do.'

Martin looked at Bonne, who had gone to sleep in his arms. 'Do you still have my manuscript? If so, I'd like to have it back. Perhaps my daughter will read it when she's older.'

'I'm sure she'll follow the recipes,' Christine said. 'But perhaps not your rules for how a woman should always obey her husband.'

'But they should do that!' Francesca cried.

'Perhaps not all women,' Martin said, looking at Christine.

Grateful that the man seemed to accept her as she was, Christine said, 'There's a lot of useful information in your manuscript, Martin. I'm sure Bonne will appreciate it.' She went upstairs to get it.

The manuscript lay on her desk and, as she gathered the leaves together, one of them fell to the floor. She picked it up and saw a passage that puzzled her. She kept that leaf separate, and when she went back downstairs, she showed it to Martin. 'You wrote here that Klara had some relatives living in Paris. Who were they?'

'She had a cousin who came from Courtrai. I thought for a while it might be good for Klara to live with her, but I changed my mind when I met her.'

'Do you think Klara had any contact with her after she was married?'

'She might have. I don't know. I hope not. She's not the sort of person a wife of mine should associate with.'

'Perhaps this cousin can tell us where Klara went when she ran away. Perhaps she had something to do with it. Where does she live?'

'Near the church of Saint-Merry. I haven't been there in a long time. In fact, I'd forgotten I mentioned her in what I wrote.'

'Did Klara have any other friends here in Paris?'

'Not that I know of.'

'Then we should visit this cousin. She might be able to help us find out what happened to Klara.'

'I don't think you would like her or her husband. They're rather crude.'

'I still think we should go and visit them.'

'You're probably right. Let's go tomorrow.'

Martin appeared early the next morning, and he and Christine walked to the church of Saint-Merry, where Martin looked around and found a side street and the house where Klara's cousin lived. But when he knocked at the door, it was opened by an old man who told them the previous owners had moved to a cul-de-sac near the rue des Bourdonnais. Martin drew a deep breath. That was where Klara's body had been found. Christine began to feel afraid.

'I know what you're thinking,' Martin said. 'I'm afraid, too.'

The man told them which house to look for, and when they found it, Martin knocked on the door so hesitantly, Christine wondered whether he really wanted anyone to answer. A woman holding a small boy in her arms appeared.

'I'm looking for a man and his wife. I'm told they live here,' Martin said.

'They were here, but they aren't here now.'

'Where did they go?'

The woman laughed. It was not a pleasant sound. 'To the Châtelet.'

'What do you mean?'

'Just what I said. They're in the prison.'

'What for?'

'Body parts.' The woman clutched her child close to her breast. 'They dug up bodies in graveyards and sold them, in pieces.'

'How do you know this?'

'I saw them do it.'

'Did a young lady with a baby ever come to see them?' Martin asked, his voice trembling.

'There was someone like that here a while ago. After she'd gone, I went to the Châtelet to get the sergeants.'

'Why?'

'Because when she left, she didn't have the baby.'

THIRTY-SEVEN

The human brain, if eaten, heals those who have lost their memory

Picatrix, ninth-century Arabic book on magic,
translated into Spanish and Latin in 1256

Martin and Christine stood dumbfounded. 'Body parts, especially brains, are valuable for healing lots of things,' the woman said. She held her child so tightly, he cried out in pain. 'I've heard the brains of babies are the best.'

Christine shuddered.

'Burnt brains can cure epilepsy. Eyes, wrapped in snakes' skin, ward off the evil eye. Arm bones for quartan fever. The burnt tips of penises for leprosy.'

Christine covered her ears.

'Sorcerers use body parts for working their spells. I've even heard the Duchess of Orléans buys them, for spells to bewitch the king.'

Christine opened her mouth to object, but Martin spoke first. 'How long have these people been gone?'

'A while. I don't know for sure.'

'Did they leave anything behind?'

'The sergeants from the Châtelet took everything. Good riddance.' The woman went back into the house and slammed the door.

Martin and Christine stood in the street staring at each other. Christine was frightened. Martin looked as though he would cry. 'I have to go back and get Bonne.'

'You know my mother will keep her safe.'

'Yes, of course.' His sorrowful expression turned to anger. 'We must go to the prison and talk to those people. Unfortunately, I don't know the provost, so I don't know how we can get in.'

'I think I know. Come home with me and get Bonne.'

Francesca was preparing dinner. 'See what I have done,' she said, showing Martin that she'd prepared a rabbit the way he said to do in one of his recipes. But he wasn't interested; he was holding Bonne to his chest as though he would never let her go.

'Let him be, Mama,' Christine said. 'He's had a shock.'

'More trouble?' Francesca asked.

'It looks that way.'

Francesca crossed herself.

Christine went to Georgette, who was sitting at the table cutting onions, and whispered, 'When you see Colin tonight, ask him to tell Henri Le Picart to come to me at the Duke of Orléans's residence as soon as possible.'

Henri appeared the next day. He bounded up the stairs – resplendent in a pleated green velvet jacket, purple tights, and a wide gold belt – and charged into her workroom. 'Do you need my help, Christine? I thought you ladies could handle everything by yourselves.'

Christine wanted to throw her inkhorn at him. 'Yes, I do need your help, Henri. There are two people in the Châtelet I need to talk to. I've heard you have connections there. Can you arrange for me to get in?'

'You've been there before. Surely you know what to do.'

'The last time, I had a letter from the queen.'

'Who are these people?'

She hesitated. She didn't want to tell him what was going on, but there was no way to avoid it. In any case, she wanted to find out how much he knew.

'The girl Marion found murdered in the cul-de-sac near the rue des Bourbonnais was Martin du Bois's wife, as you know.'

'Of course I know.'

'Do you know who murdered her?'

Henri laughed. 'I thought you and Marion had decided it was me.'

Christine clenched her fists.

'In any event, I've been trying to find out, but I haven't succeeded,' Henri said.

'I'm surprised you admit defeat.'

He glared at her. 'When I do find out, maybe I'll let you know.'

'Perhaps *you* won't be the one to find out, Henri. Martin du Bois and I think we may be able to solve this ourselves. Martin told me Klara had some cousins here in Paris. They may know what happened to her because it's possible she had some contact with them.'

'Without his knowing about it? Husbands shouldn't let their wives out of their sight. They get into trouble.'

'In this instance, I think you're right. Martin and I went to find those cousins, and we learned they're in prison, in the Châtelet.'

'What for?'

'Selling body parts.'

For once she'd been able to shock Henri. He'd turned pale and sat down on the edge of her desk. That was too close for her. She stood up and went to look out the window. Behind her, she heard him say in a muffled voice, 'You want me to write a note asking Monseigneur le Provost to let you into the prison so you can talk to these people. Is Martin going with you?'

'Of course. It was his wife.'

'Do you think they will tell you anything?'

'What have they got to lose? They'll be put to death for what they've done.'

'I don't know whether I can do it, Christine.'

'Don't play games, Henri. Marion tells me you have enough influence with Monseigneur le Provost to get prostitutes out of prison.'

Henri got up from the desk and stood looking at her for a long time. 'I'll see what I can do,' he said.

THIRTY-EIGHT

*The wise and peaceful man takes heed of the snares and deceits
of the Devil, who sees us when we see him not and tries us
grievously in more than a thousand ways.*

From a book of moral and practical advice for a young wife,
Paris, 1393

C hristine had been inside the Châtelet before, and she wasn't
anxious to go there again. But Henri had kept his promise:
she had a note for the provost. As she and Martin walked
to the prison the next morning, she told him about her earlier
visits there.

'I know,' he said. 'Klara told me how you saved Alix de Clairy
from the stake. You were courageous to visit her.'

'You say that because I'm a woman.'

Martin laughed. 'Your mother warned me about treating you as
though you weren't as brave as a man.'

'What do you think about that, Martin?'

'Actually, I think it depends on the woman. Some were meant to
cook and sew, like your mother, and some to go in other directions.'

'And Klara?'

He sighed. 'I believed I was wiser in everything and that she
should obey me in everything. Perhaps I was wrong, but I didn't
think she was strong enough to be independent.'

'Do you think that is why she may have turned to these cousins?'

'That is what I fear.'

'Tell me about them.'

'Her name is Berta, and her husband is Adam. I don't know much
about them, except that they left Courtrai and settled in Paris a long
time ago. I couldn't even find out how they made a living. Now I
know why.'

They had come to the area around the Châtelet, where the dark
walls of the prison cast a sinister shadow over the butchers', tanners',

and skinners' shops. Christine had always wondered how the people who worked there endured the terrible stench and the wrenching sounds of animals crying out in terror. She sensed that Martin was as disturbed as she was. *He's a kind man,* she said to herself, *whatever he thinks about women.* But she remembered how Klara had been so anxious to have a life of her own. In spite of the girl's faults, she sympathized with her plight. And now they were going to find out what had happened to her, and she feared that what they learned would not be pleasant.

The guards who greeted them at the entrance to the prison were not the ones who'd been there when she'd come to visit Alix de Clairy several years earlier. But they were just as nasty. They sneered when she handed them Henri's note.

'Monseigneur le Provost doesn't like anyone visiting people he's questioning.'

'Is he questioning them now?' Martin asked.

'Not at the moment. They had their time with him this morning. I don't think they will be in a very good mood.' He studied the note. *He can't read,* Christine thought.

'Monseigneur le Provost has given us permission to speak with them,' Martin said.

The guard handed the note to his companion, who opened it so brutally Christine feared it would be torn. He looked at it for a long time, then glanced at Martin. 'All right. I'll get someone to take you in.'

'The lady, too,' Martin said.

The guard studied the note again. After a long while, he nodded. The other guard went into the prison and came back with a thin, wiry man who they supposed was a jailer. He led them into a long corridor, frowning and muttering to himself and turning to look at them from time to time. Christine picked up her skirts as they stepped over dirty straw, tried not to gag on noxious odors, and put her hands over her ears to block out the moans and screams of prisoners coming from somewhere in the depths of the horrible place. Finally the jailer came to a heavy door, unlocked it with a huge key, and pushed it open.

'Step in, step in,' he said, giving Martin a shove and bowing slightly to Christine. She shuddered as the door closed with a bang and she heard the key turn in the lock. The last time she'd been in the Châtelet, there had been one sympathetic guard. This time, all she sensed was hostility.

Two people stared at them from the far side of the dingy room. 'Do you recognize me?' Martin asked.

The man shook his head, but the woman said, 'I do. You're the old man who married my young cousin. What do you want with us?' She spoke in a rough voice, with an accent that Christine knew was from the north.

The man was square and balding, with a laborer's face, and the woman was thickset and common looking, with straight brown hair that had not been combed for a long time. She bore no resemblance to Klara, who'd been plump and pretty, with red cheeks and long blond hair.

Adam said, 'If you want to talk to us, it's a good thing you came today. We won't be here tomorrow.'

'Have you been put to the question?' Martin asked.

'Of course. Do you know how it's done?'

'I do.'

'Perhaps the lady doesn't. Let me tell her.'

Martin put up his hand as if to stop his words, but Adam continued. 'First they get you nude, and then they stretch you on a trestle, and then they put a funnel in your mouth and pour water down your throat.' He smiled when he saw Christine flinch.

'And now let me tell you what's going to happen to us tomorrow. Berta here will be taken to the pig market and burned. I'll be taken to the Grève and have my head chopped off.' His voice rose and he started to shake. Martin pushed him down on to a rickety little stool.

'Don't you have any regrets for what you've done?' Martin asked.

'None at all,' Adam growled. 'Go away. We don't want to talk to you or the fancy lady.'

Berta stood sobbing in the corner. Christine went to her and put her arm around her. 'Surely you're sorry for what you did.'

'We had to find a way to survive. What's so wrong with selling the bodies of people who are already dead? Nothing can hurt them anymore.'

'Did you ever have any other kind of work?'

'Adam was once a respectable man. A friend told him this was an easy way to make money. He said sorcerers would pay well for the bodies. One just had to have the courage to dig them up. I think the friend was really the Devil.'

'That is the way the Devil tempts innocent people,' Martin said. 'But at least you can make amends by telling us what happened when Klara came to see you.'

'How do you know she came to us?'

'The woman who lives in your house told us.' He paused, cleared his throat, and asked, 'Did you kill Klara?'

'No!' Berta cried. 'We never killed anyone.'

'So what happened?'

'She came and asked us to take the child.'

'Why?'

'She didn't want to be a mother. She wanted to go away by herself.'

'Could she really have hated me that much?' Martin asked under his breath.

'What did you do?' Christine asked the woman.

'We told her we couldn't take the child. There was a man with us, and he said he'd take it.'

'Who was he?'

'I don't know. Just a man who'd come to buy some bones.'

'What did he look like?'

'I didn't pay much attention to him. He had on a big black cloak. He gave Klara a few coins and she went away. He asked us for some rags. He wrapped the baby in them and left.'

THIRTY-NINE

What excuse do we have for delivering our body, which is our castle, to its enemy, the Devil of Hell? Unless the hot tears of contrition drive the enemy from within us in this life, I don't see how we can escape being, by the good judgment of the Sovereign Judge, punished and chained to the gibbet of Hell forever as thieves, murderers, and traitors.

From a book of moral and practical advice for a young wife,
Paris, 1393

Martin was weeping as they left the Châtelet. The two guards snickered. 'Sad about your friends,' one said. Christine shook her fist at them, but Martin didn't seem to have heard.

As they wove their way through the crowds, she took his arm to keep him from wandering away, for he walked as though he had no idea where they were going, not even noticing when a man carrying the carcass of a cow on his shoulders bumped into him and nearly knocked him down.

When they came to the church of Saint-Jacques-la-Boucherie, he stopped. 'I'd like to go in there for a while,' he said.

As they stepped into church, the heavy wooden door swung shut, and the noise and stench of the street gave way to silence and the sweet smell of candle wax and incense. It was a cloudy day, and very little light filtered in through the stained-glass windows. Instead, the church was lit by candles that flickered and sputtered in the gloom. Martin walked through the dusty light to the altar and fell to his knees. Christine knelt beside him and they were silent for a long time. Then he moaned, 'Why?'

'She can't have known what she was doing,' Christine said.

'What happened to her? Why was she murdered? The officials from the Châtelet haven't been able to find out anything.'

There was nothing she could say.

'Leave me for a while, Christine. I want to pray for her, and for those unhappy people who are responsible for this.'

'They don't deserve it.'

'I pray they will understand what they have done and ask forgiveness from the Lord. Otherwise their souls are lost.'

She stayed on her knees for a moment, praying for the girl who'd been such a burden to her family and to Martin. She also begged forgiveness for herself because she'd been so impatient and unable to help her. Then she stood and looked down at the man on his knees at her side. He'd never seemed his age before, but now he looked old and bent, consumed with grief.

Leaving Martin alone to wrestle with his thoughts, she walked around the church. She'd been there with him once before, when he'd first introduced himself to her. She'd been there with Marion, too, and she felt that the statues on the pillars recognized her – Saint Catherine of Alexandria with her spiked wheel, Saint Barbara carrying her tower, Saint Dorothy offering a basket of roses. Saint Apollonia clutched a pair of pincers with a tooth in them, and she could almost hear Francesca praying to her because she had a toothache. Saint Mary of Egypt winked at her – she was sure of it

– as though they'd been partners in the effort to get Marion to change her profession.

She went back to Martin and knelt by his side. He looked up and smiled. 'I'm ready to face my daughter now.' When he got to his feet, he looked himself again – a large, hearty man who appeared much younger than he was. *Why couldn't Klara accept him?* she asked herself for the hundredth time.

They left the church and plunged back into the crowds. On the rue Saint-Denis sergeants from the Châtelet, mounted on huge destriers, thundered by, dragging behind them a group of shackled prisoners. 'Poor souls,' Martin murmured. On the rue des Lombards they found a little girl who'd become separated from her mother. When Martin picked her up, she stopped crying and rested her head against his chest.

This is how it must have been when he rescued Klara after the siege of Courtrai, Christine thought. The child's mother rushed to Martin, seized the child from his arms, and hurried away.

'Not a word of thanks!' Christine exclaimed.

'I understand,' Martin said. 'What mother would not be afraid when she sees a strange man holding her child?'

No one need be afraid of this man, Christine thought. But she changed her mind about that when they came to the rue des Escouffles and instead of continuing on to the rue Saint-Antoine, Martin went to his house on the corner of the rue des Rosiers. 'Wait here a moment,' he said. 'I need to get something.'

As she stood at the door to the house, Christine remembered going there with her mother and Klara, to get Klara's clothes. Klara had scorned the place, just as she did everything having to do with Martin. Christine couldn't imagine why, because Martin's home was furnished with everything a young wife could want.

Martin returned, fastening a dagger to his belt. 'I will not be without this again until I have used it on the person who took my child and murdered Klara,' he said.

FORTY

Berith is a great and terrible duke, and hath three names. Of
some he is called Beall; of the Jewes Berith; of Nigromancers
Bolfry . . . He is compelled at a certeine houre, through divine
virtue, by a ring of art magicke. He is also a lier, he turneth
all mettals into gold, he adorneth a man with dignities . . .

Reginald Scot (c. 1538–1599),
The Discoverie of Witchcraft, 1584

They hurried up the street, Martin encouraging Christine to walk faster. At the door to her house, they found the big black dog jumping around and wagging his tail furiously. Christine shooed him away. 'I've already brought one stray dog home,' she said. 'I don't think my mother wants another one.'

Martin strode into the kitchen, where Georgette and Francesca were at the table talking to Colin and at the same time making silly faces at Bonne, who sat laughing on Francesca's lap. Martin raced to his daughter, lifted her, and pressed her to his chest. Bonne, delighted, cried, 'Papa, Papa,' and waved for the others to look.

Francesca and Georgette were trying to get Colin to tell them what he did at Henri Le Picart's house. Christine sat down with them and tried to help them draw the boy out.

'I've heard his house is interesting,' she said. 'Tell us about it.'

'I don't see too much. He takes me to a room and asks me to keep a fire going with a bellows.'

'You haven't seen the courtyard with the fountain, or the tapestries, or the stained-glass windows?' Marion asked.

Colin shook his head. 'I'm too busy. He has important work for me to do, you know.'

'It doesn't sound too important to me,' said Thomas, who came in and stood behind his grandmother. The big black dog had followed him; it went to Francesca and laid its head in her lap.

Francesca screamed. 'Why is that beast in here? Put him out!'

'He wants to be with you, *grand-maman,*' Thomas said.

Francesca pushed the dog's head away and shifted on the bench so her legs would be as far away from him as possible.

'Where's Goblin?' Christine asked.

Everyone looked around. The little dog wasn't there.

'You forgot about him,' cried Lisabetta, who'd come in with Jean and Marie.

'Poor Goblin,' Jean said. 'He must have been frightened by this big dog.'

'He ran away!' Lisabetta wailed.

Everyone began to call for Goblin. The black dog ran around barking and wagging his tail. 'Get him out of here!' Francesca cried.

'Where did he come from, anyway?' Christine asked.

'He was at the marketplace, and he followed us home,' Francesca said.

'There's a big black dog that looks just like him hanging around Henri Le Picart's house,' Colin said.

The dog wandered into the pantry. Christine went after him and found him sniffing at a sack of flour that was spilling its contents on to the floor. Something moved inside the sack. *Probably a mouse,* Christine thought. *Maybe he can catch it.* The black dog stuck his nose into the sack and snuffled around. When he drew his head out, a floury, whimpering Goblin dangled from his jaws. The black dog dropped Goblin, unhurt, into Christine's arms.

'I think he wants to be your friend,' she whispered to Goblin. She set him on the floor, and he rolled over on to his back, let the black dog nuzzle him, and then stood up, ready to play.

Francesca came to the pantry door, saw Goblin, and let out a shriek. 'What happened to him?'

'He was hiding in a sack of flour. Your friend found him.' She put her arm around the black dog.

'My friend!'

'You brought him home, Mama.'

The black dog was sniffing at a basket of onions.

'He must be hungry,' Christine said.

'Am I expected to feed him?' Francesca asked.

'You have to. He's your dog now.'

Francesca shook her head. The dog went to her and lay down at her feet. 'I suppose he is,' she said.

Christine picked up Goblin and went back into the kitchen. The children crowded around, brushing at the flour. Bonne, seeing what the others were doing, wiggled in Martin's arms and pointed to the dogs. Martin laughed and carried her to where the others were standing.

Georgette brought a big tub of water and dropped Goblin into it. He splashed around happily, getting water all over the floor. The black dog tried to jump in, too, but she pushed him away.

Christine sat down at the table with Colin. 'Let's begin again, Colin. What does Henri Le Picart do in that big house of his?'

Colin hung his head. 'I really don't know. There's something red in the pot over the fire, and he reads a big book. I can't read, so I don't know what it is.'

'What does he use that big mortar and pestle for?' Francesca asked.

'How do you know he has a big mortar and pestle?' Christine asked.

Francesca fiddled with the strings of her apron. 'Oh, I am just guessing.'

Christine started to laugh. 'I wondered where you three had been. How did you get into his house?'

Marion laughed, too. 'We didn't. We looked in through a window.'

'Spying on me. How dare you?' Colin asked.

'We wanted to make sure you were safe,' Georgette said.

'I'm old enough to take care of myself.'

'So you are,' Christine said. 'And now that Henri has taken you on as his assistant, you can help us, too.'

Colin sat up straight, pleased to be called Henri's assistant. 'I like him,' he said. 'He's a smart man. What do you want me to do?'

Much smarter than you, Christine thought. 'Find out what he's doing with the fire and all the other things he has in that room,' she said.

Francesca gave a bowl of leftover soup to the black dog, who slurped it up, getting more on the floor than into his mouth.

'I'm sure I saw that dog at Henri's house,' Colin said.

'Is it his dog?' Christine asked.

'I don't think Henri likes dogs.'

Georgette knelt on the floor, mopping up the mess the dog had made. 'You have to give him a name,' she said.

'Let's call him Berith,' Christine said.

'What kind of a name is that?' Thomas asked.

'Appropriate for a dog that came from Henri's house.'

Lisabetta hugged the dog and tried to climb on to his back. Martin held Bonne in the crook of one arm and with the other drew Lisabetta away so she wouldn't fall. Thomas knelt in front of the dog and cried, 'Berith, Berith.' The dog licked the boy's face.

'See, he knows his name,' Thomas said. 'What does it mean, anyway?' he asked his mother.

'Berith is a god, or rather a demon.'

'Perhaps Berith is not a good name for him,' Martin said. 'Berith is the alchemist's god.'

'Do you know much about alchemy, Martin?'

'Not a lot. But I know other people who do. Or think they do. Henri Le Picart, for example.'

'Do you think he really knows how to make gold?' Georgette asked.

'Some people think so. I don't know him well. Few people do. But I have respect for him. He's a learned man.'

'Do you think he knows who killed Klara?' Christine asked.

'If he did, he'd tell the authorities, wouldn't he?'

'I'm not sure. I don't trust Henri not to have some purpose of his own that we can't guess,' Christine said.

Martin held Bonne close and gazed at her. 'All I know is I have to find out who took my little girl. If not for you, Christine, she'd be dead.'

'Not me. The duke's fools. They're the ones who found her in the palace garden and were wise enough to ask me to take her away.'

'She'd have been killed, for sure.'

Georgette made a garbled sound and started to cry. Christine went to her and whispered, 'You didn't do it, Georgette. And I'll never tell him.'

Georgette sniffled and wiped her eyes with her apron.

'The duke's fools seem to know everything that goes on at the palace,' Martin said. 'How do you know them?'

'They come to talk to me when I'm working. Sometimes they talk so much, I can't get any work done.'

'What do they say?'

'All kinds of things. A lot of it makes sense.'

'How can anything a fool says make sense?' Thomas wanted to know.

'It depends on how you look at it,' Christine said. 'Do you think everything you say makes sense, Thomas?'

'When I say things I've thought about.'

'But imagine what would happen if you said just anything that comes into your head, without thinking about it. Would that make sense?'

'Some of it might.'

'That's the point. The fools babble on and on, so we call them fools. But there is reason in some of their words. One has to know how to separate the foolish from the reasonable. Or find the wisdom in what sounds like gibberish.'

Martin set Bonne on the floor so she could play with Goblin and came to Christine's side.

'Do you think the fools know who left Bonne in the garden?'

'They think they do.'

'They're in danger if they suspect someone,' Martin said. 'Don't let them act on their own, Christine. Tell me. I'll know what to do.'

FORTY-ONE

One hardly dares go out into the streets of Paris because there one has to listen to ignorant people spouting such nonsense. If a prince falls ill, they get frightened and assume it is treason, sorcery, or poison. What foolishness! Don't they know that a prince can get sick just like other mortals?

Honoré Bonet (c. 1340–c. 1410),
L'apparition de Jehan de Meun, 1398

Christine hurried to the palace the next day hoping to avoid the malicious talk about the Duchess of Orléans. For a while, the talk had been just a murmur, but every day it had grown louder, and now it was so thunderous, it seemed to shake the whole city. She dreaded stepping out of her house.

At the palace, she breathed a sigh of relief. Things were peaceful in the library. Colart worked happily on his wall, applying a particularly vibrant shade of yellow to Horace's robe, and Gilles sat at his desk, dozing over a large book.

But Eustache had followed her in, and he strode over to Gilles and raged at him.

'No one ever gives them back! Not even *you*, Gilles.'

'What are you talking about?'

'You borrowed one of my books. How long do you expect to keep it? Or have you lost it?'

Colart threw down his brush and stomped across the room and out the door, muttering angrily to himself.

'I don't lose books, you fool,' Gilles said. He went to a shelf and came back with a large volume, which he placed on the desk.

Interested to know what Eustache was reading, Christine opened the book and saw that it was Ovid's *Art of Love*. She frowned.

'Don't you like it?' Gilles asked. 'We have other copies in the library, but this one has more beautiful illustrations.'

'It's not the illustrations. It's what he says about women,' Christine said.

Gilles slammed the book shut. 'How dare you criticize Ovid?'

'That's my book!' Eustache cried, seizing his precious volume and cradling it against his chest.

'You're welcome to it,' Christine said. 'Ovid defames women in the most disgusting ways.'

'He's a great poet!' Gilles cried.

Eustache laughed. 'If you find Ovid so offensive, why don't you write something about women yourself, Christine? Then you can defend them.'

'I might do that.'

'I hate this conversation,' Gilles said. 'Christine refuses to accept the fact that a woman's place is in the home.'

Christine wanted to lash out at Gilles, even though he'd been her friend for years. Besides managing the library at the Duke of Orléans's residence, he was in charge of King Charles the Fifth's great library at the Louvre, and she had happy memories of the days when her father had taken her there to look at the books. In addition, he'd helped her find work as a copyist after her husband had died. But his ideas about women's place in society had always clashed with hers.

To keep from venting her anger, she took the book from Eustache and glanced at several pages. This only increased her rage. She looked up and asked, 'Don't you two find this disgraceful? He tells men how to deceive women by making all kinds of false promises.'

Gilles and Eustache looked at the floor.

'And I suppose you've read about the aphrodisiacs – savory, pepper, the seeds of stinging nettles, chamomile ground up in old wine, white onions, eggs, honey, pinecone seeds. Is there anything more ridiculous than that?'

Gilles tried to take the book away from her, but she held it tightly and studied the pages. The initial letters were painted in a vermilion brighter than any she'd ever seen.

'Where did you get this book, Eustache?'

'Henri Le Picart gave it to me. He made the copy himself. He's an excellent scribe, you know.'

Henri again, Christine thought. *I suppose this is the kind of book he would like.*

Aubert de Canny came into the room. 'Where's Colart?'

'He was here,' Gilles said, looking around the room. 'Where did he go?'

'Probably to his studio,' Christine said. 'The noise in here was too much for him.'

Aubert went out. Gilles opened another book he had on his desk and pretended to read it.

'You can't get out of this argument by ignoring me like that,' Christine said. 'I don't deny that Ovid was a great poet. But his disrespect for women negates everything else.' She handed Eustache the book. 'I'm glad you got this back, Eustache. Never fear; I won't be the next one to borrow it.' She stormed out of the room.

At the top of the stairs, she heard loud voices. She peered into Colart's studio, and saw the painter talking with Aubert de Canny, who was looking at the painting of Louis and Valentina kneeling before Our Lady.

'Why have you depicted the duchess like that?' Aubert wanted to know.

'What do you mean?'

'She doesn't wear such fancy clothes. Why don't you paint her as she really is?'

'Don't tell me how to do my work!' Colart cried.

'Oh, I'd never presume to do that, a great painter like you.'

Colart raised his hand, about to strike Aubert, but Aubert started to laugh. 'You painters take everything so seriously.' He held out his hand. 'Here, I found this.' He handed Colart a silver seal. 'It's yours, isn't it? I've seen you wearing it on your wrist. I found it on the floor in the library.'

Colart took the seal and stammered thanks. Aubert took a last look at the painting of Louis and Valentina and shook his head. 'Too much gold,' he said as he left the room. He walked across the hall to the little room where Henri had said Louis practiced alchemy, went in, and closed the door with a bang.

Christine started to go into her own room, hesitated, and went back into the hall. She stood for a long time, pondering. Then she went to the door Aubert had closed and slowly opened it.

Aubert was not there.

In an alcove, a small fire burned, and on a long table lay many oddly shaped vessels – crucibles, flasks, containers shaped like gourds. She couldn't remember what they were all used for, but she knew they were alchemists' tools. She picked up a metal pot with a long, curved neck and reflected that the green, red, and yellow liquids in the glass globes she saw on the shelves had been distilled in it. There were bellows, tongs, and baskets of coal, and she could picture Colin using such things to tend the fire at Henri Le Picart's house.

The room, which had only one small window, was hot and stuffy, and the air had an acrid, ashy smell. But where was Aubert? There were several doors, and she reasoned that he must have left through one of them, but still she wondered whether he was watching her. She didn't want him to think she was sneaking around, so she decided to sit on a high-backed chair next to a large desk and wait for him to come back.

Several books lay on the desk. She opened one and saw that it was a treatise on alchemy. *Full of nonsense,* she said to herself. She fumed as she sat there thinking about how her father, urged on by Henri Le Picart, had wasted his time on such foolishness. She suspected he had lost a great deal of money on useless experiments, and she hoped Henri had, too. She opened another book and found that it contained recipes for malicious spells like the ones on the piece of parchment Hanotin had found behind the duchess's chair. *If Aubert is the one who's leaving the signs of sorcery around, he could be using this book for inspiration,* she reflected, and she began to be afraid. She stood up, looked around to make sure the big man wasn't lurking in the shadows, and went to the door. She felt something under her foot, leaned down, and picked up a walnut. *I don't remember Papa saying anything about using nuts in alchemy experiments,* she thought. She laid the walnut on the desk and went out, shutting the door carefully behind her.

Aubert was waiting for her. He smiled. 'I would gladly have showed you what we do in there,' he said. 'All you had to do was ask.'

She knew her face was bright red as she hurried into her room and closed the door.

FORTY-TWO

To make a very good vermilion, take a glass flask and cover it with fine clay. Then put into the flask one part quicksilver and two parts white or yellow sulfur, and place the flask on four stones. Pile charcoal around the flask and make a very slow fire. Cover the mouth of the flask with a tile. When you see blue or yellow vapor coming out of the flask, keep it covered. But when you see a vapor that is nearly red, take the flask off the fire, and you will have a very good vermilion.

Jehan le Begue, *Experimenta de Coloribus*, 1431

Early the next morning, it was Henri rather than the fools who came to her as she sat at her copying. 'I need to talk to you, Christine,' he said.

Do I trust him? she asked herself.

'You have to trust me,' Henri said.

'How can I? You're always around and no one knows what you're doing.'

Without being asked, Henri sat down on a chair by the window. *No manners at all,* she thought. *But does that make him a murderer?*

'I never try to hide what I'm doing.'

'Then why doesn't Colin have any idea what you do with all those oddly shaped containers you heat over a fire?'

'Colin isn't very bright.'

'Bright enough to know you're doing something you don't want anyone to know about.'

'I'm not trying to keep it a secret. I know you think those are alchemists' tools.'

'You gave my father a lot of books about alchemy. I read them. Such nonsense! One said to mix certain metals one way and the other said to mix them another way, and no matter what you do, you feed them to the fire and you end up with nothing but confusion.'

Henri got up, tugged at his red velvet jacket, and looked out the window. 'Louis is coming from the king's residence,' he said.

'Some of the men who read those books get so befuddled, they go completely mad.'

'His fools are with him.'

'Others become so obsessed, they spend all their money on materials to use in their experiments. One man thought the books said to use dung, so he used his own excrement. All he got for his trouble was the loss of all his friends, the smell was so bad.'

'The duke looks troubled. The fools are dancing around, trying to cheer him up.'

'One of those men was a goldsmith; and he was so stupid that instead of making himself richer, he made himself a pauper.'

Henri turned and faced her. 'Do you know whether the duke's fools go into that room next door?'

'Why do you ask?'

'They aren't supposed to be in there.'

'I saw Aubert go in.'

'Did you go in to see what he was doing? Yes, I'm sure you did. Your face is getting red.'

'So what if I did?'

'What did Aubert say?'

'He wasn't there, which was strange, because I really did see him go in.'

'There are several doors.'

'Do you have many doors to the room in your house where you make gold?'

'If I could make gold, would I be standing here? Why are you so obsessed with that room in my house? Do you think I invoke demons? Put spells on people? Perhaps you think I'm the one putting the signs of sorcery around here.'

'*Is* it you?'

Henri picked up the book of fables she was copying. 'These initial letters are a beautiful red, aren't they? Do you know how this red is achieved?'

'I have no idea. '

'Perhaps one day I'll tell you.' He was standing close to her now, with one hand on her desk and the other on his hip. She couldn't help thinking that in his brocaded red jacket, gold belt, and jeweled fingers, he cut a rather elegant figure. She turned away from him and said, 'As you know, Aubert was here. He had an argument with Colart, in Colart's studio. Then he went into that room. After that, I didn't see him.'

'Do you suspect Aubert of something?'

'I do wonder about him. I've been told he has a grudge against Valentina because she forces him to stay with a wife he can't stand.'

'Let's think about him a bit. He's been Louis's chamberlain for some time. A proud, solid man, a good citizen.'

'But why would he have let himself be coerced into staying in a bad marriage?'

'Expediency. He doesn't want to defy the man who supports him.'

'The duke's fools don't like him. Fripon, especially. He said he was going to follow him around and find out whether he's the one leaving the signs of sorcery.'

'Poor fool. He could get into a lot of trouble.'

'The other fools think that, too.'

Suddenly they heard shouts coming from Colart's room.

They raced across the hall and found the painter raging around his studio, brandishing a spatula and hurling imprecations at something that lay on the floor. It was the painting of the Duke and Duchess of Orléans, and Christine stared at it in disbelief. The Virgin still smiled down at the child in her lap, the angels still hovered over her head waiting to crown her, the child still stretched out his arms to saints Agnes and Dorothy, Louis still knelt. But Valentina wasn't there: she'd been covered over with a thick layer of brown paint.

FORTY-THREE

Always try to adorn with fine gold and good colors.

Cennino Cennini,
Il libro dell'Arte o Trattato della Pittura, c. 1400

'*Merde!*' Colart cried. He picked up a jar of red paint and hurled it at the wall. He saw Henri. '*Pautonnier!*' he shouted as he grabbed a palette and broke it in two. He saw Christine. '*Vilaine!*' he bellowed, stomping on the palette.

Henri went in, caught the painter's arm, and twisted it behind his back just as he was about to heave a large glass of blue liquid at Baudet. He marched him to a bench and forced him down on to it.

'Who did this, Colart?'

'God's plague and a pox on them!'

'Who?'

'Criminals! Vandals! Filthy swine! I don't know.'

'When did it happen?'

'After I left yesterday. Damned treacherous dogs!'

'I can understand your anger,' Henri said. 'But you must calm down.'

'*Allez au diable!*' Colart jumped up from the bench, stamped his feet, and tore his hair. 'My beautiful painting! Destroyed!'

'Perhaps it can be repaired.'

'Idiot!' Colart raised his arm as though to strike him. 'You think it's easy! You don't understand anything at all!'

'I do know a little about painting.'

'Do you want to try?' Colart grabbed a brush from the floor and threw it at Henri. He picked up a pot of yellow paint and would have thrown that, too, if Eustache Deschamps had not come in at that moment and grabbed his arm.

'So *now* you come,' Colart yelled at Eustache. 'The wonderful *maître d'hôtel*! How could you let this happen, you *imbécile*!'

Eustache took the pot of paint and set it on the floor. Then he saw the painting. 'When did this happen?'

'*You're* the one who's supposed to know what goes on here!'

Eustache picked up the painting and examined it. 'Only the duchess has been painted out. Perhaps you can repair it.'

'You're a moron, just like that half-wit over there!' Colart cried, pointing to Henri. 'All that work. All that paint that Baudet prepared so carefully. And some of the gold background is gone, too.'

'You can get more paint,' Eustache said. 'At least the expensive lapis lazuli of the Virgin's robe was spared.'

Henri pushed the painter down on to the bench again and sat beside him. 'You'll just have to repair it. I'm sure the duke and duchess will pay for everything. Look at it this way: it means you'll be staying here longer.'

Colart put his head in his hands and wept.

Christine took the painting from Eustache and examined it. The angels in the sky seemed to be weeping, too.

Why was only the figure of the duchess painted over? she asked herself. She looked around the room. Pots, vials, beakers, bowls, and cups spilled red, blue, yellow, green, orange, and violet paint on to the floor. Brushes, knives, spatulas, stone slabs, spoons, and ladles were strewn everywhere, and the materials Baudet ground in his mortars to make paints – oak galls, charcoal, bones, roots, crystals, and stones – had rolled into the corners. Next to the easel lay an overturned pot of brown paint, and there were brown fingerprints on the wall.

She turned to Colart and asked, 'Where was Baudet when this happened?'

He raised his head. 'He came in just after I did.'

'Then why are you throwing things at him? He is not responsible for this.'

'I didn't say he was,' he sobbed.

Everyone seemed to have heard Colart's shouts. Cooks, scullery maids, porters, *huissiers*, stewards, ladies-in-waiting, and chamberlains crowded in at the door, craning their necks to see what had happened. They pushed and shoved and trod on each other's feet, but drew back to make way for Valentina, accompanied by her two Italian maids. Gilles followed, muttering to himself.

When Valentina saw the painting, she let out a little cry and went to Colart, who was weeping so hard he hadn't seen her come in.

'Who has done this to your beautiful painting, Colart?'

He shook his head without raising it from his arms.

Valentina stood gazing down at the painter helplessly, until the duke, followed by Aubert de Canny and the fools, came in and went to her side. Aubert looked at the painting, stunned.

Colart lifted his head and cried, 'Is there still too much gold?'

Aubert hung his head. 'I'm sorry.'

'Oh, everyone is *so* sorry,' whined Colart. He picked up one of his brushes and waved it at Henri. 'Just take a magic wand and fix it!'

Henri got up from the bench and paced around the room, kicking knives and oak galls and bones out of his way. Some of the galls rolled toward Fripon, and he picked them up and began to juggle them.

'This is no time for that,' Hanotin said. The other fools nodded, and the monkey grabbed the galls from Fripon's hands.

'Aubert,' the duke said. 'See that this is cleaned up.'

Aubert didn't seem to hear. He was scowling at Fripon.

'Aubert!' Louis said again.

Aubert nodded and rushed away.

Christine expected that Louis would take charge and try to find out who had done this terrible thing. But instead the duke stood gazing at Mariette d'Enghien.

FORTY-FOUR

Make the image of a man with two faces, one face looking forward and the other looking back. Suffumigate it with sulfur and carob and say, 'You Bectue, lay waste to this place and destroy it.' Then put the image into a small bag with sulfur, carob, and some hair and bury it under the earth in that place and your wish will be granted.

Picatrix, ninth-century Arabic book on magic,
translated into Spanish and Latin in 1256

Marion sat at her worktable, surrounded by pins, needles, scissors, and colored thread. She was trying to finish embroidering a belt for the queen, but she couldn't concentrate. She laid the belt aside, went to a chest, and pulled out the beggar's clothes. She shook her head. 'These won't do this time,' she said to Babil, who was watching from the top of his cage. He flew down and tugged at the beads in her hair.

'I'm going out for a while,' she said to the parrot as she carried him back to his cage.

She put on her crimson cloak and walked to the old clothes market. This time she went to the stall where cast-off finery of the nobility – brocaded *houppelandes* with ermine-lined sleeves, beaver hats with big peacock feathers, velvet jackets with gold embroidery – was sold. The woman who tended the booth knew her well.

'What is it this time, Marion?' she asked. She held up a bright blue gown and a red velvet surcoat to go over it. 'I've got a gold belt somewhere to go with this.'

Marion shook her head and pointed to a short purple jacket with brocaded sleeves and padded shoulders.

'That's for a man,' the woman said.

'I'll take it, and those blue tights over there, too.'

'What are you about, Marion?'

'Just having some fun.'

'Well, I assume you have shapely legs, so these ought to suit you,' the woman said, handing her the tights.

'I'll have that little blue cape as well. And I need something for my head. Not just a hat. I want to cover my hair completely.'

The woman brought out a large red velvet hood. 'This is the latest fashion for men,' she said as she pulled the hood over Marion's head and arranged it so it formed an elaborate turban. She held up a mirror.

'Perfect,' Marion said as she turned her head from side to side to make sure none of her red hair showed. She paid the woman, gathered up the clothes she'd bought, and went back to her room. Babil took one look at the hood, squawked, and refused to go anywhere near her.

'I can't take it off. I'd never be able to get it right again,' she told the parrot as she put on the tights and jacket and threw the cape over her shoulders. Babil went into his cage and hung his head.

She knew that Thibault often visited the Tiron brothel, so that's where she headed. Agnes met her at the door, thinking she was a customer. Marion laughed. 'Don't you recognize me?'

'Now I do. It's your voice. Why are you dressed like that?'

'It's a secret. I'm looking for Thibault de Torvaux.'

'He's here now,' Agnes said, pointing to the leather curtain that led to one of the rooms.

'I thought you were afraid to have him here because he's a friend of Pierre de Craon.'

'He told us not worry because the Duchess of Orléans is a friend of his.'

Such a liar, Marion thought. She stepped into the communal room and sat on a bench by the fireplace. When Thibault emerged from one of the rooms, put on a big black cape, and went out the door, she waited a moment, then went after him.

She followed him down to the rue des Bourdonnais, where he went into a house she'd never noticed before, even though it was in the part of the city where Colin had been abducted and where she'd visited Mahaut. She followed and found herself in a dark hallway. There were no doors, only a narrow, crumbling staircase leading to an open door at the top. She climbed up, shuddering each time one of the steps creaked.

In a small, musty shop, Thibault stood talking to a hunchbacked little old woman. Her face was nearly obscured by a mass of white hair, and she was dressed all in black. The room, lined with closed cabinets, smelled of mold, rot, and something like rotten meat. The only light came from logs burning feebly in a small fireplace and a ray of sun that worked its way in through a dusty window.

It was impossible to hide, so she stepped in boldly, pretending to be another customer. The little woman didn't notice her at first, she was so busy with Thibault. She rubbed her hands together and bowed to him obsequiously. 'What is your desire today, sir? Have you brought me more henbane? Perhaps another baby for me to take care of?' She laughed, a shrill, grating sound.

Thibault laughed too. 'You did a good job with that. Now I want to buy something. I'm told you are the only one who sells it. Do you know what I'm referring to?'

The shopkeeper laughed nastily and unlocked one of the cabinets. 'You're right. You won't find it anywhere else.' She placed a small object on the counter. 'Look at it carefully. Does it make you shiver? Does it make you turn pale?' She saw Marion and turned to her. 'Here's another gentleman. Let's see what he has to say about it.'

Marion held up her hand and shook her head.

'The gentleman is shy. We won't press him. But see how he shakes.'

Marion really was shaking, because Thibault was looking at her closely. When he turned away, she let out a sigh of relief.

Thibault and the tiny woman bent over the thing on the counter. She looked over Thibault's shoulder and saw that the object was a little wax figure of a man with two faces looking in opposite directions. 'Lovely, isn't it?' the woman asked. She went to the cabinet and brought out two large brown pods, some yellow crystals, and a tuft of hair. 'All you have to do is put all these things together in this little bag' – she reached under the counter and produced the bag – 'and you can destroy what or whom you want.'

Thibault started to laugh. 'This will certainly frighten them,' he stammered, doubled over with mirth.

'I can make it even more frightening,' the shopkeeper said. She produced a long, sharp needle and stuck it into the wax man. Then she retreated into a back room and returned with a tiny paper crown, which she attached to the figure's head.

'Now the magic should work,' she said.

Thibault thrust the wax man and the other objects into the bag, handed the shopkeeper some coins, and left the store chuckling to himself. Marion crept after him, ignoring the pleas of the grotesque little shopkeeper to stay and see what else she had to offer.

FORTY-FIVE

A fool may sometimes give a wise man counsel.

Old proverb

Christine went back to the palace the next morning not knowing what to expect after what had happened to Colart's painting the day before. Gilles was raging around the library. 'That bastard is here again,' he shouted.

'Thibault?'

'Who else? So many terrible things are happening here, and he comes barging in like an honored guest. I don't understand why the duchess can't tell him to stay away. Especially today, when everyone is so frightened.'

'I know. After what happened to Colart's painting.'

'Now the cooks are terrified, too.'

'What happened to the cooks?'

'The master cook found a mysterious powder on some of his tarts. He was afraid it was poison, and he threw everything out.'

Christine knew the king's master cook, but she hadn't met the cook who presided over Louis and Valentina's kitchen. She felt sorry for the man, tormented merely because he worked for Valentina.

'How is Colart?' she asked.

'He's up there trying to clean his studio. He won't let anyone but Baudet help him. He says no one understands what painters do, so no one else would do it right. He says he'll destroy the damaged painting and never do another like it.'

'Do you think I can go on with my copying today?'

'I don't know why not. Just keep out of Colart's way.'

She went to her room and took out her writing materials, but before she could sit down and begin her work, the fools burst into the room. She was relieved to see Fripon.

Blondel rolled along the floor to her feet, Coquinet walked on his hands, Fripon raced around throwing balls into the air, and Hanotin did a little dance with the monkey. Giliot marched up to her and stood with his hands on his hips.

'Cooks who scream ruin the soup,' he said, shaking his shaggy mane from side to side.

'It curdles,' Hanotin added.

'And makes you sick,' said Blondel, rolling over and gagging.

'What on earth are you talking about?' she asked.

'Come and you'll see,' Fripon said.

'Follow us,' they said all together, and they headed out the door.

'What is it this time?' she called after them, remembering the last time they'd asked her to come with them. They came running back, dragged her out the door before she had a chance to put her writing materials away, and pranced around her as she went down the stairs. They led her through passages she'd never seen before and out into a small courtyard with a fountain and a garden. They raced on ahead of her, and when she stopped to look at some spring crocuses, they ran back and waved their arms, indicating that she should hurry after them. They rushed into the palace through another door and along a narrow corridor. She realized then that they were close to the storeroom where she'd first seen Bonne, and she wondered whether they had something else hidden there. But this time they led her right into the kitchen.

One of the cooks sat on a bench holding something in her lap and screaming, while scullery maids and lesser cooks stood around helplessly, patting her on the shoulder in useless attempts to calm her. They all looked up when Christine and the fools came in.

'Move away,' Fripon cried, waving his arms around to brush them aside. The women backed away, and the fools crowded around the hysterical cook. The monkey jumped down on to the bench and sat beside her, grinning and chattering. 'Get that animal away from here!' she cried, frantically putting her hands over what she had in her lap.

Christine sat down beside her. 'What is the matter? Let me see what you have there.'

'It belongs to the Devil!' the woman cried. 'The sorceress left it.'

'I don't believe that,' Christine said. 'There is no sorcery here.' She leaned over and peered through the cook's fingers.

'It's just a loaf of bread!' she exclaimed. 'Why are you so upset about it?'

'You'll see,' the cook said. She took her hands away from the bread, and it broke into two pieces. A little cloth bag fell out and landed on the floor at Christine's feet. She bent down to pick it up, and a great cry went up around her.

'Don't touch it!' everyone shouted at once, and they turned their faces away as she opened the bag. Inside she found a tiny wax figure of a man with two faces, a paper crown on his head, and a needle stuck through his breast. She shook the bag, and two large brown pods, some yellow crystals, and a bunch of hair fell out.

The cook sobbed, the lesser cooks and scullery maids wailed and moaned, and the fools sat on the floor with their heads in their hands. The monkey grabbed a dish towel and buried his face in it.

Christine drew a deep breath and asked, 'Where is the master cook?'

'He's not here yet,' the cook blubbered.

'I'm sure he would tell you there's nothing to be afraid of,' Christine said. She held up the wax figure, which caused a communal cry of terror.

'Don't be ridiculous,' Christine said. 'This is just wax.'

Giliot looked at the women and shook his head. 'They don't believe you.'

Christine snatched the bread from the cook's hands. It wasn't heavy because the inside had been hollowed out to make a hiding place for the bag with the wax image. She fitted the two halves of the bread together and saw that a strange symbol had been carved into the bottom.

'Where did you find this bread?' she asked the cook.

'On the table. Someone put it there when I wasn't looking.' The cook clasped her hands together to make them stop shaking.

'Where were the rest of you?' Christine asked the scullery maids and the other cooks.

'We didn't do it!' said a girl with a long blond braid and a flour-covered apron.

'I didn't say you did. I'm just asking where you were and whether you noticed anyone unusual in the kitchen.'

They all shook their heads.

'I know,' Fripon said. 'It was Aubert de Canny. I've seen him come in here when no one is looking.'

'So that's why my tarts disappear!' the cook explained.

If Aubert can take something, he can just as easily leave something, Christine thought. *It's possible that Fripon is right to suspect Aubert; perhaps Aubert is Pierre's accomplice.*

The cook was berating the lesser cooks for leaving the kitchen when they were supposed to be working. The girl with the blond braid started to cry. 'Sometimes we go out for a moment. We don't do anything wrong,' she wailed.

'Of course you don't,' Christine said. 'But we have to find out who left this loaf of bread here. Is it one you baked?' she asked the cook.

The cook shook her head. 'I know my own loaves! And I certainly don't make them with hollow insides.'

A large sack hung by the door, and Christine took it down. She thrust the bread and the wax figure into it. 'I'll take this away, so none of you will have to see it again. Whoever put it here wanted you to be frightened. But there's nothing to be frightened of. It's all superstition.'

She went out into the little courtyard, and the fools followed. She hesitated. She really didn't know what to do with the bread and the wax figure.

'Do you have any suggestions?' she asked the fools.

The fools sat down on the ground and hung their heads.

That was a foolish question, Christine said to herself. *Of course they don't have any suggestions. They're just fools. I'm as foolish as they are.*

'Take it to your mother,' Giliot said. 'She knew what to do with the baby.'

'That's so,' Hanotin agreed, standing up and looking at Christine with his round, unblinking eyes. 'Your mother can tell you where it came from.' The monkey sat on his shoulder and nodded in agreement.

Coquinet stood on his head. 'Yes, take it to your mother,' he said.

Blondel rolled on to his back and said, 'Mothers always know.'

'No, they don't,' Fripon said. 'Don't take it to your mother.'

'Why not?' Christine asked.

Fripon grabbed some pebbles and tossed them into the air. 'I don't know,' he said.

'It seems as good an idea as any,' she said. She slung the sack over her shoulder and headed for home.

FORTY-SIX

Make an image in his name, whom you would hurt or kill.

Reginald Scot (c. 1538–1599),
The Discoverie of Witchcraft, 1584

C hristine tried to sneak up to her room, but Francesca heard
her and called for her to come into the kitchen.
'Why are you home so early? And what do you have in
that sack?' she asked. 'Where is the pouch you usually carry?'

Christine clapped her hand to her head. She'd left the pouch and
her writing materials on her desk at the palace. *I suppose they'll
be all right until tomorrow,* she thought. But she wondered what
Gilles would say when he realized she hadn't returned the fables
of Aesop.

'It's just a loaf of bread, Mama.'

'Then why are you trying to hide it under your cloak?' Thomas
asked. He pointed to Goblin and Berith, who circled around her,
sniffing. 'They smell something,' he said.

She took the sack out and opened it so everybody could peer in.
'You see? It's just bread.'

Berith grabbed the sack in his jaws and pulled it out of
Christine's hand. It fell to the floor, and the bread tumbled out
and broke in two. The crowned two-headed figure lay at Francesca's
feet. 'Why have you brought the Devil into this house, *Cristina*?'
she screamed.

Surprisingly, Georgette didn't look upset. 'I know you wouldn't
bring anything having to do with the Devil.'

Christine picked up the wax figure. 'For once, you're showing
good sense, Georgette. This is just wax. It was in the bread.'

'Why?' Thomas asked.

'Someone thought the bread would make a good hiding place
until a superstitious person cut it open and discovered the wax king.'
Christine said. She fitted the two halves of the loaf of bread together.

'You see, they even put a mark on the bottom, so the superstitious person would think it was a message from the Devil.'

'I cannot look at it!' Francesca cried. 'Take it away, *Cristina*.'

'Georgette isn't afraid of it.'

Francesca looked at Georgette, who stood over Christine, examining the bread. 'I suppose if Georgette is not afraid of it, I should not be, either.' She took the loaf, studied it, and exclaimed, 'This is not the Devil's mark! If you paid more attention to shopping and cooking, *Cristina*, you would know that this is the mark the baker on the rue Saint-Antoine puts on all his loaves. He is proud of his work, and he does not want it attributed to anyone else.'

Christine started to laugh. 'You can't imagine how it frightened the cooks at the palace.'

There was a knock at the door. Georgette went to answer it and came back with Martin and Bonne and a man in a short purple jacket with brocaded sleeves, blue tights, and a big turban.

Goblin and Berith ran to the stranger, but the rest of the family just stood staring at him.

'I met her in the street,' Martin said. 'She has something important to tell you.'

'Her?' Christine asked.

'Of course.' Marion took off the turban and shook her head so that her red hair flew around her face.

'*Sei pazza?*' Francesca asked. She sat down on the bench by the table and tried to fan herself with the bread. Martin placed Bonne in her lap. As she put her arms around the little girl, she dropped the bread.

'Everything is *pazza*,' Jean said. 'Will somebody please tell me what's going on? Who wants to say first? You, Mama? Or you, Marion?'

But Marion didn't respond. She was staring at the little wax king on the floor. 'Where did you get that?'

'*Cristina* brought it home from the palace,' Francesca said.

'I thought that's where he'd take it.'

'What are you talking about?' Christine asked.

Marion sat down on the bench. 'Who found it?'

'The cooks,' Christine answered.

'I'll bet they were frightened to death.'

'They were. But how do you know about it?'

'Because I saw him buy it.'

'Who?'

'Thibault de Torvaux.'

Francesca let out a cry of anguish. 'Surely you were not following that criminal!'

'My disguise is pretty good, don't you think?'

'Not good enough when that man is around,' Martin said.

'Oh, Marion, you could have been killed!' Francesca cried.

Marion grinned. 'I'm surprised you would care, Francesca.'

Francesca held Bonne close and looked at the floor.

'Tell us what happened, Marion,' Christine said.

'I followed Thibault to a shop on the rue des Bourdonnais. He told the shopkeeper he wanted something really wicked, and this is what he got. She put it in a little bag with two pods and some crystals and a tuft of hair.'

'That's what was with it when the cooks found it in this loaf of bread.' Christine picked up the bread and showed Marion how it had been hollowed out.

'Clever,' Marion said. She took the bread and turned it over in her hands. 'What is this mark on the bottom?'

'We were meant to think it was a sorcerer's mark. The duke's fools told me to show it to my mother. She knew right away it was the mark the baker on the rue Saint-Antoine puts on all his bread.'

'Those fools are smarter than I thought,' Francesca said.

'Let's go to the baker's shop and find out whether he remembers Thibault,' Marion said.

'That's not necessary,' Martin said. 'We know he bought the wax figure.' He took Bonne from Francesca and held her close.

Marion clapped her hand to her head. 'I just remembered,' she cried. 'The woman who sold Thibault the wax king asked Thibault if he'd brought another baby for her to take care of. She's the one who drugged your child, Martin! I thought I smelled henbane in that shop.'

'Now I know who took my little girl and murdered Klara,' Martin said.

'But it can't be Thibault who leaves the signs of sorcery around the palace. He'd be noticed,' Christine said.

'Are you saying that Thibault has an accomplice?' Martin asked.

'Yes. And I don't think that person is merely trying to make everyone think Valentina is a sorceress. I think he intends to kill her.'

Francesca slumped against Marion and sobbed. 'I know you, *Cristina*. You are going to put yourself in danger again.' She put her hands together and started to pray.

Martin drew Christine aside and said quietly, 'Be careful if you discover who this accomplice is, Christine. And for God's sake, if you see Thibault at the palace, stay away from him!'

FORTY-SEVEN

Always remember, if you aren't on your guard, death may seize you and take you away.

From a book of moral and practical advice for a young wife,
Paris, 1393

'You must not go to the palace today!' Francesca cried as Christine started out the door the next morning.
'I have to warn them about Thibault.'
'That is not for you to do. He will kill you.'
'He doesn't know we've found him out. And besides, there will be many other people around. I'll be fine. Perhaps he won't even be there.'

The children gathered around their grandmother. 'Can't you give her something to protect her? One of your herbs or something?' Thomas wanted to know.

Francesca disappeared into the pantry and came back with a bundle of dry herbs and thrust them into Christina's hand, where they crumbled.

'It is vervain, left over from last year. It is all I have.' Francesca sat down on the bench and began to weep.

Christine put on her cloak and left the house. Marion was waiting for her in the street.

'I know where you're going, and I'm going with you. You're in trouble if you meet Thibault.'

'You're in more danger than I am, Marion. You're the one who spied on him.'

'But he didn't recognize me!'

'I wouldn't be so sure of that.'

'Nevertheless, now that I know who killed Fleur and Klara, I

want to make sure everyone at the palace knows, too. I want to
make sure they hang Thibault from the highest beam on the gibbet
at Montfaucon!'

'I do, too. Fleur didn't deserve it, and neither did Klara. I
complained about Klara a lot, but she shouldn't have died like that.
And when I think of what he did to Bonne . . .'

'When they take him to the Châtelet, I hope they put him on the
rack,' Marion said. 'I hope they keep him in a place so dark and filled
with dust that he chokes. I hope they put him in a cold room and
leave him there until he freezes to death. I hope they throw him into
the pit shaped like a funnel, where he won't be able to sit or lie down,
and he'll have to stand in water up to his knees until he dies. I hope
the other prisoners kill him when they find out what he did to a baby.'

'Those are horrible thoughts, Marion.'

'Don't tell me you don't have them, too.'

Christine remembered Bonne, half-starved, her face blackened
with grease. 'Perhaps I do.'

The racket on the rue Saint-Antoine had reached fever pitch.
They stopped to listen to a group of women who'd heard about the
wax figure in the loaf of bread. 'She wants to frighten everyone and
make us all lose our minds, just like the king,' said a crone who
was carrying several loaves of bread herself and almost dropped
them in her excitement.

'That's not true,' Christine cried.

The women turned to look at her. 'Who are you and what do
you know about it?' asked a biddy who had a live goose in a basket.

Christine took Marion's arm and led her away. They walked for
a while, and then Marion stopped short. 'Do you think Thibault put
the bread in the kitchen?'

'He couldn't have. There is no way he could have gone roaming
around the palace without being seen.'

Brother Michel came racing down the street and waved his hands
at Christine. 'Go home! You cannot go to the palace after all that's
happened there! And you, Marion, should be ashamed of yourself
for encouraging her.'

'Where is Pierre de Craon?' Christine asked.

'At the abbey, of course.'

'And Thibault?'

'I haven't seen him for a while. Why do you ask?'

'He's the one who's been bringing signs of sorcery to the palace.

Marion saw him buying the wax idol of the king with a needle through his heart.'

Michel shook his head. 'How could Thibault have managed to put those things around? Someone would have seen him.'

'He has someone helping him. That's why I have to go to the palace. I have to warn the duke and duchess.'

'It's too dangerous, Christine. Let the duke take care of it.'

'But he doesn't know what I've discovered. I have to tell him.'

'Then I'll come with you.'

'I'll be all right. Marion is with me.'

'They won't let Marion in.'

Marion drew herself up to her full height. 'Perhaps you aren't aware that I sell embroidery to the queen. *She* lets me in.'

Michel looked at her crimson cloak and beaded hair. 'If you are visiting the queen, you should at least dress more respectably.'

'*Porc de Dieu.*' Marion took Christine's arm and hurried her down the street.

At the duke's residence, all was quiet and the *portier* was about to admit Christine when Henri Le Picart appeared. 'You shouldn't be here,' he said.

'This is exactly where I should be. You can go home now, Marion,' Christine said as she went through the door and into a gallery where ancient warriors gazed down from tapestries covering the walls. Henri followed her. She turned and faced him defiantly. 'You're always telling me what to do, that women are weak. But I know more than you, Henri.'

'What are you talking about?'

'I know who's behind all the mayhem here.'

'Tell me.'

'Yesterday the cooks found an image of the king with a needle through his heart.'

'I know all about that. Everybody does.'

'Thibault de Torvaux bought that image in a shop on the rue des Bourdonnais.'

'How did he get it into the kitchen?'

'He has an accomplice who carries out his wishes. I'm going to find out who it is.'

'Women are fools. Go home! You're going to go around denouncing Thibault de Torvaux, and you don't even know what's happened.'

'What has he done now?'

'It's not what *he* did, it's what was done to *him*. He was stabbed and thrown into the Seine. The sergeants from the Châtelet pulled his body out this morning.'

FORTY-EIGHT

The second face of Virgo is of Saturn, in which you may make an image to harm tools and writing instruments.

Picatrix, ninth-century Arabic book on magic,
translated into Spanish and Latin in 1256

Christine stared at Henri. 'Do you know who killed him?'

'No one does.'

I do, Christine said to herself, remembering the times she'd seen Martin lay his hand on his dagger at the thought of what had been done to his little daughter. But she knew she would never tell Henri or anyone else about that.

Henri took off his little black cape and threw it over his arm. The ermine collar matched the ermine lining of his brocaded sky-blue *houppelande*. 'I've informed the duke and duchess,' he said. 'Soon everyone will find out. I don't think anyone will much care. In any event, now that he's dead, you can go home.'

Christine glared at him. 'Do you think I'll leave, just like that?' She started down the gallery, but Henri grabbed her arm. She pulled away and raged at him, 'Thibault had an accomplice, and that person is still here. I intend to find out who it is. Don't try to stop me, Henri!'

He stepped back and made an exaggerated bow. 'Then go right in. I'll not be responsible for what happens.' He stormed away.

She stopped at the door to Valentina's receiving room and looked in. The duchess had visitors – the king and queen. The king seemed to be having one of his better days. He even looked affectionately at Isabeau, who sat on a high-backed chair, smiling at everyone. She'd brought only one of her ladies with her, Symonne du Mesnil, who stood by her side, staring at Valentina's ladies as they huddled together on the other side of the room. *They're afraid,* Christine thought. *They should be.*

Louis was attentive to his brother, but his gaze was directed at Mariette, who fingered a gold necklace that stood out against the white skin of her breasts. She took care to stand in such a way that Louis couldn't fail to see it.

Henri had followed her in. 'Strumpet,' he said under his breath as he looked at Mariette.

Christine jumped. 'I thought you were going to leave me alone.'

He turned and stalked away.

She tried to pass the library quietly so Gilles wouldn't see her and realize she'd forgotten to return the fables of Aesop the day before. But she needn't have worried. Gilles stood with his back to the door talking to Eustache, who had obviously just told him about Thibault. Gilles was rubbing his hands together gleefully.

'Are you so glad?' asked Eustache.

'We're all glad,' announced Colart from the top of his ladder. 'He made stupid remarks about the carriage I painted for the duchess.' He turned back to Vergil and applied some blue paint to his robe.

'Is he still angry about the damaged painting?' Eustache asked Gilles.

'Yes. But now he says he's decided to repair it. I don't know why he doesn't just start another one.'

'You think it's easy. You don't know anything about painting,' Colart called down from his perch.

Christine crept away and went up to her room. Outside the door she met Aubert de Canny. He'd just come from the room with the alchemists' equipment, and he looked at her slyly. 'Don't you want to see what's in there?'

'I already know, as you are well aware. Why is everyone so secretive about it?'

'Many people believe alchemy is akin to magic. That's one of the accusations leveled at the duke. You know, of course, that he's accused of sorcery as much as the duchess.'

His straggly blond hair stuck up from his head in a most unattractive way. *No wonder Mariette prefers the duke,* Christine thought.

Aubert took a step closer to her. Too close. He leaned down and said in a soft voice, 'People say the duke used sorcery to seduce my wife.'

Why is he telling me this? she asked herself. 'It must be painful for you,' she said.

He laughed, a deep, unpleasant sound. 'Do you think I care? I'm helping the duchess. Perhaps you've heard about that.' He laughed again and walked away.

She started to go into her room but stopped when the fools came racing up the stairs.

'What did your mother say about the bread?' Hanotin asked, his voice muffled because the monkey had his tail curled around his neck and partly in his mouth.

'Mothers always know about bread,' Coquinet said.

Christine laughed. 'My mother knows so much about bread that she knew exactly where that loaf came from.'

'Did the peacock buy it?' Giliot asked.

'He did.'

'But how did he get it into the kitchen without being seen?' Giliot asked.

'He wasn't the one who did it,' Fripon said.

'How do you know?' Christine asked.

'I told you before; it must have been Aubert.'

'Let's go and talk to the cooks again,' Christine said.

So they all trooped down to the kitchen, where the master cook was shouting at the lesser cooks as they prepared dinner for everyone at the duke's residence. 'I've no time for you now,' he said to the fools, shooing them away. Then he saw Christine, and he bowed slightly. 'What can I do for you?' he asked.

'I suppose you've heard about the bread with the wax image of the king that was left here.'

'I've heard of nothing else since it happened,' he said, pointing a big spoon at the other cooks.

'Do you have any idea who left it?'

'The person who put white powder on my tarts. Who else?'

'Have you seen any strangers in your kitchen?'

'No. And they say they haven't, either; but they seem so confused about it, I don't know what to believe,' he said, brandishing the spoon at the other cooks so furiously that they all backed away. 'The truth is we don't know who's been in here, and we don't know who put mysterious powder on my tarts, and we don't know who left a loaf of bread with a wax image of the king in it, and we don't know whether we'll still be alive tomorrow – so that's the end of it. Leave us to our work.' He brandished the spoon at the fools. Hanotin's monkey, which was seated on his worktable, made an obscene gesture. The cook picked up some onions and threw them at the chattering beast. Then he grabbed a big knife. Hanotin snatched the monkey away just in time, and the fools ran out the door.

Christine wanted to say something more to the master cook, but he glowered at her and turned away. She went out into the little courtyard. Blondel wallowed on the ground, Coquinet had twisted himself into a ball, Hanotin sat by the fountain, dipping the monkey in and out of the water, and Fripon juggled the onions the cook had thrown at the monkey. Giliot stood with his mane of hair pulled over his eyes. 'God sends meat; the Devil sends cooks,' he said.

'I have to get back to my work now,' she said.

The fools scampered away, and she went back up the stairs. As she passed the library, she saw that Colart had left and Gilles was still talking to Eustache. She went in and asked if either of them had ever seen Thibault roaming around the palace.

'Not me,' Eustache said.

'He certainly never comes in here,' Gilles said.

There's no doubt that Thibault had an assistant, Christine thought as she climbed the stairs to her room. *Where will his accomplice strike next?*

She had her answer as soon as she entered the room. Her inkhorn rested on its side, spilling its contents on to the green cloth that covered the desk; the points of her quill pens had been smashed; and her handiwork had been shredded. Worst of all, the leaves of the precious Aesop manuscript had been ripped from their leather binding and thrown on to the floor.

She stood stunned, contemplating the mess, and wondering how she would tell Gilles. Then she saw a foot and realized there was someone under the desk, someone hidden behind the folds of the green cloth that hung down to the floor. At first she was afraid it might be the person who'd done the damage, waiting to accost her, but nothing moved. She knelt down, lifted the cloth, and drew back in horror.

Valentina's maid, Julia, lay on the floor. Her dress was drawn up around her neck, and her head was twisted to one side. Christine put her fingers on her throat: the flesh was cold, and there was no pulse. She pulled the girl's dress down and tried to arrange it so no one would see the full extent of the awful things that had been done to her: Julia had been raped and strangled.

FORTY-NINE

It troubles and grieves me greatly to hear men say that many women want to be raped.

Christine de Pizan,
Le Livre de la Cité des Dames, 1404–1405

A necklace of precious stones lay on the floor beside the body. Christine picked it up and found that its gold chain was broken. She looked at the dead girl and saw the marks the jewels had made on the white flesh of her neck. She shuddered, staggered to her feet, went out of the room, and stood bracing herself against a wall, trying to quiet her wildly beating heart.

Slander is one thing. Murder is another, she thought. The murder of Valentina's maid, a girl she'd brought from Italy because she loved her, was more frightening than malicious accusations of sorcery. There was a madman at the palace, a madman she was sure was out to kill the duchess herself.

The door to Colart's room was shut. She crept past it and went down the stairs to the library, where she found Gilles and Henri Le Picart examining a book.

'I need to talk to you, Henri,' she said. Gilles looked at her but said nothing when Henri followed her out into the hallway.

'Something terrible has happened,' she said. 'Valentina's maid, Julia, has been murdered. The body is in my room.'

'I'm surprised you're telling me, since I'm sure you think I'm the one who did it.'

'This is not a joke, Henri. Of course I don't think you did it.' *At least I'm fairly sure you didn't,* she thought. 'I need your help.'

'I'd better have a look.' He charged up the stairs.

Henri knelt beside the body, felt the girl's neck, and said, 'She's been dead for some time.' He picked up the necklace. 'She was strangled with this.'

'I know that.'

Christine turned away as Henri began to examine the body more closely. She heard him gasp and swear when he realized the full extent of what had been done to the girl.

'When were you last in this room?' he asked.

Christine had to think. She remembered that the day before, the fools had dragged her away before she'd had time to collect her writing materials, and that they'd taken her away again that morning before she'd even gone into the room. 'Not since yesterday morning.'

'She was killed sometime yesterday.'

He ran his hands over the precious stones of the necklace. 'This certainly isn't hers,' he said. 'In any event, I'm sure she wouldn't have worn anything, no matter how priceless, that would cover up the breasts she was so anxious to show.' He laid the necklace on the floor beside the body. A ray of light coming through the open window touched the gems, and they glittered with inner fire.

'What do you mean?'

'Haven't you noticed? Valentina's pretty little maid had been studying Mariette d'Enghien and copying her ways. I'm surprised Valentina didn't stop her. Women who wear low-cut gowns are asking for trouble.'

'Are you excusing a rapist?'

He looked up at her in surprise. 'Don't you agree?'

'I'd expect all kinds of nonsense about women from you, Henri, but not that!' She lashed out at him with her fists.

Henri stood up and grasped her hands in his. 'Calm yourself. Women always get so excited.'

This was too much. She went to the open window, looked out, and took deep breaths, trying to control her anger. Then she turned around and faced Henri. 'We have to call the guards without raising an alarm,' she said.

'For once, a woman is thinking sensibly,' Henri said. 'You wait here and I'll get them.'

When he'd left, Christine stood looking at the body. Julia had been an attractive girl who'd always cheered the duchess. She'd come from Milan, like Valentina, and she must have shared many happy memories with her. She thought of Julia's sister, Elena. She would have to be told. The news would be devastating.

Henri returned with two guards and Valentina. The duchess knelt beside the body and gently touched the girl's forehead. 'Who would do this to an innocent girl?'

'How innocent was she, always baring her breasts?' Henri asked. Christine wanted to hit him. Valentina's anger was better controlled. 'That was uncalled for, Henri. Your disdain for women does not serve you well.'

The duchess's demeanor was so dignified and her voice so gentle that Henri looked chagrined. 'I apologize, *Madame*,' he said.

Valentina picked up the necklace and gasped. 'This is mine! I lost it a long time ago.'

Christine remembered what Eustache had told her about the necklace stolen from the duchess when she was on her way to France.

Valentina looked at the marks on Julia's neck and shuddered. Tears streamed down her cheeks. 'My poor girl,' she whispered. She bent down and kissed the pale face. 'How will I ever tell your sister?'

She rose and motioned to the guards. 'There's a little staircase on the other side of the hallway. If you carry her down that way, you won't encounter anyone. There's an unused room at the bottom. Lay her carefully on the floor there. I'll call the duke. Everyone will have to know, but not right away. I must tell her sister first.'

The guards lifted the body and carried it away, with the duchess following. Christine and Henri stayed in the room, watching the sad procession. Then Henri turned to Christine and said, 'There are some things you probably haven't considered.'

'Probably not. I'm just a woman.'

'That is so. But try to put your mind to them.'

She turned to go. He grabbed her arm and pulled her back into the room. 'This is serious. If one sister is murdered, the other one must be in danger, too. And what about the duchess? Surely this was meant to be a sign for her. She is in great peril.'

'I had thought of that.'

'And have you wondered why the girl was murdered here?'

'This room is in a rather remote place.'

'Women's logic, or lack of it. It was not by chance. The murderer killed the girl here because he wanted you to know that you are in danger, too.'

FIFTY

The sapphire brings peace and harmony. It makes the mind pure, devout, and intent on doing good.

The Book of Secrets of Albertus Magnus, thirteenth century

'Go away, Henri,' Christine said.

'There's a murderer around, and you want to be left alone?'

'I suppose you think I should be begging you to stay with me.' The duchess came back. 'There,' Christine said. 'I'm not alone.'

Henri turned, made a deep bow to Valentina, and left.

'He only wants to make sure you're safe,' the duchess said.

Christine felt herself blushing.

Valentina went to the desk, sat down, and put her head in her hands. 'Someone killed Julia, but it was me they wanted to hurt.' She looked up at Christine, her eyes glistening with tears. 'Why do people here hate me so much?'

'Superstition and ignorance, *Madame*. They need to blame someone for the king's illness.'

'Next they will kill me.'

'We must find out who has done this before that happens.'

'I am not afraid,' the duchess said. 'I wish I had been strangled, not Julia.' She bowed her head. 'I am so sorry you had to be the one to find her.'

'It's not the first time I've found a body, *Madame*. It's worse for you. You have lost a dear friend.'

Valentina was carrying the necklace, and she placed it gently on the desk. The stones made a soft, tinkling sound as they touched the wood. 'It is hard to believe that someone used this to kill her,' she said.

Christine went to the open window and looked down at the street below. Two ladies stood talking. A man in a beaver hat with a large peacock feather strolled by. He took off the hat and waved it about with such a grand flourish that the feather brushed the ground. A boy threw a rock at a dog, and an old woman with a market basket stopped and shook her finger at him. Two palace guards stood watching. Everything seemed normal; no one knew there had been another murder.

She was startled out of her reverie by the duchess, who said, 'This necklace belonged to my mother. She always intended for me to have it, but she had a premonition that she wouldn't be able to give it to me herself. She was right: she died when I was only two. She wrote a letter for me to read when I was old enough, telling me about the stones.' She spread the necklace out on the desk. 'Come here and I will tell you what she said.'

Christine went to the desk and bent over the necklace. 'It is very beautiful,' she said.

'The real beauty lies in the meaning of each of the gems.' Valentina put a finger on a milky blue stone. 'This one, for example. It's turquoise. My mother said it would keep me safe if I fell from my horse.'

'She couldn't have known what a superb rider you would be.'

Valentina smiled and touched an orange-red stone. 'She suspected that one day I would travel far from home. So she gave me the jacinth to protect me on my travels.'

She caressed a sea-green stone. 'With this one she was thinking of my marriage. She didn't know who my husband would be, but she said that beryl promises a happy union.' She was silent for a while. Then she tapped a fiery red stone. 'Ruby, according to my mother, brings peace between a husband and wife.'

'And the emerald?' Christine asked, pointing to a stone that glowed with green fire.

'That will tell me whether my lover is true,' Valentina said. Then she ran her hand over a red stone that glowed orange within. 'If he is not true, garnet will take away the sorrow.' She rose, went to the window, and held the necklace up to the light. The stones glittered and flashed, as though they were signaling to each other. She stroked a blue stone that outshone all the others. 'I love the sapphire best of all. It promises everything good: peace, harmony, and a pure mind free from care.' She ran her fingers over the broken chain. 'After I lost this necklace, I could never bear to wear another one. I won't have it repaired, not after it has been used to strangle my dear Julia.'

'Perhaps its history could give us a clue as to who the killer is,' Christine said. 'Please tell me how you lost it.'

'It happened when I was on my way here, coming to be married. I brought many jewels and precious objects with me, but this necklace was the one thing I really treasured, and I wore it always. Until it disappeared.'

The duchess went back to the desk and spread the necklace out in front of her again. 'You may have wondered why I have no fool of my own. I did have a fool once. His name was Gonzo, and he was brought to me when I was a little girl. His family was poor, and there were so many children, the parents couldn't care for them all. So they gave Gonzo away.' She looked up at Christine. 'I know people think we in the nobility treat our fools and dwarfs and mutes as mere objects of fun. But that is not always true. To me, Gonzo was like a brother. He was just my age, and I loved him.'

'I understand, *Madame*,' Christine said, thinking of the queen's friendship with her dwarf, Alips.

'Gonzo was born into a family of entertainers,' the duchess continued. 'He'd learned to do all kinds of tricks, and he could entertain me for hours.' She shook her head and brushed away a tear. 'Of course, he was meant to come with me to France. I would never have left him behind. But something terrible happened on the journey. It was at Mâcon. I was careless, and one night I left this necklace on a table in the house where I was staying. In the morning it was gone. Everyone searched for it, but no one could find it.' She stroked each stone in the necklace. 'All the people who accompanied me were distraught.'

'Can you remember who they were?'

'Many people accompanied me from Milan. At Mâcon, Louis's secretary and his chancellor joined us. And Louis's good friend, Pierre de Craon. You know of him, of course.'

'Everyone in France knows of Pierre de Craon.'

'When I married Louis, he and Pierre were devoted to each other. Pierre was always polite to me; but, to tell the truth, I think he resented me for taking Louis away from him.'

'That would not surprise me,' Christine said. 'Their friendship was well known. They even dressed alike. Pierre is older than your husband, and he seems to have influenced him in many ways, not always for the good.'

'In any event, Pierre was there in Mâcon when my necklace was stolen.'

'Was Thibault de Torvaux there too?'

'No. Just Pierre and some of Louis's officials. Everyone was upset, but Pierre seemed to take it to heart more than any of the others. He raged around, claiming it was useless to look for the necklace because he'd seen Gonzo take it. He convinced everyone that my poor fool was a thief. He insisted that I question him.'

'You yourself had no reason to doubt Gonzo?'

'None whatsoever. But I thought that if I questioned him and cleared his name, people would stop accusing him. Gonzo, on the other hand, thought I really believed him guilty. He ran away, fell from a bridge, and drowned.'

'How horrible!'

'His body was recovered, but the necklace was never found. I'm sure of only one thing: Gonzo did not steal it.'

'And you never had another fool. I can understand why.'

'The duke's fools have taken it upon themselves to entertain me. They are kind, and they do make up for Gonzo a bit.'

'I've wondered about them. Eustache Deschamps says I should listen to them.'

'Eustache knows there are many kinds of fools. Blondel, for example, is truly simple. His family found him difficult to care for – he's so fat, and he eats so much. They thought his habit of rolling around on the ground would amuse the duke, and they were right.'

'I wonder whether he's as simple as people think,' Christine said.

'It's hard to tell. Hanotin, on the other hand, plays foolish, but it's obvious that he really isn't. He came here on his own and offered his services.'

'And those of his monkey,' Christine said.

The duchess laughed. 'He'd traveled a lot, but he'd run out of money, so he decided that playing the fool would be a way to support himself. He discovered he enjoyed it, and he stayed.'

'What about Coquinet? Where did he learn to twist his body into so many shapes?'

'I don't know. It seems to come naturally to him. Giliot, on the other hand, twists words and confuses people. But there's sense underneath it all; I suspect he has read a lot. It's possible he was a scholar who was down on his luck.'

'And Fripon?'

'No one knows much about him. He hasn't been with the duke for very long.'

Gilles and Eustache burst into the room, with Henri following right behind them. Gilles stopped short and cried out when he saw the mangled book of fables on the floor. He went to it and began gathering up the pages, smoothing each one with his hands, looking as though he would cry. 'You're more concerned with a book than a girl who's been murdered,' Eustache said.

'You should talk,' Gilles said. 'You're the *maître d'hôtel,* and yet you've done nothing to stop the terrible things that have been happening around here.'

Louis appeared and went to Valentina's side. 'I had to tell Elena,' he said. 'She was asking where her sister was.'

At that moment, Elena appeared at the door, rushed to the duchess, and fell to the ground, weeping. Valentina knelt beside her and did her best to comfort her, while the others in the room looked on and wept, too.

Christine listened to the duchess and Elena speaking in their native language and tried to think who could have killed Julia. She was sure the murder had something to do with Pierre de Craon. But he was confined to the abbey of Saint-Denis, and unless he'd managed to sneak away and insinuate himself into the palace without being seen, which was unlikely, there was no way he could have killed the girl. Nevertheless, his reputation as a thief was well known, and from what the duchess had told her, he was surely the one who'd stolen the necklace at Mâcon.

Which means he has someone here working for him, someone besides Thibault de Torvaux. And that person is more than a slanderer. He's a killer. She thought back to all that the duchess had told her, and she had an idea. 'Where are your fools, *Monseigneur?*' she asked the duke.

'I told them to stay away.'

'Please, *Monseigneur,* ask them to come up here.'

'Surely they have nothing to do with this.'

'If Christine requests it, it must be important,' Valentina said. 'Remember what she has done for you in the past.'

Louis scowled, but he turned and left the room, pushing his way past a group of people standing at the door. By now, everyone at the duke's residence knew about the murder, and fear gripped them all – from the humblest scullery maid to the duke's highest officials. Eustache tried to calm them, but without success. Even Gilles stopped gathering up the pages of the book of fables and stood

gazing at the duchess, as though he hoped she would know what
to do. The duchess, however, stood with her arm around Elena and
looked expectantly at Christine.

'I hope you know what you are doing, Christine,' Henri whispered.

'I told her to listen to the fools,' Eustache said. 'It seems she has.'

'Which fools?' Henri asked. He looked around the room. 'There
are so many.'

'Christine knows.'

Louis returned with Hanotin, Giliot, Blondel, and Coquinet.

'Fripon has disappeared,' he said.

FIFTY-ONE

*Piebald horses have patches of various colors. Those with
white feet are said to be weak, but those that have white blazes
are hot tempered.*

Latin bestiary, twelfth century

Colin was eager to work the bellows for Henri's mysterious
fire again, but he'd waited all day and Henri hadn't summoned
him. He grew restless. He'd hated the work at the palace
stables – shoveling dung, hauling heavy bales of hay, carrying pails
of water that overflowed and wet his shoes – but he was sorry not
to be with the horses, especially the palfrey with the missing tooth.
He decided to pay a visit to the little white horse and make sure she
hadn't forgotten him.

It was dark when he left his house, but there was a full moon.
He crept down the silent streets, alert for any signs that the night
guards were about, and approached the palace stables. The stable
master, grooms, and stable boys had left, and everything was quiet
except for the sounds of horses shuffling around in their stalls and
the rustling of rats scuttling into piles of hay. The moon – shining
through the open door, the uncovered windows, and the spaces
between the roof beams – lit his way as he crept past walls hung
with saddles and bridles and maneuvered around water pails, stacks

of blankets, and barrels of oats, being careful not to disturb anything that might fall and awaken the stable boys who slept in the lofts above. The palfrey snorted softly when he appeared and rubbed her head against his chest. 'You haven't forgotten me,' he whispered. He held out his hand with some oats, and as the horse nibbled them, he said to her, 'I know your tooth would have cured the king, no matter what the stable master says.'

Sensing his presence, the other horses stamped their feet uneasily; but they soon settled down, and the only sound was that of the palfrey's chewing. Then Colin heard the horse in the next stall kick at the walls. He'd never liked that horse, an odd-looking destrier that belonged to Aubert de Canny. He found its coat – black mottled with irregularly shaped splotches of white – ugly, and he feared its violent temper. More than once he'd been a victim, and he had bruises to show for it. The huge animal was just right for Aubert, he thought, because Aubert was also large and bad-tempered.

The destrier became increasingly restless, snorting and crashing against the sides of his stall. Colin peered in to see what was wrong.

At first, all he could see were the jagged white patches on the horse's flank shining in the moonlight, but gradually he became aware that something moved under a large pile of hay in a corner. It was much bigger than a mouse, and it was whimpering. He crept toward it. The destrier pawed the floor and lowered his head into the hay, whereupon a disheveled figure sprang up. Before he could sprint away, Colin threw out his arms, caught him, and hurled him to the floor. 'What are you doing here?' he rasped as he placed his foot on the flailing figure and held him down.

'Help me!' Fripon cried. 'I have to get away.'

'Why? What have you done?'

'Nothing. Nothing terrible, anyway.'

'Then why are you hiding here?'

'They won't believe me.'

'I don't believe you, either,' Colin said. 'I'm going to call the palace guards.'

'No!' Fripon screamed. He struggled so hard that Colin's foot slipped off his body and he was able to jump to his feet. He picked up the destrier's water pail and threw it, hitting Colin on the head. Stunned and blinded by the water, Colin fell to the floor and sat rubbing his eyes, listening to Fripon run out of the stall and unable to stop him. Then he heard sounds of a struggle and desperate cries. He grasped the side of the stall, pulled himself to his feet, and hobbled to the door of the stable.

By the light of the moon he saw Aubert de Canny laughing and holding Fripon, who writhed in his strong grip.

'Don't worry,' Aubert called out to Colin, 'I'll take care of him.' He tucked the fool under his arm and hurried away.

FIFTY-TWO

Fools go to court without being summoned.

                                                                    Old proverb

Early the next morning, Colin barged into the kitchen where Georgette was fanning the fire with the bellows. 'I caught him!' he cried.

'What are you talking about?' Georgette asked.

'The fool who ran away. I caught him.'

'You caught Fripon? I don't believe it!' Christine cried.

'Go to the palace and see for yourself. I caught him, and he's there now.'

'Then you're lucky to be alive!'

'What do you mean?'

'He's a murderer. He strangled one of the duchess's maids.'

Colin stared at her in horror and looked as though he would faint. Francesca pushed him down on to the bench by the table and went into the pantry to get him a cup of wine with valerian in it.

Colin took a large drink and said, 'I didn't know he killed someone.' He took another drink. 'But he couldn't have killed me. Aubert de Canny was there.'

'Where?' Christine asked.

'At the palace stables. That's where the fool was hiding.'

'So who captured him, you or Aubert?'

'I did. Well, sort of. I had him, but he threw a pail of water at me and got away. Aubert was outside, and he caught him.'

Georgette put her arms around her brother and started to cry. 'You could be dead, Colin.'

'Well, I'm not, so stop blubbering.' He looked as though he would faint again, so Francesca brought him another cup of wine. She turned to Christine.

'When you came home last night, you did not tell me that someone had been murdered at the palace!'

'It would have upset you, Mama.'

'You had better tell me about it now.'

'Sit down, and I will. But you must keep calm.'

'Another murder!' Thomas cried.

'Is that all you think about?' Marie asked.

Lisabetta crept close to Jean, who took her hand and said, 'Don't worry. The murderer has been caught.'

Francesca sat down on the bench beside Colin, folded her hands in her lap, and tried to look calm.

'One of the duchess's Italian maids was murdered yesterday, strangled. I found her in my workroom,' Christine began.

'*Madonna santa!*' Francesca jumped up from the bench.

'Sit down, Mama, while I tell you the rest of it.'

Francesca arranged herself on the bench again and clutched her rosary.

'She was killed by the fool Colin says he caught.'

'Are you telling us that one of the duke's fools is a murderer?' Jean asked.

'Only one?' Thomas asked.

'*Basta*, Thomas,' Francesca said. 'How do you know it was this fool, *Cristina*?'

'At first it was just a guess. Everyone was trying to think who the murderer could be, and I remembered some things I'd observed about him. I took a chance. I asked that the fools be brought to me, and they came, all except the guilty one. He ran away because he realized I'd found him out.'

'Was it the one who juggles?' Georgette asked.

'Yes. He hasn't been with the duke long, and no one seems to know much about him. But I remembered some strange things. For example, the fools are always together, but Fripon wasn't with the others when they found the baby in the palace gardens. I wondered whether he'd stayed away from the gardens because he knew the baby was there. The fools were not meant to find her.'

'Did he put her there?' Thomas asked.

'No. She was put there by the woman who was murdered. Thibault de Torvaux got her to do it. Thibault wanted the baby to be substituted for the queen's baby, because he knew that everyone would blame the Duchess of Orléans. But the rest of his plan to hurt the duchess was more difficult. Remember, someone has been leaving signs of sorcery around the duke's residence, things meant to prove the duchess is a sorceress.'

'I know,' Thomas cried. 'Wax figures with pins in them.'

'There were other things, too, some so disgusting I won't tell you about them.

'I wish you would,' Thomas said under his breath.

'The fools wanted me to find out who was doing this because they felt sorry for the duchess. They thought it was Thibault de Torvaux, all except Fripon. He kept saying it must have been one of the duke's chamberlains, Aubert de Canny. We know now it really was Thibault, because Marion saw him buy the wax figure of the king with the needle through his heart. But Thibault couldn't have put the signs of sorcery around the palace himself; he would have been noticed. So he must have had an accomplice who could do it for him, someone who lived at the palace. It was Fripon.'

'But why did Fripon do it?' Jean asked.

'That's the question. I'm going to the palace to find out.'

FIFTY-THREE

He's an ass who's infatuated with himself.

Old proverb

Henri was waiting for her at the entrance to the duke's residence. 'Fripon says he won't talk to anyone but you,' he said as he led her along a passageway to a small room next to the kitchen. 'We're keeping him here because there's a lock on the door.'

Aubert de Canny stood there with three of the palace guards. 'How did you know it was Fripon?' Christine asked him.

'I didn't. I was just annoyed that he'd been following me around. I decided to catch him at his own game. I saw him go to the stables, and I went there to find him.'

'He thought he could steal a horse and escape,' Henri said.

Valentina and the duke appeared, and they all went into the room, followed by the master cook, who burst out of the kitchen brandishing a large spoon and shouting, 'Why are you keeping the criminal in here with my spices! Don't you know how valuable they are?'

'Don't worry,' Henri said. 'He's not interested in them.'

Fripon, his thin body barely covered by a ripped tunic and tattered breeches, sat on the floor with his head in his hands. A bag of cinnamon had been overturned, and a sweet smell filled the air; but all the other boxes and sacks that lined the shelves seemed to be intact. The only other sign of a struggle was a cone of sugar that had tumbled out of an overturned carton.

The master cook gave a cry of disgust, threw the sugar back into the carton, stepped over the fool, and strode to a shelf. He grabbed a box with a lock on it and rushed from the room, calling out over his shoulder, 'At least the criminal won't get this!'

'What is it?' Christine asked.

'Gold leaf,' Henri said. 'For decorating his confections.'

Christine shook her head. Fripon, choking on tears, wouldn't be interested in gold leaf now. He looked so miserable, she almost felt sorry for him.

Valentina started to go to him, but the duke held her back. 'Don't go near him. He wants to kill you.'

'Why?'

'He thinks you killed his brother.'

'His brother?'

Fripon raised his head and shouted, 'Gonzo, your fool, the one who drowned at Mâcon.'

'Why would I have killed Gonzo?' Valentina asked. 'I loved him!'

'You accused him of stealing your necklace.'

'I never believed he stole the necklace. I only wanted to clear his name.'

'He ran away and drowned. Because of you. *You* killed him.'

The master cook reappeared, waving a carving knife. 'Don't let him shout like that! He's upsetting everyone. We have work to do!'

'*Foutez le camp, Gillebert!*' Henri said.

The cook stomped back into the kitchen.

Fripon folded his arms over his chest and rocked back and forth. 'Gonzo was my little brother.'

Valentina turned to the duke. 'How is that possible?'

'Let him explain,' Louis said.

Valentina held her arms out to Fripon. 'I only know that Gonzo came from a poor family that had a lot of children and couldn't afford them all.'

Fripon laughed. 'Someone came and solved the problem. He took one of the children away. He took him to entertain a great lord's little daughter. Gonzo was your new toy.'

'I never thought of Gonzo as merely someone to amuse me!'

'The man who brought him to you thought otherwise. Do you know who he was?'

Valentina shook her head.

'The man who is in Paris now, trying to get back into the good graces of the king. Pierre de Craon.'

'I know Pierre was in Milan many years ago,' Valentina said. 'But I was a child then.'

'He was sent by the Duchess of Anjou to borrow money from your father. One of the ways he thought he could impress your father was to bring him the gift of a fool. Gonzo and I were both offered, but Pierre chose Gonzo.'

'What happened to you?' Christine asked.

'Pierre thought I was special. He brought me back to France. My name was Filippo, but he changed it to Fripon because that's what he wanted me to be: a trickster. He was good to me. He even taught me to read and write. And he said he'd make sure I saw my brother again.' He turned to the duchess. 'Pierre went to Mâcon to meet you, on your way here. And when he came back, he told me Gonzo was dead, because of you. Can you imagine how I felt? I'd waited all those years to see my little brother again. And now he was dead.'

Tears ran down Valentina's cheeks. 'What did Pierre tell you about how Gonzo died?'

'He said you accused him of stealing a necklace. He said Gonzo ran away and drowned because he was so hurt that you would believe such a thing. After that I hated you, and Pierre said he hated you, too, because you'd been responsible for his banishment from Paris. He said we could both get revenge if I'd help.'

'Pierre wanted to get revenge on me?' Valentina cried. 'I had nothing to do with his being sent away!'

Fripon looked at the duke. 'Pierre told her about your affair with one of the duchess's ladies, didn't he?'

Louis, very red in the face, exploded with anger. 'None of this is anyone's business!'

It is everyone's business because it's the cause of much trouble around here, Christine thought.

'But I don't see what that has to do with me,' Valentina said.

'It has everything to do with you. Pierre didn't expect you to confront the duke with what he'd told you. But you told the duke, and the duke had the king send Pierre away. Pierre never forgave you for that. He planned for years to get revenge.'

'What did Thibault have to do with all this?' the duke asked.

'When Pierre learned he could come back to Paris but would have to stay at the abbey, he enlisted Thibault as his emissary to the court. Thibault would come to the palace, and I would carry out his orders. He sent me to ask you to let me be your fool.'

Louis shook his head. 'I really didn't need another fool.'

The cook came to the door. 'I need saffron.'

'You'll have to wait,' Henri said.

'*Merde!*' the cook said. He stormed away.

'Whose idea was it to bring a disfigured baby to the palace gardens?' Christine asked Fripon.

'Pierre's. He got Thibault to buy a baby, have it disfigured, and pay a prostitute to take it to the gardens and substitute it for the queen's baby. The prostitute got scared, left the baby, and ran away. Of course, Thibault had to kill her so she wouldn't tell anyone about the scheme. He had to kill the baby's mother, too.'

Poor Klara and Fleur, Christine thought.

'Things didn't work out the way they planned.' Fripon looked at the other fools and laughed. 'You fools found the child.'

'But Thibault couldn't have killed Julia. It would have been too obvious, in the palace. So he told you to do it.' Christine said. 'How could you have murdered an innocent girl who never did anything to you!'

Fripon started to shake. 'I didn't kill Julia!'

Aubert slapped him. 'Stop lying. You'll hang for what you did.'

Fripon crawled to Valentina's feet, and clutched at her skirt. 'I didn't kill Julia, I swear!'

'Who else could it have been?' the duke asked.

'Thibault,' Fripon sobbed.

'Impossible. Thibault was only a guest here. Someone would have seen him if he'd gone up to the room where Christine works.'

Christine noticed that Henri, who had been standing quietly by the door, had disappeared. *What's he up to now?* she wondered.

Then Henri was back. 'Thibault *was* up there the day Julia was killed,' he said. He stepped aside, and behind him stood a red-faced Colart de Laon. 'Isn't that so, Colart?'

Colart nodded sheepishly.

'Tell us why he was up there,' Henri said.

'I invited him.'

'What for?'

'To see my painting of the duke and duchess.'

'But you hated Thibault! He made nasty comments about what you painted on the duchess's carriage,' Christine said.

'He said he was sorry. He said he was just jealous of my talent. He said he'd heard about the painting that had been damaged, and he said he knew that I was so skillful, I'd be able to restore it. So I invited him to come up and see what I'd done.'

'Was Baudet with you?'

'No. I'd sent him out to buy supplies.'

'And were you with Thibault all the time?'

Colart looked at the floor. 'I left him for a while,' he said in a very small voice.

'Where did you go?'

'Down to the library. Some people were coming to see the paintings I'd done there.'

'Is that true?' the duke asked Gilles, who'd come in after Colart.

'Yes. He's so proud of his work, he can't keep away if there are admirers around.'

Colart bristled. 'You'd be proud, too, if you could paint as well as I do!'

'You're an ass, Colart!' Henri said. 'Because of your pride, a young woman is dead.'

Christine looked at Fripon. 'Did you know Thibault was going to kill Julia?'

'He told me that would be a way to really hurt the duchess.'

'Did he tell you how he was going to do it?'

'He just said he had a surprise.'

Christine looked at Valentina. A large embroidered purse hung from the duchess's belt. 'It's in there, isn't it?' she asked.

Valentina nodded and drew out the necklace. Christine took it and held it in front of Fripon's eyes.

'This is the surprise. Pierre was the one who stole it at Mâcon. He kept it all those years, and he gave it to Thibault so he could use it to strangle Julia.'

Fripon let out a cry of anguish that reverberated around the room.

'Can't you let him go?' Valentina asked Louis. 'He may have done some bad things, but he's not a murderer.'

'The things he's done can't be excused,' the duke said.

'*I* can excuse him,' Valentina said.

'What are we going to do with him?' Aubert asked the duke.

'Lock him in this room until I decide,' Louis said.

FIFTY-FOUR

There is no greater sorrow for women than rape.

Christine de Pizan,
Le Livre de la Cité des Dames, 1404–1405

After everyone else had left, Christine and Henri stood outside the kitchen, where they could hear the master cook stomping around in a rage shouting at the lesser cooks and scullery maids.

'He'll calm down after a while,' Henri said. He gazed at Christine. 'I have to give you credit. I would never have suspected Fripon of leaving all those signs of sorcery around.'

'Once I thought about it, it was easy to believe he was the one.'

'I could imagine him covering Colart's painting of Valentina with brown paint. But scratching words into one of Colart's frescoes and writing a recipe for demonic magic on a piece of parchment to leave behind the duchess's chair? How could a fool do that?'

'He told us just now that Pierre taught him to read and write. He might have read something in the book of spells I found in the room where Louis experiments with alchemy. I found a walnut there. I don't think walnuts have anything to do with alchemy. But I've seen Fripon juggling them.'

'How could a fool read a book of spells?'

'Fripon plays the fool, but he's not foolish. Surely you can see that, Henri; you're so smart!'

Henri laughed. 'Well said, Christine.'

'Of course, Thibault must have supplied him with the other signs of sorcery we found. He got them in places like the shop where Marion saw him buy the wax king.' She shuddered when she remembered the poison frog and the rat's tail. 'I did find it hard to believe that Fripon could be a murderer, though. And I certainly would never have suspected him of rape.'

'Fripon is not interested in women,' Henri said. 'Pierre de Craon would have known that the moment he met him.'

'But what I don't understand is why Thibault killed Julia in my room,' Christine said.

'I told you before. It was a warning to you. He knew you were trying to find out who was causing all the mischief around here. You have a reputation, you know.'

'He took a big risk taking the time to rape her before he killed her,' Christine said. 'How could he have been so foolhardy?'

'That's obvious, but I suppose a woman would never recognize it. Didn't you see the way she flaunted herself with those low-cut gowns?'

'You said that before, Henri. It means you're blaming the victim, and I won't have it!' She would have slapped his face, but the fools appeared.

'Is it true?' Giliot asked. 'Did Fripon kill her?'

'No,' Christine said. 'It was Thibault. But Fripon left the signs of sorcery around the palace to make the duchess look bad.'

'We didn't know,' Giliot said. 'But everyone will think we did.' He sat down on the floor and put his head in his hands.

Blondel started to weep. Hanotin put his arms around him and wept, too, upsetting the monkey, who climbed down from his shoulder, sat at his feet, and covered his eyes with his paws. Coquinet crept into a corner and twisted himself into a small ball of misery.

'Stop that!' Henri said. 'Everyone knows you four fools had nothing to do with Fripon's treachery. Go away so Christine and I can talk.'

The fools gathered themselves together and shuffled away, sobbing.

Christine started to go with them. 'There's nothing for us to talk about, Henri.'

'There is. We need to talk about why you suspected me of killing Klara.'

'How could I not, when Marion found you right outside the house where she was murdered?'

'Of course I was outside that house. I own it!'

Christine felt her face getting hot. *Why didn't I think of that?* she asked herself. *I should have remembered that he owns a lot of houses and rents them out.*

'The house has been empty for some time,' Henri continued. 'No doubt that's why Thibault thought it would be a good place to kill someone.'

Christine looked at the floor.

'And I know you think I'm a magician and a sorcerer, simply because I dabble in alchemy. You probably even thought *I* might be the one leaving the signs of sorcery around.'

Then Christine began to get angry. 'How could I not have suspected you, when you're so secretive? And you do more than *dabble* in alchemy. You convince other people, like my father, to try it. I'll never forgive you for that.'

Henri grabbed took her hand and pulled her up the stairs. Afraid that someone would see what he was doing, she tried to walk calmly beside him. As they passed the duchess's receiving room, she looked in and was relieved to find that no one was there. No one was in the library, either. Henri dragged her in and shut the door. He went to a shelf, took down a large book, placed it on Gilles's desk, and opened it.

'Look at these initial letters. Aren't they a beautiful red?'

'I suppose so,' she said, rubbing her hand, which had gone numb in his strong grip.

'Do you know who the illuminator was?'

She shook her head.

'It was me. And I used the finest red anyone has ever seen. The finest, I tell you. Because I've perfected it.'

'Why are you telling me this?'

'Because you condemn me for dabbling in alchemy. You don't know anything about it.'

'I know enough to be aware that men have ruined themselves because of it. And I don't see what it has to do with red letters.'

'Let me tell you, then. For years painters have been trying to achieve a red this vibrant. How did I do it? By heating quicksilver and sulfur, just as alchemists do when they are attempting to turn base metals into gold.'

Christine looked at the book and shook her head.

'Would you like to come to my house and see how it's done?'

'I think not.'

'Gilles told me you were looking at Eustache's copy of Ovid the other day. You admired the red initials, didn't you? That's my red. No one else has succeeded in making such a beautiful red.'

'So I've been wrong. But how could one think otherwise when you are so secretive?'

'That's just my way. I see you are embarrassed.'

'I am not!'

Henri sat down at the desk. As usual, he didn't offer her the seat first, just let her stand there fuming. He closed the book he'd showed her. It was the *Romance of the Rose*, a book she particularly disliked because of its shameless portrayal of women. The sight of the title on its leather cover roused in her an anger that overcame her embarrassment. Henri was looking at her and smiling. 'I know. This book makes you cross. You're so involved in your concerns about the way men treat women, you can't read it without flinging it on to the floor. Why can't you let yourself be a normal woman and enjoy life?'

'I'm past being a normal woman, Henri, now that my husband is dead.'

'We could be friends, you know.'

Christine looked at him, elegantly dressed in a short blue jacket with padded shoulders, a gold belt, a long gold chain, and jeweled rings that sparkled on his fingers. She remembered Marion's description of his magnificent house – the gold and silver floor tiles, the courtyards with fountains and flowers, the beautiful tapestries, the stained-glass windows. She could see how a woman might be tempted by all that. Perhaps it wouldn't be so bad to have him for a friend; they could at least have stimulating conversations.

Her thoughts were interrupted by shouts from below. Henri rushed out, and she followed, down to the room where Fripon was kept.

The door was open, and Fripon lay on the floor in a pool of blood. Standing over him was the maid, Elena, holding a large kitchen knife that Aubert and the master cook were trying to wrest from her hand. 'She walked right into the kitchen and took it!' the master cook cried. 'And then she followed me in here with it,' Aubert said. 'I had no idea she had it.'

Henri knelt beside Fripon, examined him all over, then looked up and said, 'It's only his arm. But we have to get a doctor or he'll bleed to death.'

The master cook succeeded in wresting the knife from the girl's hand and rushed into the kitchen, while Henri picked up a cloth that lay on the floor and proceeded to wrap it around the fool's arm.

'That won't do it,' the master cook said as he ran back in with the knife, which had turned red hot. He pressed it against Fripon's arm. Fripon cried out in pain. 'Be quiet!' the cook said. 'A knife heated in the fire is the only way to stop the bleeding.'

Christine went to Elena, who was straining in Aubert's arms. 'Why did you do it?'

'He killed my sister! And he raped her!'

'It was Thibault de Torvaux, not Fripon.'

'They told me it was Fripon.'

'When did they tell you that?'

'Last night.'

'No one has told you what happened this morning?'

'No. I've been in my room. They gave me something to make me sleep.' She sobbed uncontrollably.

'Let her go,' Christine said to Aubert. 'She won't hurt me.'

Aubert released the girl and she fell into Christine's arms.

'Don't let her get away,' Henri cried. 'She has to be punished.'

Christine stroked the weeping girl's hair. 'Have a little pity, Henri. Wouldn't you want to get revenge if someone raped and killed your sister?'

'I don't have a sister.'

'You know what I mean. Killing Julia was bad enough; but to rape her first, that's even worse. How can you condemn a sister for wanting revenge?'

'She's a murderess.'

'Fripon is not dead. Look. The bleeding has stopped. So she's not a murderess. But even if she had succeeded in killing Fripon, she should be excused.'

Feelings she didn't know she had welled up in her. For a woman to be raped was so horrible, she could hardly bear to think of it. 'Murder could be justified when rape is involved,' she said.

Henri looked at her in fury. 'You're wrong, you pigheaded woman. This girl should be punished for attempting to kill the fool.'

'Not if I can help it,' Christine said.

Suddenly, Valentina appeared. 'I heard the shouting,' she said. She saw Fripon lying on the floor, and she dropped to her knees beside him. 'Can't you do something for him?'

'I already have,' said the cook. 'I've staunched the wound so he won't bleed to death.'

'Well done,' the duchess said. She'd been holding Fripon's head. Now she went to Elena and took her in her arms. Henri looked at her with disdain. 'The girl tried to kill him,' he said. 'She has to be punished.'

'Not if I have anything to say about it,' Valentina said. 'I heard what Christine said. She's right. Rape is the most terrible thing that can happen to a woman. That's what Elena thought Fripon did to her sister. We must forgive her.'

Henri looked at the duchess spitefully.

How could I have thought we might be friends? Christine asked herself.

FIFTY-FIVE

It was commonly believed that so long as the Duchess of Orléans was near the king, he would not get well. And so, to end this slander, she had to leave Paris.

Froissart, *Chroniques,* Livre IV, 1389–1400

At the foot of the stairs, Christine met Eustache Deschamps. 'I told you to listen to the fools,' he said.

'You were right. They suspected all along that it was Thibault.'

'Pierre de Craon was behind it all, of course.'

'I wonder what he'll do now that he's lost his accomplices,' Christine said.

'He'll never take Fripon back, that's for sure. That would make his evil intentions too obvious. And he will continue to deceive everyone, of that you can be certain.'

'Do you think Pierre planned to have Thibault kill Valentina next?'

'Pierre is capable of anything.'

'At least there won't be any more dead frogs or wax figures of the king left around here.'

'That's true. You've saved Valentina from that, and possibly you've saved her life. But you haven't stopped the slander. No one can do that, the people are so set against her.'

'So what will happen?'

'I'm sorry to have to tell you this, Christine. The duke is going to send her away. She leaves tomorrow for his château at Asnières.'

Christine left the palace with a heavy heart. She was so lost in her thoughts, it took her a moment to realize that a great crowd was rushing up the rue Saint-Antoine. The people had heard there'd been another killing, and they were furious. They surged toward the palace, crying frightening threats against Valentina, because they believed her next victim would be the king. The roar was so loud, she had to put her hands over her ears.

The palace guards met the crowd and pushed it back, but she sensed they knew they would not be able to hold it back for long.

In front of the queen's residence, she met Marion.

'It's over,' Christine said. 'It was Thibault, with Fripon's help.'

'I know. I just delivered some purses for the queen and her ladies, and I heard all about it. They talk of nothing else.'

'Do they realize that Pierre de Craon was behind everything Thibault did?'

'No. They only know about Thibault.'

'As usual, Pierre will get away with his crime. There's no proof that he was the instigator of all the evil that's gone on here. It seems no one can stop his evil.'

'While I was with the queen, the Duchess of Burgundy came in and told everyone that Valentina was the evil one. She said her presence here makes people do evil things. She said the duke is sending her away.'

'It's true. She leaves tomorrow.'

'That's terrible! It's unfair! She's done nothing wrong. Is there no way you can help her?'

'I've done all I can.'

Marion reached into her sack and took out a purse decorated with a green parrot. 'This is for you, Lady Christine. You've been through so much. I used Babil as a model.'

'Do you have an extra one for my mother? She's been through a lot too, these past few days, worrying about me.'

'I have another one at home. I'll give it to her.'

Christine stood with her mother, her children, and Georgette on the corner of her street and the rue Saint-Antoine, watching Valentina's cortege go by. It was a grey, blustery day, and storm clouds scuttled across the sky, seemingly hustling the duchess away from the city that hated her. As the gusts swirled around them, men held on to their hats, women pressed their skirts down, and small children braced themselves to keep from being blown off their feet. But no matter how much the wind churned and wailed and howled, it couldn't muster a roar loud enough to eclipse the thunderous shouts of people venting their rage on the woman they believed was the cause of France's misery.

There had been no time to prepare all of Valentina's entourage, so she was accompanied by only a few carriages carrying her ladies-in-waiting and her most important retainers. Others would follow later, along with all her clothes, jewels, tapestries, and household furnishings.

Madame de Maucouvent rode in Colart de Laon's garishly painted carriage, holding the duchess's little son, Charles, on her lap. Beside her sat the maid, Elena, with her head in her hands. Valentina, tall and proud on her big grey courser, trotted up to the carriage and leaned down to speak to them. Charles, not yet two years old, played with Madame de Maucouvent's necklace and paid no attention to his mother, but Elena looked up and burst into tears. Valentina spoke to the duke, who would ride with her until she was well out of the city. He shook his head. Christine was sure she'd asked for the cortege to be halted so she could comfort Elena. It didn't happen; everything moved inexorably forward as though propelled along by the wind.

'Why is the duchess not riding in a carriage, like a lady?' Francesca asked.

'She'd rather be up on her horse,' Christine said. 'It gives her courage.'

'Is that the girl who tried to murder the fool?' Marie asked. 'Shouldn't she be in prison?'

'She did try to kill Fripon,' Christine said. 'But she did it because she thought he'd raped and killed her sister. Can't you understand how horrible that was for her?'

'I can,' Jean said. 'I would forgive her.'

Valentina turned her horse around and rode to a carriage carrying her dwarf Jacopo and a small dark man with his arm in a sling who hung his head and looked at no one. When the duchess spoke to him, he shrank back, like a dog that expects to be kicked.

'What is she saying?' Francesca asked.

'I imagine she's telling him not to be afraid,' Christine said. 'She's forgiven him and taken him into her care.'

Fripon lifted his head and nodded to Valentina.

'I think he will be all right,' Francesca said.

'I think so, too, now that he is no longer under the influence of Pierre de Craon,' Christine said. 'Pierre disavowed him. He claims he knew nothing of what Fripon had done.'

A group of frenzied boys raced by, and a gaggle of old women lurched after them, crying imprecations at Valentina. A small dog howled as he was trampled under a workman's big boots, and a little boy who had lost his mother ran sobbing to Francesca and clung to her skirt. She picked him up. 'We will find your mother,' she said as she scanned the raging crowd.

'Look! There's Michel!' Jean cried as the monk appeared. Michel didn't see them because his gaze was fixed on the seething mass of people.

'Who are you looking for, Michel?' Christine called out.

He pulled back his cowl and scratched his tonsured head. 'That demon in human shape, Pierre de Craon.'

'Isn't he at the abbey?'

'He snuck away this morning. I have to find him and bring him back.' He wandered away, scowling as he pushed his way through the mob.

A crowd of jeering people raced after Valentina's cortege. As they passed, a frantic woman ran to Francesca and snatched the boy from her arms. 'I told you we would find your mother,' Francesca called out to the boy as his mother carried him away.

Thomas cried out, 'There's Marion. What's she got on her shoulder?'

Christine looked where he pointed and saw Marion making her way toward them with Babil bouncing up and down against her cheek. 'It's her parrot,' she said.

'Why doesn't he fly away?'

Christine wondered about that, too, until she saw that Marion had made a little harness for the bird. Francesca backed away when Marion came close and shuddered as Babil let out a loud shriek.

'He won't bite,' Marion said.

'Let me hold him,' Thomas said, jumping up and down.

Marion lifted the bird and set him on the boy's outstretched wrist. Thomas giggled. 'His feet tickle,' he said.

'Hold on to the string. I've tied it to the harness,' Marion said. She reached into her sack, drew out a purse with an embroidered parrot on it, and handed it to Francesca. 'This is for you. I gave one just like it to Christine.'

Francesca took the purse, studied it, and looked at Babil. 'I suppose it looks a *little* like him,' she said. Babil nodded his head and whistled.

Then the other children wanted to hold Babil, and Marion had to accommodate everyone. Christine stood to one side, too sorrowful to take part in the fun. The last horsemen following Valentina's cortege had disappeared from view, and she felt a great emptiness. She thought about how sad the duke's residence would feel without Valentina's presence. She grieved that she would never finish copying the fables of Aesop, and that Colart would never finish the painting with Valentina in it. She grieved for the duke's fools, who would never cheer the duchess again. She grieved for Alips, who had lost her friend Jacopo. And above all, she grieved for the king, who had lost the one person who could ease his suffering.

The crowd had thinned, but a horde of drunken men came surging back, reeling and making nasty comments about the duchess. Christine had had enough. She was about to join her family and tell them it was time to go home when she felt a hand on her shoulder. She turned and found herself face to face with a man in a pleated crimson jacket, tight silver hose, shoes with very long points, and many gold chains and diamond rings. He glared at her with a wicked smile on his face and hissed, 'You succeeded in saving the duchess, but don't think that's the end of it.'

It took her a moment to realize who he was, but when she did, she recoiled as though she'd been stung by a scorpion.

'Monster,' she hissed back. But he didn't hear. Pierre de Craon had slipped away into the throng of rowdy men.